Hold On To The Hunter

The Sidhe Hunters, Volume 5

Sloane McClain

Published by Sloane McClain, 2024.

This book is a work of fiction. Names, characters, places, and incidents are products of the author's imagination or are used fictitiously and are not to be construed as real. Any resemblance to actual events, locales, organizations, or persons, living or dead, is entirely coincidental.

No Generative artificial intelligence (AI) used in the writing and creation of this work. 100% author-created content.

Hold On To The Hunter

First Edition: July 2024

Written by Sloane McClain

Cover art and design by Dar Albert of Wicked Smart Designs

Also by Sloane McClain

A Frog Knot Mystery
No Charge For Murder

A Sidhe Hunters Story
A Hunter For A Stormy Night

Sons of Pendragon
Dragon's Grace
Dragon's Heir
Dragon's Challenge
Dragon Storm
Dragon's Fear

The Sidhe Hunters
Holding Out For A Hunter
I Belong To The Hunter
I Believe In My Hunter
Take A Chance On A Hunter

Hold On To The Hunter

Table of Contents

To the readers who are enjoying reading these stories *almost* as much as I'm enjoying writing them. I hope I bring you as much joy as you bring me.

A special thank you to the health care workers at SH Medical, Novant, and Atrium.

CHAPTER ONE

Avery Beaton wished she could follow in her family's footsteps as a healer. She came from a long line of people adept in the medicinal arts. Centuries long, in fact.

Unfortunately, Avery inherited not one iota of healing ability.

Since she hadn't, she had to find another occupation. Avery loved history, so that became her focus of study. There she discovered her niche. She researched historical artifacts, tracing their provenances to make certain they stood up to scrutiny. Her specialty was the weaponry of the pre-Norman conquest era. Though Avery was also familiar with Civil War weapons. Working for a huge auction house headquartered in Charlotte, North Carolina, made that last pretty much a given.

Normally, the procedure was for the item in question to be brought or sent to the firm for analysis. On rare occasions, however, she was required to travel to a client's location. Most of the time, that wasn't a problem.

This time wouldn't have been either, except the executor of the estate whose items were up for sale gave her the heebie-jeebies. He was supercilious while pretending not to be. When he smiled, it never reached his eyes—which were too shifty for Avery's peace of mind. It was a strange, but he was *too* helpful.

Avery finished with the easiest items. A couple of swords, an article of clothing, and a diary, all from the Civil War era. She moved on to a small group of items purportedly from different periods of early Scottish history. This last batch contained a claymore in suspiciously excellent condition for its stated age, a moth-eaten piece of cloth, and a finely crafted *sgian-dubh*.

From the estate's attorney, she had photocopies of the entire list of items for sale, as well as the provenances of the items she was reviewing. Avery also had the photographs she took off each item. Once she returned to her hotel room, Avery planned to go over everything.

After extracting herself from the executor's company, Avery drove to the hotel. First, she wanted something to eat. Leaving everything but her purse in her room, she went back downstairs to the restaurant attached to the hotel.

For some reason, she was edgy. Probably a leftover from dealing with the executor. Avery hoped some people-watching would calm her down.

Just as a waitress served her meal, Avery noticed another wait person show a man to a table. She frowned as she surreptitiously studied him. There was something familiar about him.

His dark hair was pulled back in a short ponytail. Heavy dark brows slashed straight across a pair of dark eyes. A mustache, the same color as his hair, covered his upper lip. In his mid-thirties at least, he was dressed casually in a white, short-sleeved shirt and faded black denim jeans.

When he glanced her way, Avery averted her eyes. As she did, her attention caught on an attractive black man somewhere in his late twenties to early thirties. A navy t-shirt showed off muscled arms and a ripped chest. A navy and white bandana was tied around his head. As Avery studied him, she realized there was something familiar about this man as well.

She swiftly looked down at her plate as she thought back to every man she had seen that day. Except it wasn't today. She shivered a little as she remembered seeing him the day before when she stopped to refuel her car. It was possible it was a coincidence they twice crossed paths. She had driven the most common highways between Charlotte and Asheville. Rationally, it was possible. However, Avery's senses screamed it wasn't probable.

As Avery continued to search her memory, she sipped her sweet tea and nibbled her fries. She almost choked, as mid-swallow, she remembered seeing the other man. He had come into the local I-HOP that morning shortly after her. Except, at the time, his hair hadn't been pulled back; it had been loose around his shoulders. More concerning, he hadn't been sporting a mustache. The man was deliberately disguising his appearance.

Avery's stomach dropped.

She forced herself to remain calm. The last thing she wanted to do was draw their attention.

Avery's only inherited Sidhe talent was telepathy. Even that talent began to atrophy. Following her father's death, no one remained to communicate with in that manner.

At least not until the past year, when a man began to contact her telepathically, claiming to be a distant cousin on her father's side. She recently got to meet him in person. He wasn't much older than she was. He was friendly, humorous, and, on two rare occasions when she needed help, fearless. Most importantly to Avery, he was family when she no longer had any. It meant she wasn't alone. She loved that he treated her as she imagined an older brother might treat an adored little sister.

Avery wished he was with her now. Just Stiabhan's presence should frighten these guys away.

She glanced at each man, and then back to her meal. Neither appeared to be watching her, but if they were up to something nefarious, they wouldn't. Especially if they were good at it, and both men looked as if they were good at their work. If Avery hadn't trained to observe details, she might never have noticed.

If they were up to something, either separately or together, what was their interest in her? She wasn't rich. Far from it. She owned nothing that would even total ten thousand dollars. That included her eleven-year-old car.

It couldn't be her looks. She was twenty-six, overweight, and because of her work, dressed mostly in t-shirts and jeans. Makeup comprised powder and lipstick or gloss, and because nearly all of it made her eyes water, she seldom wore mascara. Her eyes were an unremarkable brown. Thick, and past her shoulders in length, her hair was an ordinary dark brown. She often wore it pulled back in a ponytail or braid.

Their repeated appearances couldn't be chalked up to them falling in love with her. Surely, they didn't work for a human trafficking ring. A terrifying thought. Which brought her full circle to their reason for trailing her. Even if mysteries were her favorite genre to read, Avery didn't think she was being paranoid to believe the men were stalking her.

Convincing anyone else, like, say, the police, that she wasn't a stark raving lunatic would be impossible without evidence. She doubted the two men would allow her to photograph them as proof.

Avery didn't know what to do. Panic wasn't her way because it almost always made things worse. This situation tested that. She didn't carry a weapon, though her employers often suggested she take a concealed weapons course. It suddenly sounded like a reasonable request. Avery knew a few basic self-defense moves—none of which she thought would work against either of these men.

If she could figure out what they wanted, perhaps she could fix things, so the object of their desire no longer had anything to do with her. Which sounded both reasonable, as well as doable. Except she had no clue what they wanted.

Suddenly she remembered she left her camera bag and her computer in her room. If there were two men, were there more?

What if these two were watching her while their partner broke into her room and stole her things?

The information and photos contained on her devices didn't concern her. As a precaution, Avery always loaded her photos onto her computer. After that, she saved a copy of it all onto a large-capacity flash drive attached to her keys. She also uploaded it to a cloud system as a second backup. If they wanted the document copies provided by the client, they could have them. She could easily get more.

Avery was concerned about her equipment. If they were stolen, she didn't have the resources to replace them.

With her appetite gone, Avery left the rest of her meal and signaled for the check. She paid as quickly as she could and headed for her room. While the two men made motions to leave as well, she hurried into the lobby. She Eschewed the elevator for the stairs and headed up at a run. It was faster, and hopefully it would confuse them long enough to buy her some time. If someone was already in her room, robbing her, then she was in trouble.

Avery reached the fourth floor. She stopped to catch her breath. It was irritating how out of breath she was. While trying to get her breathing back to normal, she peeked through the reinforced glass panel in the stairwell door. Besides an older couple just making their way into the elevator, the hall was empty. While pulling her key card from her back pocket, she sprinted to her door.

Nervous, it took her three tries to get the card to function. Avery missed the old-fashioned keys. She didn't understand it, but she always had trouble with the darned cards. Just as she closed the door behind her, she heard a ding signaling an elevator's arrival. She shoved the safety lock home.

Avery remained by the door as she looked around the room and what she could see of the bathroom. If someone had been inside, they were gone now. She walked into the bathroom to make sure.

Just in case someone managed to find a hiding place, she eased into the bedroom. Seconds later, she was confident she was alone.

First, she checked her satchel. It didn't appear to have been touched. Avery looked inside to make sure. Her computer was tucked inside its padded compartment. Next, she checked the camera. The camera bag was still in the bottom drawer of the dresser. After taking it out, Avery opened it and went through the contents. Everything was in its place, including the SD card.

Closing the camera bag and clutching it to her chest, Avery sighed in relief. She sank onto the end of the bed next to her leather satchel. Maybe she was wrong about the two men. Perhaps she was being paranoid. Avery saw no sign anyone had been in her room.

She took a deep, calming breath, and then she exhaled slowly. Avery frowned. There was something...

She took another deep breath. This time, sniffing. That's when she realized the problem. Avery smelled a scent that shouldn't have been present. Men's cologne. Very nice cologne.

A man had been in her room. Recently.

Panicked, Avery hurried to the head of the bed and reached for the phone on the nightstand. Then she stopped. She could just imagine their reactions when she told them someone broke into her room but stole nothing. Especially when she informed them the reason she knew was because she smelled expensive men's cologne. As if a man who could afford good cologne would break into a medium-priced hotel room in the first place.

Avery couldn't stay. She no longer felt safe. Avery knew she wouldn't get any sleep because she no longer trusted the locks to keep anyone out.

Avery fell back on the bed and stared at the ceiling. She needed to think.

She was due to return to Charlotte the day after next. There were only two more nights in Asheville. Her employer had paid for the room. Though Avery hated to rack up the extra expense, she would feel better if she found somewhere else to stay. At least for tonight. If she left her large suitcase and didn't turn in her keycard until Sunday morning, it might fool the two goons trailing her into believing she was still here.

Avery wished again she had inherited the ability to translocate. That would throw her shadows for a loop. The trick, since she had to do it like a regular person, was to get to her car without them seeing her. If that was even possible. But she had to risk it.

Since she had nothing to use for a disguise, Avery resorted to old-fashioned subterfuge and obfuscation. She changed into a loose-fitting sweatshirt. She's worn her hair pulled back the entire trip, so she pulled the band off the end of her braid and fluffed her hair out. For good measure, she pulled some forward around her face.

Deciding she had nothing to lose, Avery quickly packed what she would need into her satchel. She folded her coat inside out and dropped it over the satchel to hide it. Putting the strap over her head, she picked up her purse and camera bag in her left hand. After sliding the keycard in her back pocket and hooking the carabiner holding her car keys to her belt loop, Avery peered out the peephole.

Avery waited. Several seconds passed before she heard voices. She peeked out. When she saw two couples heading for the elevators, she dashed out of her room. Avery followed, joining them as they got in. No one else joined them before the doors glided closed.

When the doors opened on the ground floor, Avery stepped out after the first couple. People crowded the lobby looking for a bed now that darkness had fallen. She was glad she'd left her suitcase in her room. It would have looked weird if she was seen leaving with luggage at the time of night.

With her head down and her shoulders hunched, Avery walked out as if she was on a mission. Which she was. Mission Escape.

Once outside, she kept an eye out for stalkers, taking a roundabout route to her car. Finally reaching it, she slipped behind the wheel and locked her door. Luckily, no one was coming in at the moment, allowing her to speed out of the parking lot and head for the nearest four-lane highway. Once she reached it, she took the first on-ramp, only because it was expedient and not because she had a destination in mind.

Avery's only thought was losing two goons.

CHAPTER TWO

Darach Shanley didn't look at his partner. He didn't need to. They were both Halflings, or Daondasidhe, after all. Half human, half fairy, or Sidhe. *"She made us,"* he said telepathically.

"You're joking. She's basically a glorified librarian," Nathan Morogh replied. *"No one's ever made me before."*

"There's a first time for everything. Just because you're slipping in your old age is no reason to get surly." Darach shifted to include the third of their foursome, also their boss. *"Duncan?"*

"What?" came the immediate reply.

"The target made us," Darach informed him.

"Both of you?" His voice, heard only in their heads, sounded incredulous.

"I hate to admit it—I mean, I really hate to admit it—but Darach's right. And she's making a rushed effort to leave the restaurant," Nate said.

"Dammit!"

"How much time do you need?" Nate asked.

"None. Everything's copied. I'll have things back in place by the time she returns. I can't believe she made both of you."

"Neither can Nate. Seems it's never happened to him before. She bruised his pride." Darach's amusement came through the communication.

"It's never happened to you before either," Nate reminded him sharply.

"True, but I knew it was bound to happen sooner or later. You're upset because you never expected someone like her to be the one to do it." Darach was obviously more pragmatic.

"We underestimated her. Badly," Duncan stated with a frown. *"Peter, get out front and keep an eye on her car. We can't afford to lose her. Not until we've located the correct* sgian dubh."

"I'm on it." Peter Carey, the last member of the foursome, chimed in.

"We've got a bigger problem," Nate stated.

"What?" Duncan and Darach asked at the same time.

"We aren't the only ones tailing our girl. There are at least two other guys in here watching her, too."

"So? She's a fine-looking woman, and she's alone." Darach didn't sound convinced of his own reason.

Nate described the two men that most concerned him so that Darach could check them out. *"They're predatory, but I'm not seeing sexual interest."*

"Crap!" Darach cursed after looking them over.

"Dubh Sidhe?" Duncan asked, referring to the evil fairy.

"Beats me. Whoever they are, they'd sure love to get their hands on her," Nate replied.

"Where is Avery now?" Duncan asked.

"Paying her bill. She'll be walking out in seconds," Darach told him.

"You have to pick her up, Duncan. Figuratively. Don't think the rest of us have missed the heat in your eyes. But if she sees either of us, she is going to panic," Nate said.

"I'm heading for the lobby now. You two blanket any other exits, just in case." Duncan didn't respond to Nate's taunt. No use giving his friend more fodder.

Duncan looked over the room one last time. He had replaced her computer in the brief bag and put it back exactly where he'd found it.

He'd already returned the camera bag to the dresser drawer. Satisfied everything was in its place, he left the room as if it was his and took the elevator to the lobby.

After about thirty minutes of pretending to read magazines, Duncan began to think Darach and Nate were mistaken about her having made them. Then one set of elevator doors opened to disgorge five people. One of them an attractive young woman with dark mahogany hair, currently freed from its usual braid. Thick waves of the shiny stuff cascaded past her shoulders, threatening to distract him with thoughts of running his fingers through it. Avery might consider it a disguise, but Duncan would recognize her anywhere.

He watched her nervously glance around before making a beeline for the lobby entrance. The lady definitely felt threatened.

As Duncan rose to follow her, he noticed one man Nate described earlier. The bastard was still trailing her. Nate was right. There was no personal interest in the guy's eyes. Duncan didn't recognize him, but that didn't mean he wasn't Dubh Sidhe, or at least on their payroll.

"Heads up. Avery's heading outside with just her brief bag and camera bag. She's also got at least one shadow," Duncan alerted the rest of his team.

After giving her a couple of seconds' head start, Duncan followed her outside, heading for his own car. He was positive Avery was going to make a break for it once she reached her own vehicle. *"I'll be in position to follow her in a minute. It doesn't look like the guy shadowing her is aware of the rest of us."*

"Or he just doesn't see us as a threat," Nate suggested.

"If that's the case, I look forward to changing his mind." Duncan reached the black Dodge Charger he'd picked from the motor pool. Starting the engine, he left the lights off for the moment. *"I'm ready."*

"Good," Peter said. *"Cause now she's reached her car, she's burning rubber. Frick has joined Frack and they're going after her."*

"I see them. I'm going to follow her followers. The tracking bug is in her briefcase. It will let us know where she goes if we lose her. Follow as quickly as you can so we can switch up." Duncan pulled out behind the black Chevy Suburban containing Avery's stalkers.

He grinned. A few more large black vehicles and people might assume it was a nighttime funeral procession.

"Five by five on the signal," Peter reported. *"We'll be right behind you. Leaving now."*

Duncan and his team followed the woman and her shadows for over forty minutes before she finally pulled into a motel. Duncan eased the Charger into the parking lot, quickly turning off the lights and the engine.

Frick and Frack had already pulled into the back, parking in front of a room. One remained in the car, slinking down until his head was just visible above the dash. The other one headed to a lighted area with an icemaker and vending machines.

Avery exited her car and entered the lobby. A few minutes later, she came out and moved her car about halfway along the two-story row of rooms. Getting out once more, she froze when she spotted the man loitering in the vending area. Then she hurried to her room, fumbled a few seconds with the door before getting it open, and scurried inside.

Out of his car, Duncan headed for the lobby. *"Room number?"*

"Twenty-seven," Peter supplied. *"You'll want twenty-eight. It has the connecting door."*

"I hardly need a connecting door to enter her room," Duncan said. *"You just be ready to get her things should I have to take her."*

"Puh-leese." Even through telepathy, Duncan heard the insulted tone of Peter's voice.

Easily acquiring the room he wanted, Duncan parked his car beside Avery's. He ignored the two goons as if he didn't see them. Seconds later, he was inside the room adjacent to Avery's.

He closed the drapes, turned off all the lights save one, and moved next to the connecting door. Duncan hoped the other men weren't Sidhe. They'd be able to translocate in, grab her, and leave before he could lift a finger to stop them.

Duncan shook his head. The danger was too great to risk.

"Change of plans, lads. We're taking her now. I'll take her to the mountain safe house. Peter, give me twenty seconds, then go into her room and grab her things. Darach, don't leave the Charger behind."

"No problem," Peter replied. *"And I'll bring her car."*

"I'll get the Charger," Darach said.

"And me?" Nate asked.

"Keep your eyes on Frick and Frack. You may need to run interference, so they don't follow Peter or Darach," Duncan instructed. *"Starting now."*

Duncan translocated into Avery's room.

He appeared a few feet behind her. Something alerted her to his presence because she spun around to face him, her eyes wide.

Duncan expected her to scream. Maybe faint. He didn't expect her to pull back her right hand and take a swing at him. Using her attack to his advantage, he caught her wrist, twirled her around, wrapped his arms across her, and pulled her back flush against him. Clamping his free hand over her mouth, Duncan translocated them both to the safe house northwest of Greenville, South Carolina.

AVERY COULD ONLY DISCERN they were somewhere other than her motel room. It was too dark now to see anything. She struggled, but the man had arms like the proverbial steel bands. And why wouldn't he? From the brief glimpse she got of him, he was huge. Several inches over six feet with muscles on muscles. Yet he didn't appear muscle-bound, just solid.

"Stiabhan, please, if you can hear me, help!" Avery didn't know what else to do. There was no way she could escape this guy on her own. Stiabhan was the only person she could call who had a chance of dealing with him.

"I'm not going to hurt you. Stop fighting me."

Her captor had a baritone voice that brushed over her raw nerve endings like warm velvet. Avery shivered. She didn't think it was from fear. Could one get Stockholm Syndrome simply from hearing a kidnapper's voice?

Something else shocked Avery. He wore the cologne she'd smelled in her room. This was the man who had broken into her other hotel room. Now he'd followed her here.

Avery needed to fight both the pull the man had as well as the man himself. "You broke into my room and kidnapped me. Pardon me if I don't believe one word you say."

He didn't release his hold on her wrist, but he turned her back to face him. "Technically, I did not break into your room. There was no breaking involved." He narrowed his eyes in suspicion. Lovely green eyes like dark sea glass lit from within. "Why aren't you having hysterics? You don't seem even the least freaked out."

Was he kidding? Those were his questions? Of course, she was scared. Avery jerked her wrist, but he didn't release her. "As a general rule, hysterics are unproductive and a major waste of energy. I'll save it as an option for later. What do you want with me?"

The man was a walking, breathing female fantasy. It might have been better if he'd kept her facing away. Then she wouldn't have seen the height, the delectable body, or the face of a fallen angel. Thick, curly dark hair came just to the top of his shirt collar. Those gorgeous green eyes. A strong jawline currently sporting a five o'clock shadow. He was drop-dead gorgeous.

Wrong choice of words since he was also a kidnapper. And who knew what else?

"At the moment, I'm saving you from two stalkers."

She blinked at him, startled. "Those two from the restaurant?"

He looked taken aback by that. "The ones I'm talking about were there, too, but I have a feeling the ones you're speaking of were two of my men."

Avery frowned at him. "Just how many of you people are following me?"

"Hey, don't lump Frick and Frack in with my men," he said indignantly. "We're the good guys."

"Says you. You can't prove it by me." She ineffectively yanked her captured wrist. "Let go of me!"

He smiled regretfully. "Can't do that. Not yet. Nate pegged you for a runner, and you proved him correct. I think I'm just going to have to hold on to you for a while." He sounded entirely too pleased by the prospect.

Avery glared up at him. This close, she was in danger of getting a crick in her neck. "You aren't fostering trust here... What is your name, anyway?"

"Duncan. Duncan Kerr," he pronounced the last name as 'car.' He eyed her thoughtfully. "Do you know what a Hunter is?"

"Of course. Someone who shoots animals with a gun or a bow and arrow." Avery wasn't about to admit knowledge of anything more until she knew exactly who this guy was and what he wanted.

One dark eyebrow rose. "You're good. Someone taught you well. I think you know exactly what I mean by the term."

Avery ignored that. Her father had indeed taught her well. A tough job to teach a child who loved to talk that it was important to listen and give little away. "What do you want with me? There must be some reason I'm suddenly so popular."

"My firm needs your help in locating a specific item. And in authenticating it. It's vital we know if it's the artifact we seek."

"You could have just asked. You didn't have to kidnap me."

"We did ask. We were informed that you don't do independent contract work. Your company can't be involved. This is a very delicate matter that requires complete secrecy and discretion."

It was the first Avery heard of anyone requesting her individually. There were no rules that she and the other agents like her couldn't do outside work. It angered her that her employers hadn't consulted her. Still, she tried to be loyal. "Blackwell and Copeland are known for their discretion."

He shook his handsome head. "Too many people would be involved. More importantly for our clients, none of the other members of your firm are Daondasidhe. We checked."

Now he used the Sidhe word for Halfling. Avery still wasn't ready to admit her heritage to a stranger. Putting her free hand on her hip, hoping she looked confident instead of ridiculous, she glared up at him. With him still in possession of her right wrist, she feared the intimidation factor fell short. "I am right in the middle of an assignment. An important one for a wealthy client. I can't disappear out of the blue. This stunt of yours could cost me my job."

"You're all but finished. You've already reviewed the items. With the photos you took, as well as the documents provided to you, you have more than enough to complete your assignment. The report might be a day or so late, as unfortunately, you've come down with something. You sent an email to that effect to your employer not an hour ago."

"I did no such thing. I—you!" She stared at him in disbelief. "How did you do that? One of your goons hacked my email, didn't he? The laws y'all are breaking just keep mounting. By the time you're finished, the police will throw away the key when they lock you up."

He laughed. "You're a bloodthirsty little thing. I like that." Tilting his head to the side, he studied her. "How many times must I tell you that I'm helping you out, not kidnapping you?"

Avery tugged on her restrained arm for emphasis. "Apparently, quite a few more."

He considered a moment. "If I release you, will you promise not to run?"

Was he crazy? Of course, she was going to try to escape at the first opportunity. "Would you believe me if I say yes?"

Green eyes studied her intently. "I believe, under the circumstances, I would believe anything you choose to tell me."

He looked as surprised to have said that out loud as she was to hear it.

He continued quickly. "At this moment, no. However, I'm confident in my ability to catch you should you try it. With that being said, I'm willing to chance it."

He released Avery's wrist. Before she could celebrate her freedom, he caught her hand. He tugged her to a wall, where he flipped a switch with his free hand. Lifting her hand toward the light, he frowned at what he saw. When he faced her, honest regret showed in his lovely eyes. "I hurt you. I apologize. I didn't realize I was gripping you so tightly."

"You didn't, really." Avery stopped before she absolved him of anything else. It *was* his fault. He was the one holding her hostage.

"Release her now!" ordered a male from off to her right.

Duncan dropped her arm like a hot coal. Drawing a dirk she hadn't realized he had, he stepped between them.

"Stiabhan?" Duncan asked in surprise.

"Stiabhan!" Avery exclaimed simultaneously.

She looked at her captor and he looked at her. As one, they questioned, "You know him?"

"Yes, you both know me," Stiabhan spoke up. "I didn't know you knew one another, though."

"We don't," Avery said.

"We're in the process of becoming acquainted," Duncan said. He frowned at Stiabhan. "How did you get in here? This place is fully warded against all things Sidhe."

Stiabhan placed his hand on his chest. "That truly hurts my feelings. I thought we were friends. Have I not aided you on a mission or two?" He took a seat in a leather recliner.

"Get over it. It's not personal. I need to know how you got in here for security reasons."

Stiabhan turned his head to smile at Avery. "Avery called me. You could say she invited me."

Duncan frowned. "How did she...? She's telepathic, isn't she? I knew it."

"She *is* my kinswoman," Stiabhan replied with a shrug.

"Can she translocate?" Duncan asked.

"If I could, I'd be long gone." She sat in an overstuffed wingback chair next to Stiabhan.

Now that the lights were on, Avery took the opportunity to look at her surroundings. They were in a spacious living room of oversized, overstuffed furniture, a comfy-looking, extra-long couch, and three large leather recliners. A huge square coffee table of dark wood anchored the seating area.

Across from her, behind the couch and between sections of wall, were four windows, one story in height. Above them were four more triangular windows that stretched up to form an A-frame. The upper windows were uncovered, but the bottom ones were hidden behind thick drapes. To her left, she saw the top of stairs leading down. Next was a heavy wooden door studded with iron, and finally a fireplace. To her right, an archway opened to a dining room with a round table large enough to seat at least eight.

"Besides telepathy, what other talents do you have?" Duncan asked.

"None of your business." Avery wasn't about to admit it was the only one she had.

Duncan strolled over and sat on the couch. He turned his attention to Stiabhan. "I'm guessing she called you for assistance."

"Ha! I called him to rescue me because you kidnapped me."

Duncan shot her a look of male irritation. "For the last time, I did *not* kidnap you."

Avery appealed to the Sidhe. She pointed at Duncan. "He popped into my motel room, grabbed me, and then popped here with me. What would you call that?"

"There wasn't time to do more than that," Duncan argued.

"That sounds like kidnapping to me, my friend."

"Whose side are you on?" Duncan frowned.

Stiabhan laughed. "Avery's, of course. Kinswoman, remember?"

"I was trying to prevent two other men from taking her. None of us recognized them. I don't know if they're Dubh Sidhe or just work for them. I couldn't take the chance of them kidnapping her. As in truthfully abducting her. I felt it safer to get Avery out of harm's way."

"So you say." Avery crossed her arms, too. Partially because she felt the truth of his words.

"Damnit, Avery, you saw one of them when you got out of the car to enter your motel room. From your reaction, you thought he was shady, too."

Avery instantly knew who he meant. "The man at the vending machines."

Duncan nodded.

She turned back to Stiabhan. Avery indicated Duncan with a motion of her head. "He had two men following me, too. I hadn't seen the other man before."

"Three," Duncan corrected.

"What?" Avery looked at him in confusion.

"Besides myself, I had three men trailing you," Duncan stated. "You only saw two of them."

"You see," she said to her relative, feeling vindicated.

Stiabhan unfolded his arms. His serious expression worried her. "Avery, sweet, I've known Duncan for a few years. While his dark visage is displeasing and fearsome..."

"Hey!" Duncan protested, sitting up straight.

"...he is one of the good guys, as you people say."

Avery considered that. It eased her mind considerably that Stiabhan vouched for Duncan.

Stiabhan faced the other man. "Why were you watching her? Is it for the same reason as the others?"

Duncan shrugged. "I believe so. We're trying to locate the genuine *sgian dubh* of Accalon. It's said it can cut through both stone and iron like butter. Think how many crooks would love to get their hands on it."

Because her father was a Hunter, Avery didn't question Duncan's sanity. She had seen and heard too much during her lifetime to doubt such a knife existed. Still, "If it's capable of that, why do you need anyone to authenticate it? Just cut something with it. If it works, it's real. If not, it's fake."

"It's not that simple." Duncan frowned.

Before she could respond, Stiabhan spoke up. "Duncan is correct. The *sgian dubh* of Accalon will only work in my world. Duncan has no way to test it in this dimension."

Avery gazed from one to the other. "What age is the knife?"

"A few hundred thousand, give or take ten thousand," Stiabhan said as if he just reported it was only a few weeks old.

"How in the world do you expect me to authenticate something that old?" Avery asked.

"The same way you have before," Duncan said. "You seem to have a sixth sense about these things. I have faith in you. Before seeking you out, I had your previous authentications checked out. You've never been wrong. Not once. I don't see you breaking your record on this."

He seemed sincere in his praise, and Avery felt a warm glow inside. She shouldn't care what Duncan thought of her, but she did.

"You understand I have to see the object. I have to hold it to be able to know for sure if it's authentic," Avery tried to explain what she herself was still learning.

Stiabhan frowned thoughtfully. "You have to hold the objects?"

"Yes." She turned to Duncan. "Do you have the knife in your possession?"

"Uh, not at the moment, no," he answered sheepishly.

"Then why didn't you wait until I finished my assignment?" Avery asked, once more angry. "Just two more days. That's all I needed."

"Avery, I've seen your notes and records, remember? I saw the photographs that you took. You have everything you need to finish and make your report."

Even as angry as she was, she couldn't deny the little frisson of pleasure she derived from the sound of her name on his lips. She had to remind herself that his actions could very well cost her her job.

"No, I don't, you arrogant jerk." Avery surged to her feet to glare down at him. "Over the next two days, I was to get to examine them in person. As in touch them."

Duncan slowly stood. He met her gaze with a considering one of his own. "You're psychometric. Of course! It all makes sense now."

"What are you talking about now? What is psychowhatizit?"

"Psychometric. It means that you are able to glean information from objects by touching them," Duncan explained.

As she was shaking her head in denial, Stiabhan was nodding his in agreement.

"It is a Sidhe talent, sweet. Somewhat rare, but a talent, nonetheless," Stiabhan said. "And if those other men are working for the Dubh Sidhe, it would certainly explain their interest in you."

Avery froze. She *did* have a second talent. A rare one. She couldn't believe it. Her knees felt shaky, so she quickly resumed her seat. Avery shivered violently. She wrapped her arms around her waist and pressed back against the chair.

"Avery, are you ill?" Stiabhan asked with concern.

She looked at him and shook her head. She was fine. Avery smiled. She was more than fine. She was simply having a hard time coming to grips with the fact that she did have more than one talent and wasn't a failure as a Hunter. And she'd had it for several years. Avery just hadn't recognized it.

Avery smiled at Stiabhan. "I'm not a freak after all."

"A freak? Who dared call you such a thing? Why would you even believe it?" Stiabhan sounded affronted and ready to do battle on her behalf.

"No one called me one. I believed I was because I thought that the only talent that I possessed was telepathy. Dad had five. I've known a few other Hunters, too. They all had at least three. How could I not conclude there was something wrong with me?"

Stiabhan reached across, caught her by the arms, and pulled her over onto his lap. He cradled her against his chest. "My poor darling. I wish you had said something. I would have relieved your mind on that score. Even if you did only possess the one, we have been noticing that some females are manifesting later than normal. It doesn't mean they won't develop."

Avery rested her head on his shoulder. It felt nice to be held. Since the death of her father, there was no one to hug her. She hadn't realized how starved for affection she was until that moment.

Stiabhan pushed his feet against the floor, causing the recliner to rock gently. "Perhaps I have not previously made myself clear. I am your family, Avery. Should you ever have a problem, or even a minor concern, I want you to come to me. Call me anytime as you did tonight. Do you understand? You are not alone."

She nodded against his shoulder, fighting tears.

"I need a drink." Duncan sounded disgusted. He headed through the dining room.

Caught up in her own revelation, Avery had totally forgotten that he was there.

With her still in his arms, Stiabhan stood. He set her in the recliner. "I'll be right back."

"Stiabhan, I need to go back to Asheville. I can't afford to lose my job." She couldn't. They had done fine financially until her father's illness. It had eaten up her father's savings, and then what little Avery had. She needed her job.

Stiabhan nodded. "I shall speak with Duncan. Do not worry."

CHAPTER THREE

Three days later, Duncan stood just inside the doorway of Avery's original hotel room, watching as she packed the last of her few belongings. He still didn't understand how he not only agreed to bring Avery back so that she could complete her assignment, but also for him and his lads to act as her bodyguards. She should have been safely tucked up at the safe house while he and a few of his men did some final recognizance on the *sgian dubh* of Accalon.

As Avery slid the strap of her satchel over her head, settling it crossbody, she turned around and smiled at him. "I'm ready to go. My services are now yours."

Duncan's gut clenched in response to that pronouncement. He knew she didn't mean it that way, but his brain went there first, anyway.

This morning, she had her long hair pulled back in a ponytail. She wore little makeup. She didn't need it. Avery looked fresh and all of a about nineteen years old. In a t-shirt made so soft by many washings that it draped lovingly over her breasts, she looked like his every fantasy.

If Duncan touched her, Stiabhan would no doubt take extreme pleasure in causing him immense pain in a way that only a Sidhe could invent.

"So where is this *sgian dubh*?" Avery asked, breaking him out of his lustful thoughts.

Duncan stepped over to take the heavier bag from her. "In the private collection of a man in Houston."

"We're going to Houston? I've never been to Texas."

Avery sounded so excited. He hated to burst her bubble. "We're going to pop in, let you check out the weapons in his collection, grab the correct one, and pop back out. There won't be time for any sightseeing on this trip."

She shrugged. "Okay." She followed him to the door. "When do we do all this popping?"

"Around three AM. It's a different time zone we had to figure in." With a hand to the small of her back, he ushered her from the room and pulled the door closed behind them.

"I suppose you've done this before." Avery didn't try to move away from his touch as they made their way to the elevators. Duncan took immense pleasure in that.

"The lads and I have done it a few times before," he admitted with a grin.

"Why do you call them lads?"

"What?" Duncan was momentarily distracted by the arrival of an elevator. "Oh, it comes from my dada. That's what my brother and I call our grandfather. He was born in Scotland and lived there until he fell in love with my American Grandmother. She was on vacation with some friends at the time." Once he ushered her into the empty elevator, he pressed the button for the lobby.

Fifteen minutes later, they were in his Dodge Charger, headed away from Asheville, North Carolina, toward Greenville, South Carolina, back to the safe house.

"Are you feeling okay?" Duncan asked once they were out of the city traffic, and he noticed how quiet she was.

"Yes, I'm fine." She sounded edgy, however. "Are your friends following us?"

"Darach and Nate are. Peter is already at the cabin."

"Peter is the one that I haven't yet met?"

"That's right. Peter's one of our computer geeks, though he looks like he should be in a band. He could easily do it, too. He plays once in a while at Nightshade. It's a nightclub in Caledonia. His voice is wonderful, too, but don't tell him I said so. I don't want his head to swell any more than it already has."

When she didn't respond, Duncan glanced at her.

She noticed the look. "Are they Hunters, too?"

"Yes. Nearly everyone who works for my Dada's company and for The Pendragon Alliance is. Not everyone, but certainly most. Does that bother you?"

Her no was drawn out with uncertainty.

"Avery, Stiabhan wouldn't have put you in our care if he didn't trust us. All of us. You're important to him. He knows each one of us will protect you."

"I'm not worried about any of you hurting me. Or of you not protecting me. Despite us sort of getting off on the wrong foot, I know you are the good guys." Her smile was impish.

Duncan smiled back. "Thank you for that." Somehow, even faint praise was special coming from her.

"Do you... do you think they'll like me?" she asked hesitantly.

Duncan couldn't believe she could even ask. Then he recalled her soaking up affection from Stiabhan like a stray puppy. It was one reason that he'd needed a drink at the time. Now he wondered just how isolated a life she led.

"They'll adore you," he stated with certainty. "How could they not? Probably too much so. If they annoy you, let me know and I'll take care of it."

"Why do you believe this man in Houston has the *sgian dubh* you're seeking?"

Duncan let her change the subject. "Pritch has been trying to track it down for centuries."

"Pritch?"

"Pritchard Cathcart. A powerful Sidhe, and also one of the Old Ones. He also happens to be my ancestor through my dada."

"Is he also my ancestor?" Avery asked.

"No, thank God!" Though as far back as his Sidhe ancestor was in his genetic chain, Duncan figured it wouldn't matter if he was. "Stiabhan claims you as a kinswoman, so you're somehow related to him. And if he and Pritch are related, neither has mentioned it."

"So Pritch finally traced the knife and told you who owns it?"

"No. Pritch lost track of it during the Battle of Bannockburn."

"During?"

Duncan laughed. "Pritch is extremely old. Ancient, truthfully. Anyway, Dada picked up the first genuine lead in the late nineties. We've been slowly getting closer ever since. About five weeks ago, we got the best bit of intel we've had in years and years. After an in-depth investigation, we're as positive as we can be that we're right. That's where you come in. We can't do more than grab a *sgian dubh* and hope for the best. You, on the other hand, can tell us positively which one it is."

"What if I can't?" Avery sounded worried again.

Duncan looked at her. "What do you mean?"

She shrugged. "I mean, what if you and Stiabhan are wrong? What if I'm not psychometric?"

He laughed at that. "Honey, that shouldn't worry you. You are most definitely psychometric. When we reach the cabin, I'll try to prove it to you."

She was quiet for several minutes before she asked, "So you and your friends hunt missing objects?"

"We hunt stolen objects. When we find them, we retrieve them."

"What's the name of your firm?"

"Kerr, Limited," Duncan told her.

"I've heard of The Pendragon Alliance. They've been on the news. I've never heard of Kerr, Limited." Bless her heart, she sounded suspicious again.

"I would be surprised—not to mention a little upset—if you had. We try our best to stay out of the news. We don't have a web page, or any type of social media page. Much to Gavin's and Peter's disappointment, I might add."

"Then how do your clients find you?"

"Word of mouth. And through The Pendragon Alliance," he replied. "They are usually very rich. Which means they have their own ways of finding the help they need."

"But you said your ancestor hunted this *sgian dubh*."

Damn, but she was skeptical. "That's right. The majority of our clients are the Sidhe who hire us to recover items. They pay *extremely* well."

"And they have lots of items stolen from them?"

Duncan laughed. "You might be surprised. We also do retrieval of other things for them. Beings that either escape Tìr-dhàimh or are intentionally released into our dimension. We track them, catch them, and return them to where they belong." He left out that once in a while they had to kill the creatures.

"Things? Do I want to know what these things are?"

"I doubt it. I sincerely hope that you never need to know. But if you do, I'll tell you." Out of the corner of his eye, he saw her nod.

She was quiet for the rest of the drive to the safe house. Duncan left her to her own thoughts. He'd given her enough to think about. He figured she needed the time to assimilate.

WHEN THEY WENT UP THE steps to the covered deck of the safe house, they found a blond man stretched out on a lounger, poking away at a tablet. He surged to his feet the minute he saw them.

Avery froze.

Duncan's arm came around her waist and urged her forward as he made the introductions. "Avery, this is Peter Carey. Peter, Avery Beaton."

The guy looked to be about her age. He had shaggy brown hair and bright green eyes. He smiled, displaying a pair of adorable dimples. While holding the tablet in his left hand, he extended his right hand.

"My pleasure, Ms. Beaton."

Avery smiled as she shook his hand. She couldn't help it. He reminded her of an over-anxious puppy. "The pleasure is mine."

"I doubt that," Duncan murmured from beside her. "Let go of her hand so I can get her inside and get her settled."

Peter winked at her, but he released her hand.

Avery winked back, eliciting a laugh.

They entered through a door with a glass panel in the top half. The smell of bacon and baking chocolate filled the air. A tall, muscled black man was just pulling a pan of brownies from the wall oven. He turned and set the pan on a center island topped with some type of stone. Finished, he looked up and smiled a greeting.

"Avery," Duncan spoke up. "This is Darach Shanley. Darach, this is Avery."

"I'm sure he knows who I am since he was following me. It's nice to actually meet you." Avery shook his hand.

He smiled down at her, his eyes a warm brown and full of humor. "It's a pleasure."

Avery drew her hand back just as the other of the two men who had been tailing her made an appearance through the archway from the living room.

"It's much easier to guard you when you're not frightened of us." He held out his hand. "I'm Nate Morogh."

Avery shook his hand. "I didn't realize that you *were* guarding me. Silly me, I thought you were crazy stalkers. I was sure you didn't want me to escape before your boss got what he wanted from me."

Nate grinned at Duncan, who was standing just behind her right shoulder. "She doesn't pull any punches, does she?"

"She does seem to like to scold if you're doing something she doesn't approve of," Duncan said.

Avery shot him a look over her shoulder. "I do not scold."

He raised one dark eyebrow at her. "This last fella is Aaron Donnally. He'll be going with us tonight so Peter can stay here and be our liaison."

She and Aaron smiled and nodded greetings.

A second later, he said, "Let me show you to your room so that you can get settled."

Avery followed Duncan through the dining room and living room to a hallway. He pointed to a closed door on the right. "That leads to the basement. The door to the left is the bathroom. This second door on the left is your room. I'll be right across the hall. Nate and Darach are upstairs, and Peter's on the lower level."

Avery followed him into a simple, sparse bedroom. It had a double bed, two nightstands, and a short dresser.

Duncan put her bags on the foot of the bed. Turning, he treated her to an ornery, sexy grin. "If you need anything, and I mean anything, just let me know."

Avery grinned back. "My wish is your command?"

His green eyes flashed. "It could be, darlin'. It surely could be."

Avery was getting out of her depth. "I believe you're a tease, Duncan Kerr."

"Baby, I'm not teasing. I'm seriously interested in you. I readily and wholeheartedly admit that."

Avery nervously wet her lips. She stopped when she saw his gaze zero in on her mouth. He looked very focused.

His eyes lifted to hers. "If you don't want me to kiss you, Avery, you'd better tell me to leave. Now."

Her throat went dry, and her heart rate increased. She swallowed. Oh, how she wanted him to kiss her. But at the same time, she was afraid of where it might lead. "Perhaps it might be best if you leave."

Duncan stared at her for a few seconds. He took a deep breath and let it out slowly. "Darach will have lunch ready in about thirty minutes."

"I'll be there."

He raked a heated glance over her, causing little butterflies to come to life in her midsection. With a last nod, he left.

"YOU LOOK OUT OF SORTS," Nate observed with a grin when Duncan rejoined them in the kitchen.

"Shut up." Duncan took the beer that Darach handed him.

"You weren't gone long. Wouldn't she let you help her with...something?" Nate waggled his eyebrows.

"Shut up, Nate." Duncan knew his friend teased. There was something different about Avery, however. She wasn't the type of woman that a man joked about. "She's not like that."

If Nate grinned any wider, he was going to injure himself. "No, she's not. Avery's a lady. Glad to know that you realize it, too. I'd hate to have Stiabhan turn you into a pustule on a warthog's butt because you couldn't keep your hands off his cousin."

"He's going to do worse than that if we let something happen to her," Peter spoke up. He took a drink from his bottle of beer.

Duncan looked from Nate to Peter. "No one was tailing me after you got rid of Frick and Frack's car?"

Peter shook his head. "There wasn't any kind of bug in your car either. I checked. There were two trackers on Avery's car. They've been disabled."

"It's looking more and more like these guys are either Sidhe themselves or are working for them. Either way, they will be able to track her if they want." Nate added.

"And someone with her talent... the Dubh Sidhe are going to be tripping over themselves to get her," Darach stated what Duncan already knew, but was trying not to think about.

Duncan knew they were right. Hearing his fears stated out loud only made him hate it more. "Hopefully tonight we'll put one artifact out of their reach."

"There are hundreds of missing and stolen Sidhe relics. We can't keep Avery under wraps until each and every one of them is found," Darach said.

"Why not? We relocate her to Caledonia from wherever she currently lives. It's worked for Max, Quinn, and Kayne and their wives up in West Virginia. And for Gage and Felicity here. And Felicity's a Pure." Duncan referred to a person with no Sidhe blood. If it worked for them, he saw no reason that it couldn't work for Avery.

Providing he could get her to agree.

"Gonna marry her?" Peter asked, his dimples flashing.

"I've just met her," Duncan protested, but his heart began to pound. "Besides, I'm not ready to get married. Why do I have to marry her to get her to move to a safer place?"

Nate canted one hip against a counter. Crossing his arms over his chest, he studied Duncan. "Max readily admits to love at first sight."

Darach looked at Nate. "He said he fell in love with Ceri the moment he heard her voice over the phone. Remember?"

Nate nodded. "You're right."

"Quinn knew Olivia was his the moment he heard her sing," Peter added.

"I don't hear any of you mentioning Gage and Felicity. Why is that?" Duncan asked.

"Because he was slow on the uptake. I'm still hoping you'll be one of the quicker ones." Nate shook his head.

Duncan wasn't going to ask what Nate meant. He knew, but he didn't want to hear it.

"You sure look struck by cupid's dart to me," Peter commented.

"I think she's pretty, sure. Maybe I'm attracted to her, but that doesn't mean that I want to marry her." That was all Duncan was willing to admit.

"Pretty? She's gorgeous. Those dark brown eyes. Creamy skin. All that thick dark hair." Nate grinned at him.

Duncan shot him an irritated glance. "Drop it. You're already married. We need to talk about tonight."

"There's not much more to say on that," Darach said. "We pop in, hope Avery can grab the right knife, and we pop back here and turn it over to Pritch."

"Avery can't translocate. One of us will have to take her," Duncan told them.

"One of *us*? You expect us to believe you're not going to take her yourself?" Nate asked in disbelief.

Duncan looked from one to the other. They each grinned like idiots. What if he was attracted to Avery? She wasn't the first woman he'd ever been attracted to. And if there was something that made her stand out from the other women, well, he was nowhere near ready to admit that.

"Fine, I'll take her with me," he said.

Duncan's friends found that hysterically funny.

"I thought you might," Nate managed between guffaws.

"Shut up," Duncan told them without heat. He couldn't stop his own smile.

"Do you think she realizes the danger that she's in?" Peter asked.

Duncan sobered. "No. She's still coming to grips with learning that what she's capable of is a Sidhe talent. I don't think she's even come into her full power." Duncan gave a slight shake of his head. "I don't think she knows enough about the Dubh Sidhe world to understand the ramifications. At least her father seems to have taught her how to keep a low profile."

"That's good, but the rest isn't." Peter frowned.

"When we inform Emrys Pendragon, he'll want to appoint permanent bodyguards," Nate said.

Peter nodded agreement. "We'll guard her for now."

"I agree." Darach's gaze was serious.

Duncan held his hand up as he heard Avery approaching. "So, Darach, what's for lunch?"

"Since I didn't have much time, we're having salads and BLTs."

"Just give me a BL and leave off the T," Nate said.

"Who do you think I am? Your mommy? Your wife?" Darach retorted. "I'll put all the fixins on the table and you can make your own sandwiches."

"How may I help you?" Avery asked, walking in to join them.

"What a refreshing question. Thank you, Avery." Darach frowned at the men, before bestowing a charming smile on her. "If you would help me carry everything to the table, I would appreciate it."

Avery smiled back at him. "I would be glad to."

"I'll set the table," Peter offered suddenly.

"I'll get us each a paper towel." Nate headed for the sink.

Avery took the bowl of salad that Darach passed her. "Paper towel?"

Peter chuckled. "They're Nate's idea of a napkin. I don't know how his wife puts up with him."

Duncan went to the refrigerator. "Avery, what would you like to drink? It looks like all we have to offer is water, tea, or beer."

"Tea would be lovely," she told him.

They soon sat down around the dining room table to eat. Avery said very little, but she seemed to be enjoying their conversation. She laughed at the jokes and funny stories that they told.

After they cleaned up following lunch, Nate and Peter went down into the daylight basement to play pool and let off some pre-job nerves. Since it was Sunday in the fall, the TV was filled with pro football games.

Darach took one recliner. Avery took a seat in one of the remaining two.

"If you'd rather watch something else, let us know," Duncan said. Most women he knew didn't care for football, but Avery grinned up at him.

"I love football. I used to watch it with my dad all the time. The Steelers are my favorite."

"I'm in love. Will you marry me?" Darach asked, a sappy smile on his face.

Duncan flopped down along the length of the couch. It was either that or wipe the lovesick smile from his friend's face. It helped that Avery laughed, not taking the fool seriously.

"You'd soon regret it," Avery said, still smiling. "Most men like to eat, and I can't cook. I can't even boil water."

Duncan groaned. That wouldn't be a negative to Darach. The dude learned to cook from a friend of theirs. A guy, who, among other things, was a gourmet chef.

"No problem, sweetheart," Darach responded. "I know how to cook."

Duncan had enough. "She's not marrying you, Darach. Drop it."

Darach laughed. "I believe Duncan could use a brownie." He looked at Avery. "He needs something to help him get over this surly attitude."

Avery was looking at him as if he'd lost his mind.

Duncan questioned his own sanity. "Keep it up and I'll tell her all about your most embarrassing moment," he threatened.

Darach grinned at him before winking at Avery. "It seems our love was never meant to be, my angel. It will be difficult, but we'll have to settle for being friends."

Duncan wasn't pleased to see Darach hold out his left hand toward Avery. He became more unhappy when she smiled and placed her right hand in it.

"I'm sure we'll be great friends," Avery said.

Duncan grabbed the remote and turned the volume up. He couldn't believe that he was having such a childishly jealous reaction to a woman he barely knew. No wonder the lads were laughing at him. Over the last couple of days, he had apparently gone stark raving mad. Ever since meeting Avery Beaton in person.

He tried to focus on the game. Only when Darach and Avery stopped talking and started watching, was he finally able to do so, too.

During the last quarter, Nate and Peter made an appearance. Peter went to the kitchen and soon returned with bottles of beer for the men, and a glass of iced tea for Avery, and a large bowl of chips and nachos. He put the tray with the items on the coffee table. After grabbing a beer and a handful of chips, he found a seat.

Around six, Darach went into the kitchen. He returned about an hour later with three homemade pizzas, plates, and a roll of paper towels.

They watched football until the last game ended a little after eleven-thirty. In less than four hours, Duncan, Nate, and Darach would take Avery to Houston. He and Nate had decided on three

AM their time to allow for the time difference and give them the best chance of not being discovered.

Soon after the start of the final game, Avery had put the footrest up and reclined. Sometime during the last quarter, she fell asleep. Nate dozed off as well. It wasn't surprising for Nate who could fall asleep anywhere, seemingly at will. The rest of the men let them both sleep. They would get little enough until they returned.

Peter was to remain behind in case they needed a liaison with Kerr Limited.

CHAPTER FOUR

Avery felt as if she'd just fallen asleep when she awakened to Duncan's gentle shakes.

"It's almost time," he said. "Do you have a darker shirt you could wear?"

She considered her limited wardrobe. Avery's trips never lasted long, so she packed few extra clothes. She hadn't expected to need any more. "I have a burgundy t-shirt. Will that do?"

Duncan nodded.

Avery hurried to change. She knew they were on a tight schedule. They had carefully chosen the late time to give them the best chance of accomplishing their goal. Avery didn't want to be the one to mess it up.

She returned second later, having stripped off her light blue t-shirt and replaced it with the wine-colored one. Avery froze uncertainly upon noticing all four men staring at her. She looked down at her clothing, saw nothing wrong, and looked back up. With her hands held out to her sides, she asked. "Is there something wrong?"

"No, not at all," Duncan spoke up as the others shook their heads.

"You look good in red," Darach stated.

"Very good," Peter agreed.

Nate nodded.

Avery knew she was blushing, but she didn't care. She was too pleased with their compliments. "Thank you."

Stepping over to her, Duncan took hold of her right hand, linking their fingers. "Peter, we'll see you when we see you."

Peter nodded.

Even though Duncan had already translocated Avery twice when he'd kidnapped her, it made her uncomfortable. Her dad had been capable of translocation, too, but he'd never taken her with him. Avery touched Duncan's face with her free hand.

Duncan smiled down at her. "I'm not going to let go of your hand, Avery."

"But if it happens?" She persisted, needing to know.

"You'll still travel with me. I don't have to be touching you to bring you along," Duncan explained. "You won't get lost or dropped along the way, if that's what's worrying you. When we leave, you'll be with me. When we arrive, you'll still be with me. Okay? Are you ready?"

Avery didn't think so, but it was too late to change her mind. She nodded. The fee they were paying her was more than she made in three years. That made her committed to trying to identify the *sgian dubh* for them. After that, she would return to her nice, boring life.

A life without a tall, dark-haired, drop-dead gorgeous hunk in it.

Duncan squeezed her hand in reassurance.

In the blink of her eyes, Avery was in a room shadowed in darkness. Slices of light glowed through the center openings of two pairs of drapes over two windows on her right. As Avery's eyes adjusted, she could make out furnishings.

Nate, Darach, Aaron, and Duncan each turned on small, narrow-beamed flashlights. They cautiously played them around the room.

"Can you sense the location?" Nate asked.

Avery rolled her eyes, even if he couldn't see it in the darkness. "I'm not a scent hound. We'll have to find it the old-fashioned way, by searching."

"Sorry," Nate apologized, his teeth flashing in the darkness. "I was hoping you could lead us right to it." He sobered. "I got a bad feeling."

Appeased, Avery admitted, "I wish I could, too. We could get out of here a lot faster."

"I don't see any weapons," Darach stated.

"He would have a safe room. Someplace with security. We need to locate it," Nate said.

Avery liked it less and less. She was terrified they would get caught. Being arrested for breaking-and-entering, not to mention theft, would not look good on her resume.

"We need to find where he keeps them," Duncan said. "We don't have all night."

"Locked door here." Darach drew their attention to a heavily paneled door in the side wall. Putting his flashlight in his mouth, he placed both hands flat on the door, one over the lock. A couple of seconds later, he turned the knob and opened the door. Darach removed the flashlight from his mouth and shined it around inside. "Got it."

Avery's knees went weak with relief. It shouldn't take long now, and they'd be able to leave.

"Ready?" Duncan asked.

Avery nodded. "Let's get this over with."

Duncan still held her hand. Or she held his. Avery wasn't sure which. She didn't care as long as he didn't let go.

Going into the room behind Darach, Duncan tugged her along in his wake. Darach stepped around a glass display case and moved back near the door to give them space.

The room was small and narrow with the one lighted display case down the middle. On one wall hung all manner of swords. Along the shortest wall, guns, and rifles appearing to be from around the Civil War era were displayed. The third wall held battle axes, pikes, spears, and all other manner of long-handled battle weapons from around the twelfth to the fourteenth centuries. The central display stored the smaller knives, including six *sgian dubhs*.

As the feeling of the room began to penetrate through her fear, Avery frowned. Something was off. It was wrong. Pulling Duncan along with her, Avery moved to the nearest wall. She touched an English broadsword. Frowning, she reached out to a Scottish Claymore. It was the same. Nothing.

"What is it?" Nate asked, noticing her reaction.

"What's wrong?" Duncan asked simultaneously.

"These weapons. They're all wrong," Avery told them. "They're not old. Not at all. They're modern reproductions. Every one of them. Not a single weapon in this room is over twenty years old."

"What?" Darach asked in disbelief. "You're sure?"

"Very," Avery assured him.

"Out! Now!" Duncan no longer tempered his voice. "Get out! It's a trap."

Nate, nearest the door, spun around and back to the main room.

Darach headed for the door from his side of the case. Aaron followed behind. On the other side, Duncan did too, pulling Avery along beside him. Darach barely made it through the door when it slammed shut, leaving the three inside.

"Duncan!" Nate shouted from the opposite side of the door.

"Go home!" Duncan shouted back. "Hurry. If we don't show up in ten minutes, contact Pritch." Looking around the room, he told Avery. "We can't translocate out."

Avery held onto his hand with both of hers. As a bright light filled the room, she moved closer to him.

"Get a weapon," Duncan urged Aaron as he grabbed a broadsword from the nearest wall. "Hold on to me, Avery."

Avery grabbed a dagger. "Believe me, I have no plans to let go. But can you use that if I'm holding on to you?" She hoped the answer was yes, because she needed to touch Duncan. However, she also didn't want to hinder him in a fight.

"Yes, I can, so hold on."

The light became so bright it blinded her. Avery turned her face into the back of Duncan's left shoulder.

The air seemed to vibrate. To Avery, it was a similar feeling to that when Duncan translocated her, only more intensely. This was so strong it made the hair on her arms stand up.

It also made her sickeningly dizzy. Avery leaned heavily on Duncan.

"My bait seems to have caught three mice. I should have expected the lion cub to be guarding the treasure."

It was a man's voice. Deep, gruff, and smug.

"I could have done without ever seeing you again," Duncan responded. "Where are we?"

"Such rudeness, cub," the unknown—at least to Avery—male admonished sharply. "Show the lass to a seat before she faints."

Avery still hadn't managed to open her eyes. The bright light disappeared. The dizziness and resulting nausea did not. She felt Duncan turn as Aaron moved in behind her.

"Let go," Duncan whispered.

Avery released him at once. The moment she did, his arm came around her waist to pull her against his side. Avery wouldn't fall now, even if she did pass out. Which she had no intention of doing.

"We're fine. What do you want, Omaon?"

"Àrdrìgh Omaon to you, cub. You're a smart lad. In spite of your lineage. You already know, I am sure, but for the benefit of your companions, I will tell you. I want the lass, of course. I have been informed of her ability, and I have use of it."

Avery opened her eyes a slit. She turned her head just enough to take a peek at their captor. He was a large man, though several inches shorter than Duncan. He had straight, shoulder-length, light reddish brown hair showing signs of graying. The top part pulled back and somehow fastened behind his head. Sharp blue eyes watched Duncan with a mixture of amusement and threat. A short beard and mustache covered the lower portion of his face. He was heavyset, mostly from muscle but starting to go to fat. A leather jerkin studded with metal covered a forest-green shirt. Dark brown trousers were tucked into knee-high, brown leather boots.

He looked as if he'd stepped out of the Middle Ages.

Rather like Duncan might if he wasn't wearing modern clothing.

"Avery, can you hear me?"

She tried not to jump at the sound of Duncan's voice inside her head, but she didn't know if she'd succeeded. *"Yes."*

"Do not let him know what you're capable of. Right now, he's going by word of mouth. You're going to have to bluff your way. Convince him you can't do what he's been told you can."

That was easier said than done. Duncan had never seen her when she touched an artifact. It was the reason she always made it a condition that the client leave her alone with the item. *"I don't think it's going to be possible. When I touch an artifact, I sort of zone out for a moment or two."*

"Form all the plans you want, cub. You will not fool me. I know the lass has the ability to discern a true object from a fake one. You are aware that many of our weapons and special items have been stolen. I want them back."

"They're not yours. Avery can't help you find any of them, even if they were."

Avery dropped her forehead against the soft material of Duncan's t-shirt. The three of them were in the middle of a nightmare.

"You have no say in the matter, Duncan. If you want to remain with her, you will behave. Give me problems and I have no compunction about killing you," the king threatened.

Avery didn't care that she'd known Duncan for less than a week. She didn't care if she was being forward. She slid her arms around Duncan's waist and held on. When one was terrified, extreme measures were allowed. Avery didn't raise her head or turn to look at their abductor when she made a threat of her own. "You harm them at all, and I won't help you with anything. You'll be right where you are now."

Duncan stiffened. Avery tilted her head back to look up at him. He gave an imperceptible shake of his head and frowned at her.

The king laughed. "The kitten has claws. She thinks to protect the lion cub. Does she not know lions—even cubs—eat kittens? It seems she cares for you, young Duncan."

"I would hope so," Duncan replied. "She's my wife."

It was a good thing they were holding on to each other so tightly. Without it, Avery would be sitting in a heap on the floor.

"Go with it, Avery. Hopefully, it will keep them from separating us."

"Really? It must have happened recently. Very recently," the king's voice dripped skepticism.

"Two days ago," Duncan replied, without missing a beat. "A quiet Sidhe ceremony. You've forced a temporary postponement of our Cruinne one."

Avery knew enough words to recognize the Sidhe word for the human dimension.

"Who married you?" The king stared at her.

"Tell him Stiabhan," Duncan instructed.

Avery turned her upper body to face the king. "Stiabhan."

The king's eyes narrowed to slits. "He is your ancestor?"

"No. He's related to my ancestor. Stiabhan is a cousin or an uncle." Avery felt his question was to test her.

Omaon turned back to Duncan. "The old lion must be pleased that one of his cubs has wed. He now has the potential for great-grandchildren. It is sad he will never get the chance to see them. Your lovely wife will not be leaving Tìr-dhàimh."

"Continue to believe that, Omaon," Duncan said.

The older man's eyes narrowed once more. This time in anger. He jerked his head toward Aaron. "Who is your companion?"

"I'm Avery's cousin," Aaron lied.

Why not? Avery thought.

"None of you will leave here, Duncan. Not unless I have you tossed over the balustrade into the sea. In case that is unclear, none of you will leave unless you are dead."

"We'll see," Duncan stated.

The man's face turned purple with rage. "I am king."

"You're not my king," Duncan reminded him.

Avery dug her fingernails into Duncan's back. *"Please, don't goad him."*

"There is only one way back to the mainland. One which is well guarded. Nor is there a tairseach anywhere near."

"We're supposed to trust your word on that?" Aaron asked.

The king suddenly smiled. It chilled Avery's blood as he motioned with his hand.

Avery felt a whoosh of air at her back. She heard a noise she couldn't identify. Liquid spattered her back as Aaron's head bounced off her left shoulder and hit the floor. Avery cried out in horror. As she felt Aaron's body begin to fall against her, Duncan spun her away. One hand at the back of her head pressed her face into his chest. She shook violently, Avery knew she couldn't stand without Duncan's support.

"You rat bastard," Duncan growled.

"You required a lesson of my seriousness."

"There was no need to kill him," Duncan said.

Avery had never fainted in her life, but she feared she might. Her brain seemed to be trying to float free of her skull. If she shook any more violently, she feared she would break a bone.

"There was every need. You and your wife now understand I will not be gainsaid. If she does not aid me, what just happened could easily be your fate, cub."

Avery couldn't contain her whimper.

Omaon walked away. "Allow me to show you your new home."

Duncan turned her toward the tall door their captor walked toward. He kept his body between her and the horror behind them.

They were in a circular room, furnished with a table for four. Six large chairs sat placed around a fireplace in a semicircle.

Omaon headed for the door in the center of the circular wall. He opened it to a strong, chilly sea breeze and stepped outside.

Duncan caught her right hand. *"Do not look back. Don't look down."*

Avery shuddered, fighting a wave of nausea.

Duncan followed the king, and Avery stuck as close to him as she could. They walked out onto a balcony about ten feet across. It circled around the building like a wrap-around porch. As they stepped away from the wall, the wind intensified.

Suddenly, Avery understood why Omaon wasn't concerned about them escaping. She felt as if she was flying. The circular balcony projected out over the edge of a rocky promontory at least seventy feet above the roiling sea. If she suffered from vertigo, this place would cause a major attack. There was a narrow bay to their left, and a wider but shallower one to their right. Before them was water as far as the eye could see.

Cold air consistently buffeted them. Avery tugged free of Duncan's hand so she could wrap her arms around herself. Her short-sleeved t-shirt was no match for the wind.

"Look around you, Duncan," Omaon invited. "I believe you will admit that I have chosen a perfect place for you to be contained. This is now your home. You will live here. So will your wife between the times I require her assistance. Behave, cub, and you may remain. Cause problems and you will end as your friend."

Avery looked at Duncan with concern. He hurt over the murder of his friend, and he was angry. If he challenged Omaon, however, the king would no doubt toss him over the balustrade without a second thought. Avery placed her hand on his forearm. "Please, Duncan. I need you."

Angry green eyes turned on her. Avery met them with pleading ones. Slowly, the anger receded. Reaching out, Duncan cupped the back of her neck with his left hand. He used it to draw her closer to his side, where he encircled her with his arm.

Duncan was a healthy male. He threw off heat like a furnace. Between the sea breeze that seemed to get colder by the moment and the shock of having someone she knew murdered right beside her, she was thankful he was. Avery needed all the heat she could get. She wondered if she would ever get warm again. She snuggled against him.

Duncan turned back toward the building. Despite her trying to dig in her heels, he ushered her back into the room they'd just left. He must have known that they had removed Aaron's body. Avery looked around in trepidation. Her horrified gaze caught on a pool of congealing blood and blood spatter. Black spots danced before her eyes. She barely heard their captor enter behind them and close the door.

Putting his hand against her cheek, Duncan pressed her face against his chest once more. "I trust you have appropriate clothing for us. Or do you believe Avery can work if she's frozen to death?"

The king snapped his fingers.

Avery jumped as a fire burst to life in the fireplace.

"Clothes for Avery are waiting upstairs in the bedroom. Some will be sent for you. If you remember, I was not expecting you," Omaon reminded them.

"I can wait."

Avery heard the anger in Duncan's voice.

"I shall leave you to settle in. In two days' time, I shall return to collect Avery for her first mission."

She squeezed Duncan's waist as she felt him stiffen. *"Duncan?"*

"Don't rush on our account." Duncan couldn't seem to stop needling their captor.

This time, the king didn't take the bait. Omaon gave that wintry smile once more. "Plot and plan all you wish, cub. You will not escape." With a nod to her, he left through the inner doorway.

Avery took a deep breath. Even with the king gone, she couldn't stop shaking. Aaron was dead. Omaon had him murdered. She had never been around anyone so cold-bloodedly evil. He hated Duncan. So far, the king hadn't harmed him, but how long would that last?

A couple of seconds after the king left, Duncan let go of her hand. "Don't move." He headed for the inner door.

Avery ignored his directive and followed him.

He paused long enough to take her hand and bring her to his side. "I just want a look at the rest of our prison." He cautiously opened the door.

They entered a large rectangular room more lavishly furnished than the round tower room. Thick carpets covered the stone floor and heavy drapes hung over the windows. The furniture, several chairs and two couches, was upholstered in soft materials. In the fireplace, a fire burned, heating the room. A staircase against one wall led up. Beneath it, more stairs went down. In the outer walls straight opposite each other were two sets of floor-to-ceiling arched windows. Through partially open drapes, Avery could see the water and across to the far sides of both bays.

Duncan headed for the door straight across from the one they'd come through. Avery stayed on his heels. When he opened it, they walked out onto a terrace which doubled as the roof of another portion of the fortress. When looking toward the mainland, they had a clear view of the connection to the narrow rock outcrop the small stone fortress perched on. They currently stood on the second floor.

Stretching across the narrow band of land that led to the mainland was a stone wall about four stories tall with three guard towers, one at each end and one in the middle. As Omaon informed them, it was well guarded.

"Crap!" Duncan's eyes narrowed. He slowly surveyed their surroundings. After several minutes, he turned to her. "You shouldn't have followed me out here. You're freezing." He led her back inside the building.

"Where are we?" she asked.

"Tìr-dhàimh, or less formally, the Realm." Duncan closed the door behind them.

A violent shiver wracked Avery. "Are you telling me we're no longer on Earth?"

Duncan rolled his head from side to side, stretching his neck muscles. "Yes, and no. From what we understand—and believe me, that's not much—it's sort of an alternate dimension."

"Can you translocate us home?" Avery asked hopefully, though she feared she knew the answer.

"No, honey. Only a powerful Sidhe can translocate out of the Realm. For the moment, we are well and truly trapped. We need to escape and locate a tairseach." Duncan used the name given to the stone circles through which Halflings and Sidhe could move from place to place. His hands cupped her shoulders as he bent to look directly into her eyes. "I know you're scared, but I promise you, I will get you home."

Scared was woefully inadequate to describe what Avery felt. Dark, breath-stealing terror seemed more appropriate. However, Duncan already had enough pressure on him. "I know you will." Avery tried to give him what she hoped was a confident smile.

It wasn't Duncan's fault they were trapped. It was hers. She was the reason Aaron was dead.

"Hey, don't faint on me, sugar. Let's go upstairs. Maybe you can get a hot bath and then get into something warm."

Avery allowed him to lead her upstairs. She would love to change clothes. Especially if she could get a shower. She tried not to think about it because she feared she would be ill. Avery knew some of Aaron's blood was on her back. The thought of it was almost more than she could bear.

She hadn't known Aaron long. She didn't need to do so. He was sweet and funny, and like her, he hated the taste of zucchini. He enjoyed teasing his buddies, and now he was gone. His life snuffed out by an evil bastard who wanted to make a point and show his power.

"Don't think about it, Avery." Duncan seemed to once more read her mind. "There's nothing either of us could have done."

Rationally, Avery understood. It didn't make Aaron's death easier to accept.

Her greatest fear was that on Omaon's whim, the same thing could happen to Duncan. It was horrifying. Avery was glad Duncan held her hand. As long as they touched, she could keep the fear at a manageable level.

The stairs led to the third floor of the round tower. A huge bed, its frame carved into a bas relief of seashells, was near a wall that separated the bedroom from another room. On each side of the bed was a small table. Next out on each side was a large wardrobe. The other three quarters of the tower walls were studded with at least a dozen six-feet tall by four-feet wide windows.

Releasing her hand, Duncan walked to the nearest wardrobe and peered inside. It evidently didn't have what he wanted because he shut the door and crossed the room to the far one. Opening it, he looked inside.

"This will do." Duncan opened the wardrobe doors wide so she could see it was stuffed with women's clothing.

Joining him, Avery looked over the contents. Most appeared to be gowns, but there were also shirts that looked to be thigh length, and trousers in a soft, fluid material.

"Do you think they'll fit?" Avery asked, reaching out to touch a pair of trousers.

"They'll fit," Duncan confirmed. "Omaon is nothing if not thorough. I imagine he knows everything about you there is to know."

"I don't like the sound of that." Guilt ate away at her. She looked up at Duncan. "The king wants *me*. I mean, he wants what he thinks I can do. It's my fault we're here. You and Aaron wouldn't have been here if not for me."

"Hush." Duncan kissed her to stop her from berating herself. "None of this is your fault. I brought you into this. My company fell for the bad intel. This is all Omaon's fault for being a greedy, evil bastard. I should have recognized sooner that it was a trap. When we see Stiabhan again, he's going to kill me for not taking better care of you." He winced at his poor word choice.

"Taking care of me isn't your job," Avery argued.

Duncan gave her a get-real look. "Of course it is."

Avery disagreed by shaking her head. “No, it’s not. But there’s no point arguing with you, is there?”

“None.” He looked at her seriously. “There should be a bathroom in the room behind the head of the bed. You should be able to get a bath, or at least a shower. Change into something warmer. I’ll wait in the stairwell. Unless you want me to stay.”

Avery didn’t want to be a coward, but she didn’t want to be too far away from Duncan. “I don’t mind if you stay here in the bedroom.”

Duncan nodded, his gaze gentle. “I’m not going to leave you alone, Avery. Pick out some clothes and get cleaned up. I’ll be here when you’re done.” Walking over to the stairs, he sat on the top step.

Avery looked at him for a minute before turning her attention to the clothing. Gowns were out. She focused on the tunics and trousers. Obviously, Duncan wouldn’t stop looking for a means of escape. She planned to be ready when he found one. Trousers were definitely the better choice.

Considering the weather and the terrain she’d seen, she picked out dark gray slacks and a thigh-length gray-green tunic. Avery didn’t keep up with fashion or material, so she didn’t know what the material was, but it was soft and thick, and felt as if it would be warm. They reminded her of a well-worn pair of sweats.

On the bottom of the wardrobe were several pairs of shoes and one pair of sturdy ankle boots. She then looked into the drawer across the base where she found socks. Choosing a pair of thick, soft ones, she took them and picked up the boots.

Taking everything, she went behind the bed and found the door in the wall. It led to a small room that resembled a modern bathroom. Against a wall was a stone basin. Across from the door was a stone stall. Avery hoped it was a shower, because nothing she saw looked in any way like a bathtub.

Avery quickly removed her clothes while she avoided looking at them. She rolled her t-shirt and jeans into a wad and put them on the floor in the corner. She put her sneakers on top, soles up.

When Avery stepped into the stone cubical, the water began to automatically shower down on her. It was like stepping into a warm rain. A carved-out niche in the wall held a fresh bar of soap. Not knowing how much time she had, Avery washed as fast as she could. Including her hair.

When Duncan called, she was putting on the last of her clothing, "Hurry, Avery. I hear movement below."

"I'm coming." Drying off, Avery braided her wet hair and dressed in the new clothing.

"Avery," Duncan called in warning.

"Coming." She tied the laces on her second boot and hurried into the bedroom.

Duncan, standing two steps down, glanced at her. He nodded his approval. When she reached him, he caught hold of her hand before descending the stairs.

No one was in the large room, but they heard noises from the tower room beyond. Avery followed Duncan as he crossed to the door. He stepped into the room and stopped.

Avery stopped behind him. She was afraid to look. If she saw any of Aaron's blood, she feared she would lose it. When Duncan stepped forward, she had no choice, as he tugged her along.

Thankfully, there was no sign of blood that she could see. She was glad, but simultaneously horrified that nothing remained to give evidence of Aaron ever existing.

A woman was setting out plates, cups, utensils, a pitcher, and a large bowl of food from the tray she carried them in on. She turned at the sound of their approach.

The woman was thin with little shape. Brown hair reached to just above her hips. Because of the color of her hair, the woman's age surprised Avery. The lines on her face placed her somewhere in her seventies. Over an ankle-length dress of light brown, she wore a floor-length, long-sleeved coatdress of deep russet. Her hair was parted in the middle, pulled severely back, and fastened at the base of her skull.

She lifted her lips into a smile, no doubt meant to be welcoming. Except there was no welcome in her eyes. They were alive with cunning. The same shade of blue as the king's. All of which put Avery on edge.

"I've brought something for you to eat. My brother wants you to be comfortable during your stay here," she said.

Avery clamped her mouth shut to keep it from dropping open. The woman pretended they were on some sort of vacation.

"Your brother? Omaon?" Duncan asked.

Anger flashed so briefly in the woman's eyes that Avery couldn't swear she saw it. But the uneasy feeling wouldn't leave.

When the woman answered, her voice was soft and gentle. "That is correct. Àrdrìgh Omaon is my brother."

"And you are?" Duncan asked.

"I am Dealla Heregeat." She eyed Duncan up and down, an appreciative gleam in her eyes.

Avery couldn't blame her for that. Duncan was a beautiful sight to behold, but this woman's perusal was creepy. It was predatory, arousing all of Avery's protective instincts.

"You are Angus' grandson, are you not?" Dealla asked.

Duncan's reply was a curt nod.

"I met him years ago when he was about your age. He, too, was a find specimen of man. How is Angus?"

"We aren't friends, woman. I have no intention of exchanging pleasantries with you and pretending your brother isn't holding us against our will." Duncan's layered his response with anger and impatience.

Anger definitely flared in Dealla's eyes at that. "It is a shame Angus was not able to teach you manners. You may have inherited his fine features, but nothing else."

Duncan smiled coolly, letting her know his views of her opinion. Through their linked fingers, Avery felt his tension.

Dealla's gaze swung from Duncan to her.

Avery returned her look squarely, but said nothing. There was nothing for her to say. Avery was less eager to converse with the woman than Duncan.

After a couple of awkward moments of silence, Dealla spoke. "I will leave you to your repast. Should you require anything further, tell one of the guards in the room below the solar." With that, she left through the door they had just come through.

Duncan released her hand. Walking over to the table, he inspected the food in the bowl before pouring liquid from the pitcher into both goblets. He pulled out a chair before looking at her. "Aren't you hungry?"

Avery pointed to the food. "Are you serious? Do you honestly think we should eat that?"

Duncan grinned. "It's safe. I promise. Omaon wants you very much alive and able to help him. He won't poison you. That would defeat his purpose."

"What about poisoning you?"

"Oh, he'd love to do that. No doubt. But the food is in one bowl. He can't very well poison the cups or utensils. There's no way to guarantee which ones you'll use. Omaon won't chance killing you just to do away with me."

"What about his sister? She doesn't seem to like me. And except for thinking you're a stud muffin, I think she hates your guts."

Duncan's eyes widened a moment before he threw back his head and laughed. "Where do you get the idea that Dealla thinks I'm a—what did you call me—a stud muffin?"

Avery's cheeks heated. "Because the woman looked at you like she'd love to jump your bones. But then you got rude and ticked her off."

Duncan sat in the seat he'd pulled out. "The woman's Dubh Sidhe. She's an evil, cold-blooded bitch."

"Then making her angry seems like a foolish chance to take."

"She won't kill me, Avery. As much as she might like to, Dealla has the hots for my grandda. She would find herself very much out of favor if she murdered me."

Relaxing slightly, she took the chair opposite Duncan. "Is that why the king calls you cub? Because he knows your grandfather?"

"That and simply to pi—make me mad." He scooped some food from the bowl and dropped it onto her plate. He waved his spoon at it after he'd served his own and taken a taste. "This is good. I don't know what it is, but it tastes a lot like buttered grits."

Avery picked up her spoon and stirred the food around on her plate. "You're not frightened?"

Duncan reached across the table and covered her wrist with his hand. "Angry as hell, yes. Frightened? Not much. You don't need to be either. I'm not going to let anything happen to you."

"You're just one man, Duncan. Look what happened to Aaron. As you said, neither of us could have stopped it. While I appreciate the gesture, I don't want you putting yourself at risk because of me."

"It's not a gesture, Avery. It's a vow. One I mean to keep."

Avery shook her head. "I'm a big girl. Not some fragile flower that needs protecting. I've been taking care of myself for several years."

Duncan's gaze turned thoughtful. "When did your father die?"

"About five years ago."

"When did Stiabhan show up?"

"A little over a year ago. Why? What does that have to do with anything?" Avery had a hard time concentrating since he began rubbing his thumb slowly back and forth over the pulse point of her wrist. Who would have thought it was an erogenous zone? His simple touch was making other parts of her anatomy come to attention.

Duncan suddenly smiled. A pleased smile. A smile filled with heat and sexual prowess. He pressed his fingers tighter against her wrist. "Your heart rate has increased." There was satisfaction in his voice.

Avery didn't want him to realize he was the cause. Duncan was arrogant enough as it was. "Of course it is. These people terrify me."

His smile turned even more sexy. "You have the same effect on me."

While she was still trying to absorb that amazing statement, Duncan released her wrist, cupped the back of her neck, and leaned across the table to kiss her. Avery's nerve endings instantly went into sensory overload. Her brain short-circuited. The first thrust of his tongue into her mouth froze her. Then, as the deep kisses continued, the wonder of them overcame her shyness. She began kissing him back, giving herself up to everything Duncan offered.

And he offered a lot.

Later, when he pulled back, they were both out of breath. Caressing her cheek, he gently pressed the other against his shoulder.

It was only then that Avery realized she was no longer sitting in her chair. Startled by her new location, she pulled back further. "How did I end up in your lap?"

That too-arrogant grin appeared. "Magnetism."

"Duncan, I can't... I mean... I don't think it's a good idea for us to... um..." Avery waved her right hand in the air as if that would make her crazy rambling make sense.

"To what? Kiss? Have sex?"

Avery got out of his lap as if he was on fire. She returned to her own seat, once more putting the table between them. "Any of it. All of it." Her ability to articulate her thoughts clearly had obviously deserted her.

For Duncan, it would no question be a lark. Undoubtedly, she was only the latest in a long line of female conquests. Avery wished she could be carefree about sex. Especially when the man in question was Duncan. Unfortunately, she couldn't. She was naturally shy. Intimate relationships had always been difficult for her. And the only one she managed hadn't ended well.

Since her father's death, Avery became even more of a recluse. It was one of the reasons she liked her job. She didn't come into contact with that many people. At least not in person.

She'd certainly never encountered anyone like Duncan before.

Avery barely knew him, and she was already half in love with him. She couldn't take that next step and make love with him without becoming emotionally invested. It would break her heart if it meant nothing to him except another notch in his belt or whatever he put notches in. Avery simply didn't feel brave enough to risk it.

"Avery, have you ever made love?" he asked gently.

She choked on the swallow of the drink she'd taken. She waved him off when he started to come to her aid. She finally managed to say, "Of course I have. I've been in relationships." Well, only one that counted, but he didn't need to know everything.

For once, she shocked him. "Seriously?"

Avery frowned, feeling insulted. "I went to college. I didn't spend all my time studying. Why? Don't you think some guy could find me attractive enough to have sex with?" Avery's gut clinched. Now why had she asked him that?

"I can see any number of men wanting to have sex with you. It's too easy to envision. With your curves and that long, thick hair, I would find it hard to believe some man hadn't taken you to bed. What I find unbelievable is that you gave in. But even more, why the hell the man you trusted didn't hang on to you with everything he had?"

"I had a short-term relationship during college. It just didn't last once we graduated. Neither did the relationship with the guy I dated first." Avery clamped her mouth shut. Why was she doing exactly what she hadn't wanted to do? "Besides, I thought men preferred skinny, flat-chested women these days."

Duncan laughed. He shook his head. "Some might. But not any of the ones I know."

Avery blushed. She wished she didn't. Quickly, she looked down at her bowl. She wanted the topic of conversation changed before her cheeks burst into flame. The sooner the better.

"Do you have any idea how we escape?" She picked up her spoon and took a small bite of the food Duncan had put on her plate. It did taste like buttered grits. Suddenly, she was hungry.

Duncan's look told her he knew exactly what she was doing. "I have a few ideas."

"Good."

She had eaten half of her meal before he spoke again. "You do realize that we're going to have to share the bed."

Avery looked up sharply. She wanted to tell him that was never gonna happen, but there was only one bed in the one bedroom. "That shouldn't be a problem. It's an enormous bed. I doubt we'll even know the other person is there."

Duncan raised one dark eyebrow in a you've-got-to-be-crazy look. "Your lover, or god forbid lovers, must have been awful. Otherwise, you'd remember what you're missing."

"Duncan!"

He laughed. Just as quickly, he sobered. "You're safe with me. At least as safe as you wish to be. But I'm giving you fair warning. The only man who is going to take you to bed from now on is me."

Avery looked down, her cheeks heating again. She was afraid that he would too easily be able to read the pleasure his words brought her. She'd had guys flirt with her since college, but none had made it plain that they wanted her. None made her feel so incredibly special. Perhaps it was only because he wanted to get her in bed, but at least Duncan made her feel as if he specifically wanted her and not just any random female.

She glanced up to find Duncan still watching her, heat and hunger in his gaze. Just when she thought he would say something more to make her skin tingle, he resumed eating. Avery felt simultaneously relieved and disappointed.

Avery returned to her meal. By the time she finished, Duncan was pacing back and forth in front of the bank of windows. He turned to face her as she stood.

"Come outside with me. I want to get a good look at our surroundings."

"You need a jacket. Unless the sun has heated things up considerably, it's freezing out there."

"We won't stay long. I just want to check out the shoreline." He held out his left hand.

Out on the stone balcony, the wind slapped at them. Duncan led her around to the left. He studied what he could see of the steep, high cliff beneath them and then studied the shoreline of the bay and the opposite cliffs. Leading her back around to the right, he repeated the process.

"Okay. I've seen what I needed to see. Let's go up to the bedroom."

"What?" Surely he wasn't thinking what she thought he was.

Duncan tugged her against him. He lowered his head to kiss her. When he raised his head, he grinned wolfishly. "Hold that thought for later, princess. The bedroom is round and full of windows. I want to see what I can see of the promontory behind the castle."

He wasn't contemplating what she believed he was after all. And that was not disappointment she felt.

Inside, they found the king's creepy sister supervising the removal of the meal's remnants. Avery shivered. There was something about the woman that terrified her on a visceral level.

Two girls in their early teens were the ones picking up the dishes and silverware. Duncan's and her sudden appearance through the balcony door startled them. The smaller one dropped the earthenware mug she just picked up. It fell to the stone floor, shattering into several pieces.

Before Avery could guess Dealla's intent, the older woman grabbed the child by the front of her worn gown and slapped her forcefully across the face. The girl cried out in pain, her hand flying to her abused cheek. A small trickle of blood slipped from the corner of her mouth.

Avery started toward the child, but Duncan put his arm in front of her waist and shoved her partially behind him.

Dealla noticed the movement. She looked coldly at them both. "You must be firm with them. Otherwise, they don't learn that they cannot be careless."

"Leave it, Avery," Duncan warned. Out loud, he said, "If you will excuse us." He slid his hand down her arm until he caught her wrist, then pulled her along with him.

Avery turned her head to keep an eye on the older woman until they were in the next room and out of her sight. "There is something seriously twisted about that woman," she whispered when they reached the turret room.

"You're no doubt right. Which means she's even more dangerous than the run of the mill evil Dubh Sidhe. Don't challenge her, Avery. She has power here. And I'm talking about more than the magical kind. We don't. I want you to stay as far away from her as possible."

"But, Duncan, that poor child."

He nodded. "I know. I get it. But we'll be doing her no favors to champion her. Once we leave, it will be worse for her."

CHAPTER FIVE

Duncan knew how Avery felt. He'd wanted to slap Dealla, too, but he couldn't risk it until he better understood what he and Avery were up against.

He moved slowly from window to window, checking out the land the castle was constructed on. From a vantage point near the door to the small bathroom, Duncan could see over the guard wall. What he observed wasn't encouraging. Beyond the outer wall, the rock split into fissures, reminding him of the slightly spread fingers on a hand.

Whoever had built the castle, small though it was, had picked the perfect site. Constructed with both defense and offense in mind made security easy.

But it also meant it would be damned difficult to escape.

Looking back into the room, Duncan saw Avery had curled onto her side on the bed. She appeared to be sound asleep. He couldn't blame her. So far, they'd gotten very little rest. At least she was currently warm. Avery wasn't safe by any stretch of the imagination, but at least he'd managed to see her more suitably clothed for the local weather conditions.

Duncan turned back to studying the views outside the windows. He had to find a way for them to escape. His first priority was to get her away from the king. He'd be damned if he would allow Omaon to use her. He needed to get Avery back to their world.

Duncan's memory wasn't photographic, but it was close enough. He had studied a few maps of Tìr-dhàimh. He was almost certain he knew where they were. Unfortunately, it meant that the nearest tairseach was at least a week away on foot. They would be hunted the entire way. Plus, Omaon would expect them to head for the nearest gate. Which meant that they would have to make their way to a different portal. One even farther away.

The northern border would be guarded. South wasn't even an option. So, it was either north and take a chance on slipping past any portals, or head west and try to find a way across the Inland Sea.

After much consideration, Duncan came to the conclusion that there was only one way that they could possibly escape. They would never be able to get past the wall at the mainland. They were going to have to go by sea. It was a long way down, but not impossible. Duncan had made similar dives before. With the air temperature cold, the water was no doubt even colder, but at least it wasn't freezing yet. Still, if they survived the jump, they ran the risk of hypothermia setting in before they reached shore.

It wasn't a good plan, but it was the only one he had. Providing Avery could swim. He should have asked her. He hoped she would agree.

Duncan had until sunset to convince her. In the meantime, it would behoove him to get some rest, too. They both had stressful days ahead.

Avery partially awoke as he shifted her to the middle of the bed. "Duncan?"

"Go back to sleep," he urged softly. "I need this side of the bed." It was a testament to how tired she was that his little Puritan didn't come fully awake at that. Otherwise, she would either have shoved him from the bed or left it herself.

Duncan lay on his back. Glancing sideways, he checked on Avery. She had once more turned on her side. He listened to her breathing. She was asleep.

He turned his ears to the rest of the building. The only sound was that of the muffled waves crashing against the cliff about seventy-five or eighty feet below. He hoped that meant the king's crazy sister had taken her two whipping girls and gone.

Finally, Duncan allowed himself to sleep. He was confident that if anything moved anywhere below, he would awaken.

"YOU WANT TO DO WHAT?" Avery's brown eyes widened with shock.

"It's the only way to escape." Duncan tried to sound confident. Avery needed to believe they could do it. "If there was another way, I would take it."

"How far down is it? Would we even survive the jump? What if there are rocks beneath the surface? There are probably rocks."

"It's a long way, but I've done similar dives before." Duncan wasn't going to give her the exact distance, even if he knew it. "We can make it. I've been watching. Even at low tide, I couldn't see any rocks. The tide is already coming in. By the time we jump, it will be full. We time it so we jump as a large wave rolls in. It will shorten the distance of the jump even more."

Avery didn't look convinced, but she nodded. "Okay."

"Okay? You're agreeing that easily?" Duncan didn't know why he questioned her. She'd agreed. He should be grateful and just let it go.

"You have the experience here. I have none. The thought of jumping off a balcony terrifies me. But I trust your judgment. I'll follow your lead as best I can."

Duncan was in awe of Avery's bravery. The faith she placed in him both humbled and frightened him. The pressure of protecting her weighed heavily. So did not disappointing her.

The witch, as Duncan thought of Dealla Heregeat, had brought them both lunch and supper. Duncan saved cheese and fruit from both meals to take with them. It was food that exposure to saltwater wouldn't damage.

The sun was setting. Dealla and her workers once again disappeared to wherever it was they came from. In Dealla's case, Duncan suspected a dark corner where she could spin her tangled web. She wouldn't be catching Avery in it.

"What will you do about clothes?" Avery asked as she rifled through the wardrobe.

"I'll be fine. What I have on will dry soon enough once we reach shore." Omaon had yet to supply clothes for him. The old goat probably hoped Duncan would freeze to death during any escape attempt.

"Duncan, you can't go traipsing through the woods in this weather in nothing but a t-shirt. And those jeans will take forever to dry." She turned back to the wardrobe. A moment later, she pulled out a dark gray cape with a hood. She tossed it to him. "Try it on."

"Avery, I don't ne—,"

"Try it on!" She looked adorable with her hands on her hips, trying to intimidate him.

Duncan, shaking his head, followed her instructions. On Avery, it would reach her calves. On him, it barely covered his butt. It would keep the wind and rain off, however.

Duncan rubbed the material between his thumb and forefinger. He wouldn't know for certain until he tried it, but if this was made from *forabuige caora* wool, it would be waterproof. They could put their food and extra clothing for Avery inside and bundle them up.

"There'd better be a second one for you or you'll be wearing this one."

Instead of a second cape, Avery pulled out a dark-green, thigh length cloak. It, too, had a hood.

"How will we carry these and the food?"

"We'll put the food in a pillowcase. Pick out a change of clothes. We'll put everything, including your cloak on my cape, wrap it up tightly and then bundle it in a bedsheet. I can tie that across my chest and back, so I don't lose it during the dive."

Avery immediately stripped a pillowcase off the nearest pillow. Putting the foodstuffs inside, she tied a knot at the open end. Duncan folded Avery's cloak and put both in the middle of his laid-out cape. Once Avery's change of clothes and both of their shoes were added, he wrapped them tightly in the cloak. Duncan rolled that in the bedsheet and tied the two catty corner ends together, rolled it into a long tube shape, and then tied it around his chest, cross-body.

Duncan held out his hand. "Ready?"

"No," Avery answered honestly, but she slipped her hand into his, lacing their fingers together and gripping tightly.

He felt her trembling.

Cautiously, they descended the stairs to the second floor. Duncan had studied everything carefully. The balcony of the round tower over the left bay offered the best chances for success—and survival. On that side, the balcony extended out over the cliff several feet, affording them the best chance of avoiding the rocks at the base. That bay also had a small beach, allowing them an easy exit from the sea and escape into the woods just beyond the shoreline.

Duncan led her to the balustrade, the stones frigid beneath their bare feet. He mulled it over until he had the best spot possible. At the moment, he was thankful for the moonlight. Once they dove into the water, he wouldn't be. If the guards spotted them, the gig was up before it began.

First, he and Avery had to survive the dive. He gave her instructions on how to position her body when they dove. If Avery didn't do it correctly, she could end up badly injured. Or dead. Duncan had to believe she was tough enough to do what they had to in order to escape.

At its highest peak, the tide would begin to turn in moments. They had to go now.

The railings had wide, flat tops. Duncan climbed up and pulled Avery up to stand beside him. "Remember what I told you. And whatever you do, don't scream." He urged her to sit on the railing and cautiously climb over to stand on the shallow ledge on the cliff side.

Avery nodded. Her mouth appeared clamped shut in terror as she gazed at the waves rolling in below. Rather than give her more time to dwell on it, Duncan spotted a high wave and jumped, pulling Avery with him.

Duncan slammed into a cresting wave. As he did, the moon slipped behind a cloud. The water was colder than he anticipated, and the currents were stronger. He started to panic when he couldn't see Avery, after having lost hold of her when they hit the water. Then his grasping hand encountered a flailing arm. Duncan latched onto it with bruising force. He would worry about hurting her once they safely reached the shore. Until then, he wasn't about to chance losing his grip on her.

From her movements, Avery swam. Or tried.

Duncan struck out for the center of the shoreline to get away from the waves rolling over them after crashing into the cliff base and bouncing back. It took longer to swim than he'd hoped. The icy temperature of the water was draining his energy.

About two-thirds of the way to the beach, Avery's movements turned sluggish. Hypothermia was setting in.

By the time they reached the rocky shore, Duncan was towing Avery, who barely managed to keep her head above the swells. Once he could stand, he scooped her up and headed for the trees.

"Can walk," Avery whispered through teeth chattering so hard he could barely make out the words.

"You can walk later. Omaon's overconfidence in our prison will work to our advantage. They shouldn't miss us until we don't appear for breakfast. That gives us all night to get ahead of them."

After a couple miles of walking, Avery either fell asleep from exhaustion or passed out from hypothermia. Finding a clear spot at the base of a large oak, Duncan eased her down on the ground. There was no time to change clothes, but dry socks and shoes, as well as the cloak and cape, would go a long way toward keeping them from getting colder.

Duncan pulled on his own socks and shoes. As his feet began slowly thawing, he put socks on Avery and then her ankle boots. Leaving the cape and cloak out, he wrapped the rest of their supplies back up and once more fastened the sheet across his body. After fastening the cape at his throat, he wrapped Avery's shivering form in her cloak. It was the best he could do at the moment.

Duncan lifted Avery, shifting her over his shoulder. It enabled him to walk faster, plus it left a hand free. It made him feel better, even if he didn't have a weapon to wield.

He walked at a steady pace through much of the night. The sun would rise in less than two hours. He needed to find shelter. And soon. Avery's shivering was getting weaker. With the cold air whipping around them, he doubted it was because of her warming. Duncan feared her core temperature was dropping dangerously low.

What he wouldn't give to be able to call Pritch, or any of the others, for aid. Something was still blocking communication. He hoped it was only for a certain distance and once they passed it, he could call for help.

Over an hour earlier, he had begun climbing into the mountains. Duncan searched for a cave or overhang. Something for shelter. It was nearly impossible to do in the almost complete darkness of the evergreen forest. It took what he guessed was a good twenty minutes more to find a shallow cave about twelve feet deep and eighteen to twenty feet wide.

Laying Avery near the back wall, Duncan unwrapped her from her cloak. Her skin felt like ice. Her shivering was down to intermittent tremors.

Leaving the sodden sheet containing their supplies on the cave floor, Duncan hurriedly gathered nearby twigs, moss, dry leaves, and anything else he could use to get a fire started. He located a couple of iridescent rocks the Sidhe called fire stones. They were similar to the flint rocks found in his native South Carolina, except these were easier to use to start fires. Once he had the kindling cracking, Duncan began adding larger and larger limbs. Soon, a pleasant fire was blazing, and the cave began to heat.

Duncan spread their damp outerwear over some rocks to dry. Unwrapping the sheet, he also spread out Avery's spare clothing, which had gotten damp from being wrapped in the wet sheet. Once that was done, he pulled off his boots, socks, t-shirt, and jeans. The air was frigid against his damp skin. At least he could feel the heat from the fire.

He turned his attention to Avery. Ankle boots and socks came off first. Her trousers next. Lastly, Duncan pulled off her tunic. He would have removed her damp underwear, but Avery wouldn't appreciate finding herself naked when she regained consciousness. Her bra and panties didn't seem that damp, anyway. They should dry quickly.

With both of them stripped down, Duncan lay down with Avery between him and the fire. He pulled her chilled body against his warmer one, chest-to-chest. Finger-combing her long hair, he spread it out toward the fire. He kept doing that with one hand, hoping to aid in its drying.

Warmth returned to him faster than he expected. It took longer with Avery, but she gradually lost the icy feel to her skin. Her shivering began anew and became violent. Wrapping both arms around her, Duncan held her tightly. It soon eased, and he loosened his hold.

"Where are we?" she murmured after a while.

"In a cave in the mountains behind the fortress."

"Aren't you worried about someone seeing the fire or the smoke?"

"I was more concerned with you freezing to death. The sun's already up. The fire's not producing much smoke, so we should be good for a while." He waited for her to mention their state of undress, but she remained quiet.

Perhaps it was that portion of his anatomy pressing against her thighs that had her mute. Duncan wasn't going to apologize for his body's response to being this close to her. His condition was her fault. No other woman brought his body to full need like Avery did. It was damned irritating that the woman didn't even seem to realize the state he was in.

"How do you feel?" he asked more sharply than he meant.

"Fine. A little chilly, but then I am... A little chilly."

"You're nearly naked. Is that what you were going to say? Yea, I noticed."

That was enough to get her to tilt her head back and face him. "You should notice since you're the one who no doubt undressed me. I know why you did, though."

"Good." Rolling over slightly, Duncan threaded the fingers of his left hand through the hair at the back of her head. He slid the fingers of his right hand around her lower jaw and tilted her face up to his. Duncan couldn't make love to her, even if she allowed it, but he could sure as hell kiss her senseless.

What he hadn't counted on was his reaction to her. Avery was like an incoming tide that he couldn't stop. Not that he wanted to. Finally, he raised his head to tuck her head beneath his chin, holding her tightly to him as he rolled onto his back. "Get some sleep. We'll let the sun rise some more. Then we'll have to get dressed and be on our way. If they haven't discovered it already, they'll learn of our escape the moment the witch brings our breakfast."

Avery shivered. Whether from fear or chill, Duncan didn't know. It didn't matter either way, because she snuggled closer to him. Avery was almost right where he wanted her. For the moment, it was enough.

Cupping the back of her head in his palm, Duncan pressed her cheek to his bare chest. Wrapping his other arm around her back, he cupped her bottom and held her tightly to him.

Duncan half expected her to pull back, even to struggle. He was prepared to release her if she did. Avery surprised him yet again. After an initial stiffening, she tucked one small hand against his chest. She slipped her other arm around his waist, holding him as tightly as he held her.

An unfamiliar wave of tenderness crashed over him. The sexual tension was still present, simply muted to a manageable level.

"Sleep while you can, sweetheart," Duncan whispered above her head.

CHAPTER SIX

Avery didn't expect to fall asleep. Not with Duncan's erection pressed hard and hot against her. He was warm all over. He held her as if she was precious. If she could ignore Duncan's mind-blowing kiss—and it would take a much more experienced woman than her to be able to do that—Duncan was a comforting presence. His kiss, however, was anything but calming. Blood-firing. Breathtaking. Soul stealing. Any or all of those described it more accurately.

She thought she would remain awake reliving the terrifying jump. The dive into the frigid ocean happened so quickly, she didn't have time to fear. Hitting the water felt like what she imagined being in a wreck might be like. It hurt. It also knocked the breath from her. Without Duncan's care, she knew she would be dead.

Because she remembered little else between the jump and now, and thankfully they both survived, Avery easily fell asleep to the tingling aftereffects of Duncan's kiss and the encompassing warmth of his body.

When she awoke several hours later, Avery wasn't nearly as warm. She was still in her underwear. Duncan was gone, but she was covered in both her cloak and Duncan's cape. Even together, they didn't do the work of one healthy male.

Avery had to push herself to a sitting position. She was stiff, sore, and bruised in numerous spots. But she was grateful to be alive. She was chilly, but it no longer felt bone deep. The fire still crackled merrily, heating the small cave. She could see it much better now that the sun was up, and had been up for a while by the brightness of it.

She started as a shadow crossed the light. Duncan stood at the entrance, already dressed in his boots, jeans, and navy t-shirt. Walking over, he squatted at her side. Catching a tendril of her hair, he rubbed it between his fingers. His smile rivaled the sunlight behind him.

"Good morning, sunshine," Duncan greeted her. "I hate to rush you, but we've got to get moving."

Avery clutched the wool to her chest. "Where are my clothes?"

"Right here." He pointed to a neatly folded pile of clothing between her and the fire. "Your boots may be stiff from any water they came in contact with, but they'll soften up as you walk."

Avery nodded. When he remained squatted beside her, playing with her hair, she cleared her throat and gave him a pointed look. Duncan didn't move.

"If you'll give me some privacy, I'll get dressed."

"I've already seen you in nearly nothing."

"If you're in a real hurry, you'll turn around."

"It astonishes me how shy you are." Dropping her hair, Duncan rose fluidly to his feet. "I'll be right over here." He took the cape she threw to him and walked over to stand on the lip of the cave, facing outward.

Avery grabbed her clothing and dressed as fast as she was able. Her boots were a little tight, but not uncomfortable. She put on her cloak and walked up to Duncan.

Duncan picked up the tied sheet and slung it over one shoulder before refastening the cape at his neck. He put out the fire, scattering the hot remains as much as he dared. After kicking some dirt over most of it, he looked at her. Pulling an apple from his pocket, he handed it to her. "We won't be able to stop often."

"Don't worry. I can walk forever." Avery smiled at him.

"Okay then. Let's go." Turning, he left the cave. Heading into the woods, he began climbing up the mountain.

Avery struck out on his heels.

It took eight days for them to wend their way through the mountains and come out on the inland side. Duncan kept them near streams, so they always had water to drink. Food was more difficult to come by since it was late fall in this part of Tìr-dhàimh. The berries and nuts they found helped. Duncan even did a little fishing and hunting. He prepared, cleaned, and cooked so that Avery didn't even know what animal they ate. Though she recognized fish when she saw it.

It was late afternoon, and they walked toward the glow of the setting sun. Ahead of them, Avery saw a break in the trees. Rays of light shown through in ever wider and brighter paths. Several minutes later, they came to the edge of the forest. Before them stretched a golden grassland as far as the eye could see. Wind ruffled the thigh-high grass, making it bend and sway like women dancing.

Avery only took a couple of steps forward when Duncan reached out and stopped her.

"Wait."

"Don't we have to cross this?" After days of pushing her, his hesitation confused her.

"Yes, but the minute we step out there, we're going to be exposed to anyone who might be watching. We'll camp here for a while, get some rest, and cross after the sun sets."

"We passed a pool in the stream a short way back. If we're going to be camping for a while, can I get a bath?" Avery hadn't had one since the fortress. After days of walking, she stank. Her hair was lank, and her scalp itched. She might not be able to wash her clothes, but she would feel better if she could wash herself.

Duncan didn't respond. He seemed to be mulling it over.

"You could use one yourself," she told him. "Your hair's greasy and you stink."

Duncan's eyes twinkled. He got that sexy, impish look he had mastered. "Why, Ms. Beaton, are you suggesting we take a bath together?"

"No! Not together. I will take a bath and then you take a bath. Or vice versa." Avery wished she could blame her flaming face on the rays of the setting sun.

"It's together or not at all."

"That's blackmail."

He shrugged. "I prefer to think of it as a negotiation."

"That is not negotiation." Duncan wanted to negotiate. Okay, Avery would give him a negotiation. "Fine, but we keep our underwear on."

"Fine, my little Puritan."

Avery reveled in what she considered a win as she led the way back to the pool. Taking off her boots, she shucked out of her bra and panties.

"The water is going to be cold," Duncan warned.

"I don't care if it has ice chunks in it. I'm getting a bath." She was also going to wash her clothing as best she could. Avery couldn't stomach putting dirty clothes on after getting clean. Picking her clothes up, she took them to the edge of the pool to wash them.

"You're going to freeze." But after stripping down to his boxers, Duncan kneeled beside her and washed his clothes, too.

Finished with those, Avery got her change of clothes from the pack and also washed them. "My clothes will dry a lot faster than your jeans," she observed.

"I'll survive. But you're right. We both stink and neither of us wants to put on dirty clothes."

When the clothing was washed as well as it could be, they spread them out on nearby shrubs so they could dry.

Duncan wasted no time wading into the pool. When he reached thigh deep, he dove forward into the water.

Avery followed him, gasping at the temperature. Somehow it hadn't felt quite so cold when it was only her hands in it. Right after she was deep enough, she, too, dove under. When she resurfaced, she swam around until she became accustomed to the water's chill. Then she washed her hair and bathed. By the time she felt clean, her skin pruned, and her teeth were chattering.

Suddenly, powerful arms wrapped around her waist from behind and pulled her against a solid chest. Against her bottom, she felt something else firm.

"I thought cold water was supposed to have a shrinking effect on the male anatomy."

Duncan chuckled near her ear. He rubbed his bearded cheek against hers, softly tickling her. "Normally it would, darlin', but now I have you. With you in my arms, even ice water can't make me flaccid."

"Is that supposed to be some kind of weird compliment?" Putting her arms over his, Avery snuggled back against his warmth.

She couldn't believe she had this amazing man all to herself. Duncan was kind and considerate. He looked out for her without treating her like a child. He was a warrior with a warrior's heart who made her feel like a princess. Though she wanted to get home, she wished their time didn't have to end.

Avery was no longer used to male attention. Certainly not of the sexual kind. The more time she spent with Duncan, the more she enjoyed his company. He was witty and clever, and those gorgeous green eyes of his missed nothing of their surroundings.

"Take it any way you want, darlin'," Duncan replied. "I merely stated a fact."

She gave a startled squeak as he unexpectedly scooped her up.

"We're clean so we're getting out of this freezing water before we catch pneumonia." He strode onto the bank, slowly let her feet drop to the ground, and stepped back.

Avery turned to face him. Duncan's eyes weren't looking at her face. She followed their direction to her breasts. Her nipples pressed against her wet bra like hard buttons. She raised her arms to cover herself, but Duncan stopped her.

"Please don't." He looked into her eyes then. "You're beautiful, Avery. Don't hide. Not from me. I love looking at you."

She blushed. Avery knew she wasn't, even though Duncan made her feel he was telling the truth. She had lost weight during the days of walking, but she was still overweight. And always would be. She had some pleasant features, but that didn't make her beautiful.

Duncan slid one arm around her waist, lifting her completely off her feet. He threaded the fingers of his other hand through the wet hair at the back of her head, holding her still as he kissed her senseless.

This kiss was like neither of his previous ones. This one contained both hunger and need, but it also had something deeper. Duncan kissed her as if he'd never get enough.

Neither could Avery. She might be new to going after what she wanted, but Avery knew what it was. Wanting Duncan, she kissed him just as hungrily. She wasn't ready when he pulled back. Avery looked at him in confusion. "What's wrong?"

"We have to stop." He shook his head.

"Why? I enjoy kissing you." What was she saying? Like was too tame. Avery *liked* Key Lime Pie and mac-and-cheese. What she felt when Duncan kissed her was more. So much more.

"Aw, honey, I love kissing you, too." To punctuate his statement, Duncan gave her a quick brush of his lips. "But if we don't stop now, I'm not going to want to stop. I know it's cliche, but this truly is neither the time nor the place. When I make love to you, it's going to be where and when I can take my time and savor every second."

He released her and walked to the bushes where they'd spread their clothes to dry. He touched the jeans and cursed. "I need to find someplace to get a different pair of pants."

"That's going to be a little difficult, isn't it? Not least of your problems is your height."

Duncan grinned at that. "Actually, that's the easy part. Most Sidhe are tall. Between six-two and six-eight."

"We haven't passed a single house, let alone a village or a town. And if we do find one, what you plan to do, steal them? We don't have any local currency."

Duncan shrugged. "I'll decide when the situation presents itself."

Avery pulled on her tunic. Though it was still damp, it wasn't wet enough that she couldn't wear it. Neither were her trousers when she checked. She quickly pulled them on. "I don't know what this material is, but it's amazing."

"It's a type a wool made from a special breed of llama-type animal they raise here. One of the best features is how quickly it dries. Also, how durable it is. Better than denim." He checked his t-shirt. It must have been dryer because he pulled it over his head.

Avery watched as he put on his socks and boots. He put on the sheet, fastened his cape at his neck, and threw his jeans over his shoulder.

"What are you doing? Are you planning to travel without pants?"

Duncan wrapped her cloak around her shoulders and fastened it beneath her chin. "I am until they're a lot dryer. If I put these on now, I fear I'll come down with some dread, shrinking disease." He grinned at her. "The sun will be down in a few minutes. No one will see me except you, and maybe some night creatures."

With his cape on, he reminded Avery of a Roman soldier or a kilted Scotsman. He possessed a fine pair of legs. A really, really fine pair of legs.

"You're going to be cold," Avery said, still worried.

"Not as cold and uncomfortable as I'd be if I wear them. When they dry, I'll put them on." He caught her hand in his and started walking. "The creek we've been following runs into a river before long. There's bound to be some form of civilization somewhere along its banks. Maybe we'll even be able to catch a ride in a boat bound for the Inland Sea."

"How often have you been here?"

"This is my fifth time in Tìr-dhàimh. I've never been to Orithea before."

"Then how do you know so much about the geography?"

Duncan gave her a sheepish look, as if embarrassed. "I've studied a few maps of each kingdom."

Avery had looked at maps of North and South Carolina lately, but if she was plunked down in the country somewhere, she wouldn't know which stream fed into which river. Then she remembered a comment one of his partners had made. "You have an eidetic memory, don't you?"

Again, the embarrassed sideways glance. "Not exactly, but close enough. I have very good visual memory retention."

Duncan was amazing. Gorgeous to look at with brains to boot.

DUNCAN HATED TO WAKE Avery because it was the first good night's sleep either of them had in over a week. It took them about four more days of walking before they came across a small farmstead. It belonged to an old woman named Orla, which made her ancient by human standards. She welcomed them, delighted for the company.

She also had a trunkful of clothes that belonged to her late husband. With a little altering, they fit Duncan perfectly. The lady fixed three pairs of trousers for him and five tunics. She also cut down two more tunics, fitting them for Avery.

Once she showed Avery how to milk the cow and the goat, and how to feed the smaller livestock, Avery performed those tasks for her as payment. Avery even learned to churn butter and make cheese.

For his part, Duncan cared for the large livestock. He also chopped wood, stacking enough firewood near her cottage to see her through the winter. He patched several leaky spots in her roof and repaired a couple of loose boards in her small corral.

Duncan was uneasy about staying so long, but they had been with her for about a week. Avery didn't say a word, but the old woman did. Avery started her period. Duncan figured it would be easier on Avery if they stayed with another woman.

Only one patrol had come by so far. The old woman hid them until the warriors departed.

That night at supper, Duncan informed Orla that they had to leave. "More patrols will come. We're putting you in danger."

The old woman laughed. "Son, at my age, a little danger charges up the old heart."

Avery reached over and covered Orla's hand with her own. "I don't like leaving you here alone."

Orla leaned sideways into Avery, resting her cheek against Avery's upper arm. "You are a sweet child, Avery. I have lived here alone for centuries. I have family and good neighbors. Do not worry about me, I will be fine. You and your young man need to return to your world without delay. Àrdrìgh Omaon will not stop until he captures you once more. You are not safe in Orithea."

Duncan nodded. "I agree. We had to bypass the nearest tairseach on the way here. I figured that Omaon would have people there before we could arrive."

Orla lifted her head. "Wise. There is a tairseach about a day's walk from here. It is your best option. It is in a sparsely populated area. So much so that it is often overlooked."

That peaked Duncan's interest. "You think Omaon and his warriors have forgotten about it?"

Orla shrugged, her eyes sparkling. "I cannot be certain. I believe it is worth investigating, do you not?"

Duncan looked at Avery. He wanted to get her back to their world as soon as possible. She didn't know it yet, but he was going to move her to Caledonia and ward her new house out the wazoo.

"Yes, it's definitely worth investigating."

Pulling her hand from beneath Avery's, Orla rubbed her hands in glee like a child. "I have not been on a trip in ages. This will be fun."

"You're coming with us?" Avery smiled.

"Only to the tairseach, my dear. Only to the gate. I have to return. My animals need me."

Avery looked at Orla worriedly. Duncan's little Puritan was a saver, a rescuer. She wanted to help everyone.

"Orla will be fine, Avery. She most likely got about three hundred or so more years to live. The Sidhe live exceptionally long lives. We can't force her to go with us."

Orla chuckled. *"No, you cannot. This is my home, and this is where I shall stay until I die. My family is here."*

"You can hear us," Duncan stated the obvious.

"I have learned a great many things in my time, Duncan. Including how to eavesdrop on others' telepathic communications." Intense eyes stared into his. *"You are in more danger here than you realize."*

"I take it Avery can't hear you."

"No, she cannot. The child is frightened enough without hearing what I have to say."

Duncan swallowed. *"What?"*

"I overheard the warriors. They have orders to kill you on sight. The àrdrìgh knows that without you, Avery would not have escaped. He has also told his son to take her."

A chill slithered up Duncan's spine. He looked at Avery. She frowned back at him.

"What does that mean?"

"It means that Vreis will take her to bed. He will breed her, and they will try to raise their own people capable of psychometry."

"The hell they will. They touch her over my dead body."

Orla arched one white eyebrow. *"I believe I stated that was their first order of business."*

Duncan frowned as he caught Avery's hand. "We leave here at first light. One way or another, we're going through that tairseach."

CHAPTER SEVEN

The three of them set off before dawn the next morning. Though they hoped they wouldn't need them, Avery packed their extra clothes in a leather satchel Orla gave her. Avery carried it, bumping lightly against her bottom, the strap across her chest. Duncan had a broadsword about four feet in length strapped to his back. It had belonged to Orla's late husband.

Duncan and Avery walked. Orla led the way, riding her small pony. They reached a forest soon after lunch. The brush was fairly thick, slowing them, but they still reached the double circle of waist-high standing stones well before dark.

Orla dismounted. Walking to the edge of the circle, she held her hand out to Avery, who immediately took it.

Duncan stepped closer to Avery just as the older woman released her hand. Orla pulled a white-gold chain from around her neck. Stretching up, she put it over Avery's head. Duncan lifted the pendant from his palm and looked at it. It was an intricately carved tree of life surrounded by a narrow circle filled with carved Celtic symbols.

Orla met his gaze. "For protection."

"This is lovely." Avery looked from the pendant to Orla. "But I can't accept it. It should go to a family member."

Orla faced her gravely. "You can and you shall. It is mine to give to whom I choose, and I give it to you. Promise me you will *never* take it off. Ever."

Duncan nodded when Avery turned to him. He wanted her to have all the protection she could get. And if Orla believed it would protect Avery, then he figured it had more power than anything he could get his hands on.

"I promise." Clasping the older woman's hands, Avery begged, "Come with us, Orla. Please. You can live with me. I'd love to have you."

This wasn't the time to tell Avery, but during the walk, he'd decided that she would be living with him, Gavin, and Darach until he could guarantee her safety. He had room for Orla, too, but he knew she wouldn't leave her home.

Orla pulled her hands free to cup Avery's cheeks between her gnarled fingers. "Oh, my darling girl, I cannot leave here. This is my home. I have children, grandchildren, and great-grandchildren here, and I am happy here. I know how to protect myself. Truly. There is no reason to concern yourself with me."

Duncan knew Avery wasn't convinced. Still, she nodded. After another hug, she stepped back.

Duncan removed the broadsword and scabbard from his back and tied it to the saddle. He bent and gave Orla a gentle hug. "Thank you for everything."

She smiled up at him, her eyes twinkling merrily. *"Give your firstborn daughter my name for her second name and I will be well repaid."*

"My firstborn daughter?"

"Avery is your mate, Duncan. Your soul recognizes this fact. You will have beautiful, strong children together. Maybe someday you shall bring them to visit an old woman."

Orla's words shocked Duncan speechless. Sure, he'd considered making love to Avery. A lot. However, he hadn't considered marriage and children with anyone—including Avery. After hearing a few sentences from an old woman he hadn't known long, it was now all he could think of. In his mind's eye, Duncan could envision Avery ripe with their child.

"And does Avery's soul recognize it as well?"

Orla merely smiled. "Safe journey, my children." Duncan lifted her into the saddle, and she set off at a trot for her home.

"You know telepathy is rude when one person is excluded from the conversation," Avery chastised gently. She stood with her arms folded beneath her breasts. If she wanted him to pay attention to what she said, she needed to find a different way to show her displeasure.

"Yes, I know." Wrapping an arm around her shoulders, Duncan walked her into the circle. "Let's go home."

AVERY DIDN'T HAVE TIME to grab hold of him. One minute, they were standing in the stone circle in the forest near Orla's home and in the next blink of her eyes, in a stone circle in a different forest.

"Where are we?" she asked.

"Just outside Caledonia, South Carolina." Duncan took hold of her elbow and ushered her out of the stones.

Avery wanted to sag with relief. "What do we do now?"

"I take you home."

Before she could ask how he knew where she lived, he translocated. Only it wasn't to Avery's house. She and Duncan stood in someone else's hallway.

"Welcome to my home." Duncan spread his arms wide.

Avery looked up at him, a little unsettled. "Are you going to drive me to my apartment?"

Duncan's smile faded. "No. I can't do that, Avery. I thought I'd have more time to discuss this with you."

"Discuss what?" she asked suspiciously.

"You're going to have to move to Caledonia."

She shook her head before he finished. "No. I don't want to move. I like my apartment."

"You can't go back there. I'm sorry, Avery, but you'd be a sitting duck. Omaon still wants you. Don't think he hasn't found out exactly where you live. If you return, they *will* take you back to Orithea."

"Stop trying to frighten me, Duncan Kerr. I don't like it." She glared at him. Avery didn't want to be manipulated into moving because of fear, but Duncan was doing a good job of it.

"I'm not trying to frighten you, damn it! I'm stating pure fact. I'm sorry, truly, but your life will never be the same. You can't go back."

Avery didn't want to give credence to his words, but in her heart, she knew he was right. "That's not fair. I didn't even find the dagger."

"Yet. You haven't found it yet. But you're one of the few who can. Probably the only one Omaon knows of. Darlin', few things involving the Dubh Sidhe are fair. That's another fact. You can't go back, but you can go forward. And who's to say your life won't be better?"

"How am I any safer in Caledonia?" Avery hated change. She'd had entirely too much upset in her life.

"All of Somerset County is warded. Caledonia is what you might call triple warded. Sidhe powers are muted here."

"But you translocated us here. Isn't that a Sidhe power?"

"It's also Halfling magic." Taking her by the arm, he ushered her through a doorway into a casual dining area in front of a bank of floor-to-ceiling windows, and a large, airy kitchen with a long bar area. "Take off the satchel and have a seat." He waved his hand to the right. "In fact, go into the den and make yourself comfortable. I'll get us something to drink. What would you like? I can make you a glass of tea, or I have coffee, hot tea, or something alcoholic."

"Coffee's fine. Cream, or milk if you don't have it. No sugar." Avery walked past a large, round dining table and into an enormous room.

A large L-shaped sectional of dark blue micro-suede sat across the room in front of a bank of windows. Three large, dark burgundy leather recliners formed a sort of semi-circle with their backs to the kitchen area. All the furniture faced toward a curved wall with four floor-to-ceiling windows separated in the middle by a huge fireplace with a flat-screen TV of at least sixty-five inches hanging above the wooden fireplace mantel. A square coffee table of teak anchored the seating. The wall to her left was floor-to-ceiling bookcases filled with books and historical artifacts.

After walking around the chairs, Avery sat in the middle of the couch, facing the fireplace and television. It was heaven to be able to sit and know that they didn't have to get up again and walk for days.

Sliding the satchel over her head, she laid it on the floor at her feet.

Suddenly, bone-weary, Avery sank back into the soft cushions. While they had been running, she had been able to keep the exhaustion at bay. The moment she relaxed, it hit her like a semi running over a sub-compact.

Rolling her head on the back of the couch, she watched Duncan moving around his kitchen. After weeks in another dimension, it seemed strange to be watching him in a modern house. Duncan fit, no matter where he was.

Avery managed to keep up with him in Tìr-dhàimh. Barely. As much as she wished it was different—that she was different—she didn't belong in Duncan's world. She wasn't strong. Avery didn't understand how the Sidhe world worked. She was proud she hadn't been a burden or a hindrance to him, but that was about all she could claim.

Now Duncan was trying to tell her that she couldn't go home. He wanted her to move to a new town. Even if she still didn't understand why it was supposed to be safer. She didn't want to think about moving, about being uprooted yet again.

Avery was also hot now that they were home. She took off her cloak, and then her boots and socks. The air conditioning was on, but the wool clothing was warm.

Avery wiped her hand over her face. She was exhausted and trying not to sink into a self pity party. After all, she was alive. She was home—well, sort of. And for the time being, she had a gorgeous man to ogle.

A handsome man who was bringing her a cup of coffee. "Thank you." She took the mug Duncan held out to her.

"You're welcome." He sat down in the nearest recliner, toed off his boots, and flipped the footrest up. A relieved sigh escaped.

Avery sipped the coffee. It was good. Bold, but not bitter. "I didn't realize how much I missed the normal, everyday things."

"Good. I ordered pizza. It'll be here in about twenty minutes."

"When did you do that?"

"While I was making the coffee. It's a local place that has a standing order for whenever I call." He reached for a cordless phone. "Speaking of calling, I need to call my family, or they'll be over here en mass before long."

"How would they know you're home?" Avery asked as he dialed.

"Dada is amazingly tech savvy for his age. He had Peter rig my house and security system feed so that he can access it whenever he wants. Dada's no doubt been monitoring it since he learned of our disappearance." He held up his finger to signal the call had been answered. "Yes, it's me... Fine. I'm fine... Avery is tired, but otherwise okay... Omaon wants her. He's damned angry that we escaped. He'll be sending people to try to take her back... I've got it covered for the moment... Yes, send Gavin and Darach home... I'm glad we're home, too, Dada. Give Aunt Josey a kiss for me and tell her I'll see her soon. Love you, old man."

Duncan looked at her. "Why don't you go into the bathroom and at least change into your t-shirt. I'm going to do the same. We'll get your clothes as fast as we can."

It sounded like a good idea to her. When Avery returned, she said, "I still don't understand how Caledonia is safer."

"Because it's heavily warded by some of the strongest Sidhe magic there is. Some very powerful Sidhe wizards set it up centuries ago. Somerset County, too, but Caledonia and a five-mile radius around it are specially warded. No Dubh Sidhe can use their power at full force here. At least not unless invited in by a human. Or Halfling, and we don't do that."

"So what? I move here and then I can never leave. That's not a home. That's a prison. I sometimes have to travel for my work. You know that. It's when you kidnapped me," Avery reminded him.

"I did not kidnap you." He frowned at her. "With some planning, you can still travel." Duncan didn't sound pleased by the idea.

The enormity of her situation sank in. Avery didn't like it at all. "Free run of a town—or even a county—still sounds like being in prison."

"There's a shop in Caledonia that you'll love. And Iona, the owner, will adore you." It seemed Duncan was switching tactics. "In fact, I'll be surprised if she doesn't offer you a job. And I can guarantee you'll make more money than you're making now."

Avery was being bombarded with so much she didn't know what to think. Going into an alternate dimension was shocking enough. What happened after their return was stunning. And not in a good way. More like a zapped-with-a-taser way.

"Do you enjoy traveling around? Staying alone in different motels? Being paid only a fraction of what your ability is worth?"

Avery smiled weakly. "You're a regular spin doctor."

"Just trying to give you a different perspective. Is it working?"

"I don't know," Avery answered honestly. She was confused and scared. There were so many things to think about. "Maybe."

"I'm also here."

Avery looked at him in surprise. Duncan looked serious. She couldn't believe he was, however. No, she wouldn't let herself speculate on his meaning. It would hurt her too much if she was mistaken.

"What do you mean?"

Duncan looked frustrated. "I think you know what I mean."

She shook her head, feeling frustrated herself. "No, I'm sure I don't. Tell me what you mean. I'm not going to guess and take the chance of being wrong."

"Okay, fine." It was strange. Duncan seemed nervous. He released a breath before continuing. "There's something between us."

"Like you wanting to take me to bed?"

"And you wanting me to. But it's more than that. I think we've become friends over the last few weeks. I think we could be more."

"What if that is just the result of the intense situation we were put in?" Avery needed to know he was certain.

In the blink of an eye, Duncan was beside her on the couch. His arms came around her and he pressed her over into the cushions. "Tell me if this feels like it was just the damned situation," he demanded right before his mouth covered hers.

It felt like heaven. It felt like an eternity.

Avery would much rather concentrate on kissing Duncan than on her fears of moving. She wanted to touch him, so she pulled his t-shirt until she could slide her hands beneath it to run her fingers up and down the firm muscles of his back.

Duncan rose and looked down at her. "Don't move." He yanked his shirt off over his head and tossed it somewhere into the room. "Better?"

"Much." Avery smiled as he came back to her.

Duncan was a master kisser. It was easy for Avery to imagine that he was a master at all he did.

"Ah-hem."

Avery barely registered the sound, but Duncan shot off the couch in a flash. He faced away from her as Avery scrambled to a sitting position.

"Dammit, Dada! I'd have brought Avery around to meet you all tomorrow. You didn't need to ambush us." He caught his t-shirt one-handed as someone tossed it to him.

"Don't worry. I ordered more pizza on the way over," a male voice stated.

Duncan quickly pulled on his shirt. He then held out a hand behind him.

Avery took it and let him pull her to her feet. Peering around his shoulder, she got her first look at the four people who stood at different levels of the steps to Duncan's den. The only one she recognized was Darach, who winked at her.

There was a middle-aged woman with brown hair and green eyes. She was about Avery's height, but even more Rubenesque. She smiled warmly. Deep laugh lines at the outer corners of her eyes indicated she laughed often.

Avery liked her on sight.

The woman walked over and elbowed Duncan aside. "I tried to get them not to come, at least Dad. Since it's nearly impossible to stop bull-headed Kerr men from doing exactly as they please, I decided to add some estrogen to all the testosterone."

"Aunt Josey," the youngest man in the group groaned.

He appeared to be anywhere between twenty and twenty-five. Nearly as tall as Duncan, he had the same dark brown hair, only his was longer and curling at the ends. Instead of Duncan's green eyes, his were a brilliant blue.

Duncan waved a hand in the younger man's direction. "My baby brother, Gavin Kerr. My Aunt Jocelin, whom we all call Josey. And finally, the instigator of this ill-timed gate-crashing, my grandfather, Angus Kerr. Who obviously turned off the chime feature of my security system." He turned to her. "Though I'm sure I don't need to introduce her, this is Avery Beaton."

Duncan's grandfather was not what Avery expected. He was only a bit shorter than his two grandsons. His tanned skin appeared darker because of the snowy white of his hair and short beard. Some black remained among the gray of Angus' mustache and his eyebrows remained mostly dark. His hair was still thick, much longer than Gavin's, and pulled back in a ponytail. Avery couldn't begin to guess his age, as he was in great shape. Obviously, the progenitor of his daughter's and Duncan's green eyes, his had crow's feet, and he had some deep lines etched in his forehead.

"It's a delight to meet you, Avery." His voice sang with a strong Scottish burr. Stepping forward, he caught her left hand and raised it to kiss her knuckles.

Avery blushed.

"Back off, old man. I saw her first," Duncan fairly growled.

"Duncan!" Avery couldn't believe he was being so rude to his grandfather.

"Don't fash yerself, love," Angus said with a smile. "It's my grandson's insecurities speaking."

Realizing that it was some form of teasing between them, Avery relaxed. "I'm sure you're a hard act to follow."

Angus winked at her. Avery felt she was getting glimpses of Duncan in forty or fifty years.

"Don't feed his already engorged ego," Duncan groaned affectionately as a doorbell rang.

"I'll get it. That should be the pizza." Gavin headed down the nearest hallway.

"This is not the night for a party. Avery and I just got here. We've spent weeks trudging around Orithea trying to find a tairseach to get home. We're exhausted."

One of his grandfather's dark eyebrows lifted in an expression so like Duncan's that Avery smiled.

"Aye, we could tell how tired when you didna hear the chime that I didna disable," Angus agreed knowingly. "And we're well aware of how long ye've been away."

"Didn't look conducive to sleep to me," Darach piped up. He waved his hand toward the couch. "You know, what you two were doing when we arrived."

"Keep it up and I'll rent your basement crash pad to someone else," Duncan threatened.

Darach grinned in response.

Angus clapped Duncan on the shoulder, his demeanor suddenly serious. "I wasn't planning on staying. I just needed to see you with my own eyes. To make sure for myself you're unharmed in truth."

Duncan hugged his grandfather. "I'm fine, Dada. Not even a scratch."

Angus patted Duncan's cheek when they separated. "I like the beard. You might want to consider keeping it."

"And look even more like you?" Duncan's eyes twinkled. "I'll have to think hard about that."

Angus turned to her. "Avery, it is a pleasure to meet you. I'm sure we'll be seeing a lot of each other," he said enigmatically. "Josey, honey, are you ready to leave?"

Josey smiled at her. "I hate to leave you with so much maleness, but I have the feeling you can handle them. If it gets to be too much, my number is on Duncan's speed dial. Give me a call and I'll come rescue you."

Avery nodded as she smiled back.

"Good night, Aunt Josey." Duncan wrapped an arm around her shoulders and shepherded her to the front door just as his brother returned carrying three large pizza boxes.

His aunt wrapped her arm around his waist, hugging him. "We're going, Duncan." She looked over her shoulder at Gavin, who was setting the boxes on the kitchen table. "Well, Dad and I are leaving. I'm afraid you're stuck with the others."

Duncan kissed the top of her head. "Them I can handle. It's him I don't trust." He nodded toward his grandfather before grinning.

Josey laughed. "Smart man." She stepped into the hall. "Call me if you need me, Avery. We'll meet again soon."

"Thank you so much," Avery responded, stepping up into the dining area so she could see down the hall.

Darach, who had grabbed a beer from the fridge, walked over to put his arm around Avery's shoulders and urge her toward the kitchen table. "Get some pizza before Gav eats it all."

"Hey, I would never leave a lady unsatisfied," Gavin said with a grin. It was nearly as devastating as his older brother's. He pulled out a chair and held it for her.

Just as she started to sit, they heard something slam against a wall in the entry. "Where the hell is she?"

Avery recognized the angry voice. "Stiabhan!"

"Oh, hell." Darach followed her as she ran to the front.

Stiabhan heard her because he met her at the entry to the den. He caught her in a bear hug, lifting her off her feet.

Wrapping her arms around his shoulders, Avery held on tightly. It had been a while since she'd had anyone to worry about her.

After a few seconds, he set her on her feet. Holding her by the shoulders, he put her at arm's length and looked her over from head to toe and back. "You've lost weight. Are you injured?"

"I'm fine. In my case, losing weight is a good thing."

"It is not a good thing. I don't like it. Nor do I like that I was unable to communicate with you." He shot a glare at Duncan, who stood a few feet away.

"I tried to call you but couldn't." Avery looked at him.

"Why not?"

"We were in Tìr-dhàimh. Orithea, to be precise, you arse," Duncan spoke up from behind Stiabhan.

Keeping one hand on her arm, her cousin turned toward Duncan. "You were to guard her. Not take her on an excursion to the Realm."

"Take her? Take her! I didn't take her there on some lark. We were kidnapped, you fae jackass. Omaon grabbed us because he wants Avery," Duncan growled.

"Omaon? Shite. Then he knows of her ability."

"Ya think? He's already got an agenda worked out on how to use her."

That was the first Avery heard that the king had worked out plans. How did Duncan know? And what did he mean? It couldn't be good, because if she didn't know him, the ferocious expression on his face would put the fear of God into her.

Stiabhan hugged her to him. "You will come home with me."

"The hell she will. She's staying here with me where it's safer."

"Avery will be safer with me," Stiabhan argued.

"I can't go with you. My work is here. My life is here." Besides, going back to Tìr-dhàimh scared the crap out of her.

"Come with me and you'll never have to work again. You will live like a princess," her cousin said.

Avery placed her palm flat against his chest and smiled up at him. "I love my work. And this is my home. This dimension, I mean."

Stiabhan looked from her to Duncan. "I would speak privately with you."

Duncan waved a hand to an open doorway to his right.

"If this is about me, I should be present." This wasn't the Middle Ages where her male relative got to decide her fate. "You two are not going to decide what I do. Only I am going to do that."

Stiabhan tried to look innocent. "I merely have some matters to discuss with Duncan."

"Go get some pizza, angel. This won't take long. I promise," Duncan said.

Avery glared at them both. Chauvinist jerks. They could plan and plot all they wanted, but if they thought to dictate her life, they were in for a big surprise.

She turned toward the kitchen. Darach and Gavin were unashamedly eavesdropping. Catching them each by the arm, she turned them back around and pulled them along with her. If she couldn't listen, then neither could they.

CHAPTER EIGHT

Duncan allowed the Sidhe to precede him into the study. He closed the door and went behind the desk, facing Stiabhan across the shiny beech surface. "Avery stays with me. She sure as hell doesn't return to Tìr-dhàimh."

Stiabhan's emerald eyes blazed in anger. "A Dubh Sidhe kidnapped her on your watch. It is obvious you cannot protect her."

"I got her home without her being harmed." Duncan thought it best not to mention their cliff dive. "She remains here in Caledonia."

"No. I trusted you with Avery's care once. I shall not do it again. Omaon took you. Omaon! I know what that evil bastard is capable of."

"You think I don't? But it's not your decision to make," Duncan reminded him, and taking pleasure doing it. "It's Avery's."

Stiabhan crossed his arms. "You think she will choose to remain with you?"

"I don't know what she'll choose, but I'm willing to let her. To a point. Are you?" Duncan was concerned about her choice. He feared she might go with the Sidhe. Duncan knew how frightened she was.

"I have already lost family to the Dubh Sidhe. I do not plan on losing anyone else. Certainly not Avery."

"I've lost people to them, too. They killed a friend of mine right in front of us. I'm not going to lose Avery to anyone."

Stiabhan's eyes narrowed as he uncrossed his arms. "I see what this is about. You want Avery for yourself. You want to bed her."

"I don't only want to take her to bed. It's more than sex." Duncan didn't want to try to explain himself to her kinsman when he hadn't figured it out himself.

"What more?" Stiabhan demanded, like an irate father.

"I don't know yet. That's something Avery and I were working on discovering before the entire world descended on us."

"You will not bed my cousin until and unless you are wed to her. Do you dishonor her? You will beg for death to release you from the purgatory I will rain down on you."

"Don't threaten me, Stiabhan. I have no intention of ever hurting Avery."

The Sidhe sat down. "When shall we perform the binding ceremony?"

"Damn you. Give me some time. I'm trying not to scare her off." Duncan glared. "Why the big rush? What aren't you telling me?"

Stiabhan didn't answer. Instead, he got to his feet once more and began wandering around the room. He picked up a knick-knack, looked at it, and put it back. A book was slipped from a shelf, the spine read, before it was replaced. He walked to the window, moved the shutter and peered out. A few seconds later, he closed it.

"If it's that bad, then the sooner you tell me, the better." Duncan sat in the chair behind his desk and rocked back.

"You say Omaon seeks her." Stiabhan faced him. "You know what they want of her. What they will do to her. To protect her the best I can, I must see her bound to someone."

"A moment ago, you didn't trust me to care for her. You were threatening to take her to Peadaran. Now you want me to wed her?"

"I had to be certain you were sincere."

Duncan was still missing something. "How will being bound to a mate help?"

"Right now, we can communicate telepathically with her. If they kidnap her and take her back to Orithea, that tenuous link will be broken. If she is bound to a mate, the mate will be able to communicate with her. Even over great distances."

Duncan frowned. This was news to him. "If Avery and I go through the binding ceremony, even if Omaon kidnaps her again, he wouldn't be able to block us from communicating with each other?"

"Sharp as a tack, as they say, aren't you? There are still ways to block you, but I can pull in a favor. During the binding ceremony, the connection can be strengthened. It is not foolproof, but it is the best chance we have." Stiabhan glowered. "But perhaps I should speak with my cousin. There must be a more worthy Halfling man somewhere. Perhaps that Darach fellow. He seems capable enough."

Darach was plenty capable. Duncan was on his feet in an instant. "Over my dead body, you elf."

Stiabhan crossed his arms. "I am Sidhe. Elves are a different race."

"If the wings and pointy ears fit."

"I possess neither pointy ears nor the appendages you mention. Perhaps if I were to beat you within an inch of your life, you might learn some manners."

"Only when you leave Avery alone."

"She is my kinswoman, Halfling prick. I will see to her care as I see fit."

Both men turned as the study doors opened and the subject of their argument poked her head in. "Enough, you two. The pizza is getting cold. Your discussion... argument... whatever you want to call it, is canceled until further notice."

Duncan grinned as Stiabhan frowned. "As you say, she is your kinswoman." He walked around his desk, past Stiabhan, and wrapped his arm around Avery's shoulders. "If you behave, you can have one of the spare bedrooms for the night."

"How many bedrooms do you have?" Avery asked as they walked to the kitchen.

"Seven. One on this floor. Four upstairs, including mine and Gavin's, and two downstairs. When he's mooching off my largess, Darach claims one of the basement rooms," he said loud enough as they approached for his brother and friend to hear.

"I'm your only sibling," Gavin spoke up. "You have to take care of me. Besides, you love me and want me near."

"You're a pain in my—"

"Hey!" Darach yelled. "Language. There is a lady present."

"—rear," Duncan finished smoothly, eliciting a smile from the lovely woman tucked against his side. Neither mentioned that Avery had heard much worse from him during their escape trek.

"I will take a room near Avery's." Stiabhan followed them.

"I figured you might."

DUNCAN SHOWED AVERY to a spacious bedroom on the second floor. It was next to Gavin's room; it's door straight down the hall from Duncan's. She had a private bath complete with tub and detached walk-in closet. In the bedroom, a lovely, upholstered window seat looked out a pair of large windows. Through them, she could see a garden two stories below. The ground sloped from right to left, allowing the basement to open into the back and side yard.

Stiabhan was given the fourth bedroom on the second floor, on the other side of Gavin's, on the front of the house.

Later that night, Avery crawled between the softest sheets she'd ever felt and snuggled into an amazingly comfortable bed for a guestroom. Going to sleep didn't worry her. She was exhausted. Avery fell asleep almost the moment her head touched the pillow.

Avery slept as she hadn't slept in years. Since her father's death, she had become a light sleeper. That night, she slept deeply. She felt both safe and protected. It was sad how easy it was to take those feelings for granted. Avery didn't think she would ever do so again.

She slept so soundly that she didn't remember dreaming. Which was good because Avery had been having nightmares since Aaron's murder. She woke up feeling refreshed for the first time in ages.

After showering and washing her hair, she toweled most of the moisture from it and left it to dry on its own. Returning to the bedroom, she found her luggage from the Greenville cabin sitting on the floor just inside the door. She would have to remember to thank Darach. Having her own things, especially her own clothes, was wonderful.

Dressing in jeans and a plum-colored, cowl-neck sweater, she pulled on socks and her brown leather ankle boots. Popping back in the bathroom, she put some powder on her face and ran a brush through her damp hair. Studying herself in the mirror, Avery sighed. She reached for her lip-gloss and then put it back. It wasn't as if Duncan hadn't seen her for days with no makeup whatsoever. She wished she was more adept at using it, but before Duncan, she hadn't cared.

Putting on makeup at this point might lead Duncan and the others to believe she was after him. Not that Avery wouldn't be if she thought she had half a chance. Duncan, however, was beyond her reach on many levels. No matter what he'd tried to say the previous night.

Avery would enjoy looking at him while she had the opportunity. She would soak up impressions and memories to pull out and enjoy when she returned to her own boring life. In the meantime, she would do her best to keep her heart out of the equation.

No one was in the kitchen, the dining area, or the great room when she arrived. The coffee was brewed. A mug and carton of cream sat on the counter near it. As she poured her coffee, Avery heard voices from the front of the house. Coffee in hand, she went down the hall and crossed the foyer to the living room.

Similar to the den, the living room furniture was centered on a fireplace. A loveseat sat to the left, facing the bay window at the front of the house. A matching couch faced it. With their backs to the archway were two club chairs. They were occupied by Duncan and Stiabhan, who seemed to be getting along better than the night before.

Both men stood the moment they realized someone was behind them—which was immediate.

Stiabhan smiled. "You look rested."

"I am. How late did I sleep?" Avery hadn't thought to look for a clock.

"Not that late." Duncan's eyes sparkled with laughter. "What would you like for lunch?" He pointed to the mantel where a lovely casement clock ticked away.

Avery looked at the time and blinked in embarrassment. "Twelve-forty-five! I've slept for over twelve hours. Why didn't someone wake me?"

"Because you needed the sleep, darlin'," Duncan replied. "There was no reason to make you get up before your body was ready."

"But according to you, I need to find a home here in Caledonia. And a new job. I need to get on with that. I can't waste time sleeping."

Duncan's eyes lost their merry twinkle. "Look for a job if you wish. For the time being, it would be better if you live here."

That wasn't a good idea. The longer she was around Duncan, the more she fell under his spell. Oh, who was she kidding? She doubted she could get any more under his spell. She very much feared she was already head over heels in love with the man.

"Duncan is correct. Caledonia is warded, but it doesn't keep Sidhe from entering. Or even from using our powers. Though they are severely limited unless we're invited in. I would prefer it if you are serious about remaining here instead of coming home with me, that you remain under Duncan's protection."

Avery looked at her cousin in surprise. "You *want* me to stay here with Duncan? That's definitely not the impression I got last night."

"My preference would be that you return to Peadaran with me, but I understand your reticence. My world is not yours. But you would be welcomed and loved there."

Tears burned the back of Avery's eyes. She slipped her arms around her however-many-times-removed cousin's waist and hugged him tightly, her cheek pressed against his chest. Strong arms hugged her in return.

"Thank you very much for the offer."

"But you are turning me down." He didn't sound surprised.

She leaned back to face him. "I don't like change. I need a routine. Having to move to Caledonia is hard enough. Going to Iartha would be..."

"Not anything she wants to contemplate," Duncan finished when she hesitated.

Stiabhan frowned at him before turning back to her. "If you remain here, you remain under Duncan's care. It is the only way that I will consent to leaving you behind. I am not trying to take charge of your life. It is your safety that is my utmost concern."

After that, Avery couldn't very well remind him it was her life. He was her family, and she knew he only wanted what was best for her. Avery knew that if Stiabhan wanted her to go with him, he would have no trouble taking her. Whether or not she wanted to go. It was good for her that he was considerate.

"I need to find my own place," she argued. Though her whole heart wasn't in it. "I need to get settled."

"When we find some way to keep Omaon and anyone else of his ilk at bay, then you may move out of Duncan's house."

Avery was horrified. "That could take months. I can't possibly impose on Duncan's hospitality for that long."

"It's no imposition," Duncan stated. "In fact, I insist on it."

With everything else, that rubbed her the wrong way. "You insist? You have no right to insist on anything in my life." Who did he think he was?

"I'm taking the right." Duncan crossed his arms over his chest.

"It's Duncan or me, love," Stiabhan said. "It's your choice."

Avery stepped back and glowered at both of them. Their idea of a choice wasn't one.

Duncan apparently thought she couldn't decide. Uncrossing his arms, he caught her up against him, threading the fingers of one hand through her hair and holding her still for a passionate kiss. It left her knees weak and her thoughts jumbled.

When he raised his head, intense green eyes bored into hers. "That gives me the right, princess. Don't you think it would be a good idea to stick around and find out what it means?"

It took Avery a moment to realize she was nodding in agreement, her arms around his neck. She froze. The thought that Duncan wasn't just toying with her, that he might seriously want a relationship, both terrified and thrilled her.

Though she hadn't answered him, Duncan nodded. The tenseness eased from his muscles. "Good. It's settled."

Stiabhan shook his head. "I don't know. Avery said nothing. She looks as if she's in shock."

"She didn't have to say anything out loud. I got the message. And Avery may be in shock. A little. My kisses have that effect on women." Duncan's grin was brash and confident.

Avery rolled her eyes. She tried to put the thought of how many women—beautiful ones, no doubt—Duncan had had in his life.

"If you're that concerned about a job, let's go see if we can at least find you one you'll love. We'll go into town and after I see about feeding you, I'll introduce you to Iona."

"Iona?" Stiabhan perked up. "Iona Gruffydd, Mer—"

"Yes, Emrys Pendragon's sister," Duncan interrupted. "She owns an antique shop called Time Passages. I predict she's going to adore Avery. And if I'm correct, she'll offer her a job."

Stiabhan nodded. There was an enigmatic look on his face that Avery couldn't begin to decipher. Except she did comprehend that there was something her cousin and Duncan shared they weren't letting her in on. If they didn't want her to know, they wouldn't tell her and nothing she said or did would change their minds.

"I'm not exactly dressed for a job interview."

Duncan raked her with his gaze. "You look perfect. Iona will love you. I promise." Removing the coffee mug from her hand, he set it out on the nearest surface.

A LITTLE OVER AN HOUR later, Avery was towed into a quaint shop that took up a quarter of a city block. Instead of shadowed and musty, as many antique shops were, this one was light and airy. It smelled faintly of lemon and lavender.

Avery loved it.

She frowned as she began to sense something. Something—or rather many somethings—that was beyond ancient. When she first began learning her talent, she'd had to touch objects. Now, she could sense the age without handling it. The objects in this place were all old. Some were so old that she doubted there could be a true provenance on them.

And they all called to her.

Avery pulled against Duncan's hold on her hand. She should have considered her reaction before so blithely agreeing to just walk in with no preparation. But then she'd never experienced this reaction before.

Probably because she'd never been around so many ancient artifacts at one time.

"Duncan, wait."

He immediately stopped. Looking at her, she saw the alarm in his eyes. "What's wrong? You're pale."

"What is wrong, you moronic males, is that she was not prepared for a large number of ancient artifacts gathered in one area. Bring your woman, Duncan, and I'll get her some fortified tea."

Avery saw a lovely older woman with white hair and bright blue eyes making her way toward them.

Avery's smile turned to surprise as Duncan easily scooped her up in his arms. "Put me down! I'm perfectly capable of walking."

Being Duncan, he ignored her. "You look like you're about to faint."

"I do not faint."

"Relax and enjoy, my dear. Anytime a big, strong, handsome man wants to carry me about, I find it's always best to let them. You know where to go, Duncan. I'll be along in just a minute."

It wasn't that Avery objected to Duncan carrying her. Not exactly. It was more that her weight embarrassed her. Though Duncan didn't seem to notice. He carried her as if she weighed no more than thistledown. Since her head spun, she took the lady's advice and relaxed.

Duncan took her into an office decorated as much for comfort as function. It was located at the back of the shop. He gently deposited her onto a fainting couch. Before she could move, he sat down beside her hip, preventing her from doing so.

"Please remain in a prone position for the immediate future. You're too pale. And fainting women upset my digestion. Since I enjoy eating, that's bad." He caught her nearest hand, holding it between both of his.

"I'm fine. And I repeat, I don't faint." Avery explained, "I didn't consider the effect of so many ancient artifacts all at once. I've never been around so many simultaneously before." She let her senses fan out for a second before she quickly snapped them off. "There are so many timeless antiquities stored here. Each with its own long historical story. It was as if thousands of videos began playing all at once. It can be overwhelming."

Duncan's eyes widened. He looked at Stiabhan, who had followed them in, and then back at her. "Good god! That's what it's like for you?"

"Yes." With her head still spinning, Avery wasn't about to nod.

"This was a bad idea. Why didn't you tell me? No wonder you work for a company like you do. Let's get out of here. I'll call back and explain to Iona."

Avery caught his arm as he started to stand. "No, wait. It's fine. Really," she added when he looked dubious.

"You don't look fine." Duncan looked at Stiabhan again. He had taken a seat in a large armchair. "She's your kinswoman, as you keep reminding me. What's your take?"

Stiabhan frowned. "My take? I have taken nothing."

"Damned elf."

"Fairy, if you please."

"It means I want your opinion on the situation."

"Ah." Stiabhan nodded. "I see now. Yet another American idiom. I think that if Avery believes she can handle the situation, then we must trust that she can."

Duncan glared at him. "I see it now. Your entire raison d'être is to torment me."

"I do enjoy my hobbies." Stiabhan grinned.

"How long have you two known each other?" Avery asked.

"Too long," they said simultaneously.

Avery laughed. "You two like each other. A lot."

"I don't like him," Duncan denied.

"He's a pain in my arse," Stiabhan stated. "No one likes that."

The door opened and Iona walked in. "How are you feeling, dear?"

"Much better, thank you. I just hadn't prepared myself for the potential of sensory overload. I have it under control now." Well, pretty much.

"Excellent. I shall order some tea and we'll talk." She picked up the phone and made a call, and ordered a pot of tea and scones from a nearby shop.

"You're a woman after my own heart, Iona," Stiabhan spoke up.

"And you are an outrageous flirt, Stiabhan Iorworth." The old woman smiled at him.

Duncan laughed.

So did Avery. The look on her cousin's face was priceless. He looked like a boy who'd been caught with his hand in the cookie jar. The merry glint in his eyes told them he was certain if in trouble, he could talk his way out of it.

Duncan became serious once more. "Iona, I'm not sure this is a good idea. I didn't understand how Avery's talent works or how it affects her. She can't be around this much history at one time."

"Nonsense," Iona stated, dooming Duncan to disappointment. "I'm sure Avery has learned to control her gift. And if she hasn't, this is the perfect place for her to hone that skill."

"I tried to explain to him that I just wasn't prepared. I've never been in the presence of so many historical artifacts at once. It's simply taken a little more getting used to." Avery smiled confidently when Duncan shot her a disbelieving look. "Honestly, I can handle it."

"Let her be, Duncan," Iona ordered. "Avery is a strong woman."

"I'm well aware of that. I've just spent several weeks traipsing through Omaon's damned countryside with the woman. Believe me, I know how strong she is. And how brave. That doesn't mean she should be subjected to this kind of stress if she doesn't have to be."

So startled by his praise, Avery barely registered the last sentence. She savored the warm rush of pride from his words, wrapping it around her heart like a warm blanket. She would hold on to the feeling and the words for when she was once more alone and on her own.

Avery looked into Iona's knowing blue eyes. Perhaps she wouldn't be alone after all.

Provided Iona offered her a job.

"I don't believe working here with me will cause Avery stress," Iona replied. "Do you, my dear?"

Avery shook her head. She felt like a kid at Christmas. "No, ma'am, not at all. Does that mean that you have a job opening?"

"Not anymore. I believe I just filled the position. If you accept it, that is."

"Yes! Yes, of course, I accept." Avery tried to wiggle past Duncan to get up. He stood and held out a hand to assist her. Once she was on her feet, she held out her hand to the older woman.

Iona smiled. She ignored the hand and instead wrapped her arms around Avery, hugging her tightly. "Welcome home, child."

Avery fought tears as she returned the embrace. She felt as if she had come home. Peace settled over her. Something she hadn't felt since her mother's death.

Iona released her. The white-haired woman grinned at Duncan. She then gave him a quick hug. "I will take good care of your woman. You don't need to worry about her when she's here."

Avery waited for him to correct Iona's misconception, but he didn't. She decided to wait until a later time when she and Iona were alone to set her straight on her and Duncan being a couple.

"Why don't you go next door and get my order from Lena?" Iona phrased it in the form of a question, even if they all knew it was not a request.

Duncan leaned over and kissed Iona on the cheek. He then surprised Avery by turning and kissing her quickly on the lips before leaving the office.

Avery blushed when she saw Iona's knowing smile. "We're just friends."

"Ha!" It was the first sound Stiabhan had uttered in several minutes.

Avery would have been happier if he'd stayed silent. "We are," she stated emphatically.

"No doubt, but that's not all there is to it," he said.

"Stiabhan!"

"What? I have eyes, Avery. I know what I see."

Avery shook her head. Stiabhan would use any further denial on her part to make it worse. So she turned to Iona. "May I look around?"

"Of course you may." Iona waved a beringed hand toward the door into the shop. "Look wherever you wish."

Avery barely refrained from rubbing her hands together in glee. With her mental barriers firmly in place, she went into the antique shop.

WITH A FOND SMILE, Iona watched through the open door as the young woman began to peruse the items for sale.

"I thank you for employing Avery, Ganieda," Stiabhan said.

"They know me here as Iona," she reminded him sharply. "I advise you to remember that."

Stiabhan inclined his head. "My apologies. I am still getting used to the fact that you and..."

"Emrys. Emrys Pendragon."

He nodded. "I didn't know to which time period you had been sent. Safer for everyone involved, I know. I was surprised when I met the princes. Pleased to know that the swords are appearing." His eyes lit with excitement. "I was with Connor and Brenn when they turned their locks."

"Yes, we are all pleased by that. I'm sensing another sword, but it is not yet in the prince's hands."

"At least it has begun."

"It began the moment that Mordred killed Arthur and the Dark thought it could defeat the Light."

"As you say," Stiabhan agreed.

"I am pleased that Duncan is infatuated with Avery. They will be good for one another."

"Aye. She feels the same for him, though she is afraid to show it." Stiabhan caught her nearest hand and raised it to his lips for a quick kiss on the knuckles. "Again, I thank you for hiring her."

"Don't thank me. It is I who should thank you and Duncan. Avery will be a wonderful assistant. Duncan was right to bring her to me."

"He is concerned that Omaon will send people for her. Rightfully so."

"He will try. Someone has provided Avery with a powerful protection amulet. Whoever did it knew what they were doing. It is extremely powerful. It should keep her safe." Iona looked at Stiabhan. "There are at least four more Daondasidhe women out there with Avery's talent. We must spread the word among our allies to be on the lookout for them. They need to be identified and protected without delay.

"I will certainly spread the word among family and friends, but how do you propose we identify them?" Stiabhan asked.

"I should be able to sense when they come into full power. How do you think Duncan knew to contact Avery? I am sensing one now. Eavan Douglas is showing signs. I am keeping an eye on her. The moment I know anything for certain, I will inform the other Mother Guardians. It will not do for Omaon or any of the Dubh Sidhe to get their hands on any one of them."

"No, it won't. As soon as they're identified, we'll put protection on them. For the present, however, my only concern is Avery."

Iona smiled. She patted his forearm. "Your concern for her is commendable."

Stiabhan glanced sideways at her. "You seem surprised."

"Perhaps. A little. For so long, you held yourself aloof. It pleases me to see you becoming close to others again."

He was quiet for a moment. "I will never forget them. I will never forget how they were taken from me. Or that I did not protect them." He held up a hand to stop her when she would have commented. "Yes, yes, I know it was not my fault. But they were mine. My family and I failed them. Avery is my cousin. It doesn't matter how many generations removed. She has no other family left. It is my responsibility to step in for her deceased parents."

Iona was pleased. "You see her as a daughter. I'm glad for you both. What do you think of Duncan?"

"Hah!" Stiabhan rolled his eyes. "As if it matters what I think. Avery has chosen him, whether or not she admits it."

Iona agreed. "I believe Duncan realizes that Avery is his mate."

"He realizes he wants her in his bed," Stiabhan grumbled.

She gently slapped his arm. "He is honestly concerned for her. Solicitous of her. I truly believe he recognizes her importance to him. Even if only subconsciously at the moment."

Stiabhan nodded. Reluctantly. "Aye, he does. He kept her safe and got her out of Oirthea. He is a warrior through and through."

"Which is excellent, considering Avery's special talent."

Stiabhan nodded.

The shop door opened. Duncan entered carrying a tray containing a teapot, four cups, and a large sack. He stopped when he spotted Avery, watching her for several seconds before continuing toward them.

Stiabhan watched with a frown as he approached. "If he hurts her, he'll wish he was dead."

Iona laughed.

DUNCAN COULDN'T BELIEVE that Stiabhan was irresponsible enough to allow Avery to wander around the shop alone. He hurried to the private office to set the tray on the desk.

"Are you insane?" he demanded of Avery's cousin. "You're supposed to be looking out for her."

"Avery is fine," Stiabhan snapped, but he said it to Duncan's back.

Duncan was already back in the store portion of the building. He walked over to where Avery stood, studying a rack of vintage dresses. She turned to him at once, her brown eyes shining with delight.

She caught hold of his upper arms. "This place is marvelous! I love it here!"

Avery's smile was contagious. Duncan smiled, too. Still, her initial reaction continued to concern him. His hands went to her waist to hold her. He wanted to wrap her in his arms, but they had a nosy audience watching through the open door to the office.

He tilted his head around to indicate the store. "You're sure you're feeling well? None of this is bothering you now?"

Her eyes sparkled as she looked at him. Unhappily, he discovered he was jealous. Of a stupid store. He wanted to be the cause of the joy in her eyes, not a bunch of dusty antiques.

"Not much. I can control it. At least, I'm learning to control it, Duncan. And I'm getting better at it."

Avery's hands kneaded his upper arms as she spoke. She was unaware of her actions, but he certainly wasn't. Duncan didn't mention it. He wasn't sure he wanted her to discover how easily she could affect him with a touch or a look. It was bad enough he knew.

"No more headaches? No more nearly fainting?" Duncan needed to be sure. If it truly made her happy, and she could control her reactions, he would be able to be happy for her.

"No. None. This is perfect. No more traveling. No more nights alone in hotels and motels." Letting go of his arms, she put her arms around his neck and stretched up on her toes to hug him.

Duncan didn't want to settle for a mere hug. Wrapping his own arms around her waist and back, he lifted her off her feet, holding her to him. She felt good in his arms. Right. As if she belonged there. He didn't want to release her.

What he wanted was to carry Avery inside the office, run Iona and Stiabhan out, lock the door behind them, and then make love to Avery on the fainting couch.

It seemed Avery wasn't of a similar mind. She put her hands on his shoulders and leaned back. Her cheeks flushed a becoming pink. "Duncan, put me down."

He complied. But slowly. Very slowly. Letting her body slide down his.

The moment her feet touched the floor, she hastily stepped back. Avery avoided looking at him, but he could see her cheeks had turned an even darker shade of rose. He followed on her heels as she walked back to the private office.

"Have a cherry-almond scone, dear. Lena makes them herself. They're delicious." Iona held out a bag.

"It's about time." Stiabhan's gaze was fixed on Duncan. "Your tea is getting cold."

Duncan grinned. He took a scone from the sack when Iona offered it to him. He then picked up the last cup and saucer from the tray and sat next to Avery on the fainting couch.

CHAPTER NINE

Avery started work at Time Passages the following Monday. She wasn't pleased that Duncan insisted on driving her to work and then picking her up afterward, but to refuse him would have been childish. Especially, since he was driving to work himself, and her vehicle hadn't been retrieved from the Greenville safe house yet.

It was the following Tuesday before she was able to drive herself to work. Even though her car had been delivered on Sunday, it took her another day to convince Duncan—with Stiabhan surprisingly on her side—that she was perfectly capable of driving herself.

On Friday evening, during the drive to Duncan's house, Avery wished she hadn't been so quick to fight for her independence. She was tired. In a good way, but still tired. A chauffeur would have been lovely. There had been customers in the shop until well past closing. When she and Iona finally locked up, it was almost eight. That meant it was dark by the time she headed home.

Avery had just reached the city limits when she noticed the shadow following her. It was strange that she could see it in the dark. It was blacker than the night, which was terrifying in itself.

"Duncan? Stiabhan?"

She waited, but there was no answer. The only thing Avery could figure was the shadow might be responsible. It was creepy and otherworldly enough to be the cause.

Pulling out her cell phone, Avery hit speed dial.

"I was just about to call," Duncan answered. "But why are you using the phone?"

"I'm being followed."

"What? Avery? Avery, talk to me?"

She *was* talking to him. "Duncan?"

"Damn it, Avery! Answer me."

Why couldn't he hear her? Avery could hear Duncan clearly. She waffled between fear and anger.

"Okay, I can tell the line's open. Don't hang up, honey. I can track you. I'm on my way."

That was the best news she'd heard all evening.

Suddenly, the shadow enveloped her car. Avery slammed on brakes, but she was disoriented. She felt the tires leave the pavement. The vehicle tilted forward and began sliding downward. Tree and shrub limbs snatched at and broke against the car. The vehicle crashed into something she couldn't see hard enough to cause the airbags to deploy. That would have helped if the car hadn't hit on the driver's side and her head hadn't hit the side window first.

PUTTING THE PHONE ON speaker, Duncan snatched up his keys as he headed for the garage. "Stiabhan, are you able to connect with Avery?"

Bounding to his feet from his seat in front of the TV, the Sidhe shook his head. "What is going on?"

Darrach, who was stirring a pot of vegetable soup in the kitchen, immediately went on alert.

"Avery called. She said something about being followed and then nothing. The line's open, but if she's saying anything, I can't hear her. Something's blocking communications. We're going to find her."

"Excellent. How do you propose we do that when neither of us can reach her telepathically and neither of us is a tracker?" Stiabhan asked.

Duncan tapped his phone with his index finger. "With this. Her phone has a GPS tracker in it. I made sure it was on."

"A what?"

Duncan headed for his vehicle. "GPS. Global positioning system. Suffice it to say, it means her location will appear as a tiny dot on a map." Duncan got in as Stiabhan rushed to get in the passenger side. Duncan whipped out of the garage, barely missing the still-rising door. "What I don't understand is why we can't connect with her."

"You already know why. You just do not want to give it credence."

"If it is Omaon, or his people, he won't be able to take her."

"Do not wager on that."

Duncan didn't respond. He put Avery's phone number into his special, in-dash GPS. He was only somewhat relieved when the dot representing Avery showed up. It showed the location of her phone. Until he reached the spot, Duncan wouldn't know if Avery was with it.

The way Duncan drove, it took less than four minutes to reach the place where Avery's car, or at least Avery's phone, should be. There was no visible sign of either. If Avery's phone had been tossed, she could be anywhere.

"I don't see her vehicle. There is no sign of Avery here." Stiabhan sounded as panicked as Duncan felt.

"I'm not hanging up. Use the phone I gave you and call the office. Tell them to get people out here now. They can pick up her GPS from my SUV." Duncan rocked the truck to a stop.

There had to be something. Some clue.

Jumping out of the SUV, he headed across the two-lane road, flashlight in hand. If someone tried to run her off the road, there should be signs. Something. Anything to tell him where Avery was.

Duncan heard a metallic ping in the darkness. The type of sound engines made as they cooled. It came from down in the deep gully off the edge of the road. That's when he saw the broken branches.

"Oh, God!" Terrified of what he would find, Duncan yelled, "Stiabhan! Down here." He shoved his phone in his pocket and took off down the steep slope as fast as he dared. He would be of no help if he broke his own neck. "Avery!" he shouted as he spotted the car. There was no reply, which only alarmed him more.

Shoving branches out of the way, Duncan made his way to the passenger side door since the driver's side was against the side of a three-feet diameter sapling. The front left corner crumpled against the trunk of an old oak. It made it impossible to enter from that side.

Duncan shined the light through the window. He saw Avery slumped over the center console. It took several wrenching jerks to get the passenger door open. Climbing in, he grabbed her wrist and checked her pulse. If he hadn't already been kneeling, his legs would have buckled in relief. He began carefully checking her for injuries. He didn't find broken bones, but he found a nasty bump on the left side of her head.

Moving her carefully, Duncan eased Avery from the car and lifted her into his arms. He turned just as Stiabhan slid to a stop beside the trunk.

"Is she...?"

"She's alive, but she's got a knot on the side of her head. Grab her purse from the floorboard and then call the office again. Tell them to get Haldis and ask her to meet us at my house." Duncan translocated back to the top of the road. Most folks had headed home over two hours before, so the traffic on this secondary road was few and far between. He raced across the road to his SUV.

"The healer will be awaiting us," Stiabhan said when he joined them.

"Can you drive?" Duncan asked. He didn't want to let go of Avery, even for the short drive to the house.

"No, though I have requested to learn. However, few of you seem willing to teach me," Stiabhan groused.

"I'll get someone to teach you tomorrow. Get in the backseat. I'll hand Avery in to you."

Duncan broke a few laws getting home. It didn't matter that Avery regained consciousness just moments after he put her in the Sidhe's arms.

"I can walk," Avery stated when Duncan opened her door after parking in the garage.

Duncan let her exit the SUV before sweeping her up in his arms. "The hell you will."

Forty minutes later, Avery had been checked out by the healer and pronounced fine. Duncan waited outside her room while she showered. When she was dressed in her gown and robe, he led her to a recliner in the den. Darrach had a mug of hot cocoa on the table next to her chair. Once she was seated, he brought her a bowl of vegetable soup.

"What happened?" Darrach asked.

Avery shivered so violently that if Duncan hadn't snatched the bowl from her hand, she would have spilled it in her lap. "A shadow. A huge black shadow. It followed me as if it was alive. I called Duncan. I could hear him, but he couldn't hear me. Then the shadow just grew until it covered the entire car. I couldn't see. I thought I was stopping on the road, but the car went down an embankment or something."

"Brollochan," Stiabhan stated.

"What?" Avery asked as both Duncan and Darrach cursed.

"Wait. Why didn't it take her?" Darach asked.

Good question, Duncan thought. Then he remembered. "Orla's necklace. The Sidhe woman we stayed with gave Avery a necklace and told her to never remove it. She said it would protect her."

Avery pulled the necklace out from under her shirt and fingered the pendant.

Stiabhan looked at it, nodding. "Iona and I could feel it at the shop. It contains strong protection powers."

"That's great to know, but what is a brollochan?" Avery asked, still holding the pendant between her fingers.

Stiabhan faced her. "Brollochan. It is a creature capable of changing shape at will. Most often they appear as dark shadows, only their forms are more solid. They are a favorite tool of the Dubh Sidhe."

"That makes no sense. Why would Omaon try to kill Avery if he wants to use her talents?" Darrach asked.

"Omaon did not send it," Stiabhan replied.

"Cernach Runcie or one of the others," Duncan surmised. "If they don't think they can grab her, then they'd rather see her dead."

Stiabhan inclined his head. "That is my guess."

"Wonderful," Avery said.

"Can the ceremony be performed tonight?" Duncan asked the Sidhe. He wasn't about to go through the fear of not being able to contact Avery again. Perhaps it was the shape-shifter wolf part of him, but he recognized his mate, and he wasn't about to allow her to be harmed.

Stiabhan nodded. "It can. *If* she is amenable."

Avery looked from Stiabhan to Duncan. "What are you talking about?"

"A binding ceremony," Duncan responded fast enough. "Nothing can block communication between us if we're bound. It's a simple ceremony."

Ignoring the bowl Duncan held out to her, Avery surged to her feet. "Only a simple ceremony? Do you think me naïve? A binding ceremony is a Sidhe wedding. My mother made sure I knew because that's how my father tricked her into marriage."

Duncan stilled. That didn't sound good. "Weren't they happy?"

"Deliriously so. That's not the point. She said male Hunters often trick their women into marriage by suggesting a binding ceremony first." She shook her head. "You asking it of me makes no sense. Surely you have other options."

Grabbing her by the hand, Duncan tugged her along with him. Going down the hall, he spun her into his office and closed the door. Before she could say anything, he pressed her between his body and the door. His lips claimed hers.

Every rational thought in Avery's head turned to dust and blew away on the sultry breeze of rapidly rising passion. When Duncan finally lifted his head, allowing some semblance of sanity to return, Avery was startled by her new position.

Avery was on her back on a couch. Her calf-length skirt was hiked to her waist, and she had wrapped her legs around Duncan's waist, opening her to the male member pressing against the juncture of her body. Her panties and his jeans were the only separation. He held himself above her on his elbows, which only served to press that hard, very male portion of his anatomy more firmly against that very female portion of hers.

"Now, does it make sense?" he asked, before he breathed deeply.

"I understand that you want to have sex with me." Grabbing her courage in both hands, Avery admitted. "And I would love to make love to you."

Duncan's eyes heated at that pronouncement.

"But that's not a reason to get married. Especially in this day and age."

"It is to me. I want you, Avery. Now I know that you want me as well. I believe we can have a great life together. You get along with my family. They all adore you. Besides, I don't want to just live with you. I want us connected on a deeper level. I feel more for you than that. And I want the universe to know that we belong to each other. Give us a chance."

Avery felt as if she was being offered every dream she had ever had, plus ones she'd never allowed herself to dare. She looked up at the beautiful man above her, waiting for her answer. She was going to have to ignore her insecurities and take a leap. Avery quaked inside.

She was surprised Duncan couldn't feel it and wasn't commenting on it. It was time to go for it. That proved to be one of the most difficult things she'd ever had to do. She closed her eyes for a moment to muster her courage.

Duncan, being Duncan, wasn't going to let her shut him out. He kissed her again, a hand moving up to cup her breast. He began to trail kisses across her cheek and down her throat as his hand worked its own magic.

"Give us a chance. Give me a chance, Avery. Trust me to take care of you."

She opened her eyes to look directly into Duncan's.

"We can be married tonight. Say yes," he urged.

Staring in his beautiful green eyes, Avery threw her reservations out the window and went for what her heart wanted. "Yes."

Duncan froze. It seemed that he couldn't believe that she agreed. "Yes?"

Avery laughed joyously. It was nice to know she wasn't the only one unsure. "Yes." Capturing his cheeks in her palms, she pulled his head down for a kiss.

Duncan looked at the beautiful woman in amazement. He was so relieved, he felt like crying. And wasn't that a sorry state for a grown man to be in?

He looked at his watch. It read nine-thirty-six. Duncan couldn't believe half the night wasn't already gone. But it meant that they had time. That he had time to try to make a hurried union something special for Avery.

"Tonight, at midnight." He wasn't going to allow her the chance to think about it and change her mind.

"What? No, I can't possibly be ready by then."

"Yes, you can. What are fairy relatives for? I'll take care of the officiant. Stiabhan is your family. He would be delighted to walk you down the aisle, so to speak. If that's what you want?"

She nodded dazedly.

"I'll ask him to make a dress for you."

"How is he going to do that between now and midnight?"

"Fairy. Magic, remember? For tonight, think of Stiabhan as your fairy godmother." Duncan kissed her again. He couldn't help himself. Carefully moving off of her and getting to his feet, he held his hand down. When she placed hers in his, he pulled her to her feet. Right into his arms. Duncan was so happy. He kissed her again, holding her tightly to him for a moment before reluctantly releasing her.

Despite what he told her, there was a lot to get done if they were to be sealed at midnight. It wouldn't be easy, but he could manage to keep his hands off his bride for a little while. At least until they were sealed.

As his emotions calmed, Duncan thought of something else. He caught Avery's shoulders, garnering her full attention once more. "We'll have a regular Pure wedding, too. As soon as you want to plan it. Whatever you want. I'll help."

It bothered him she looked away from him at that. He hated she seemed to have no idea of her worth. What had he said to upset her?

"I don't need a church wedding, Duncan? A justice of the peace will be fine."

He was cognizant of the fact she said *need* instead of *want*. Avery might not need a church wedding, but he would bet his favorite claymore she wanted one. "All right. We've got plenty of time to discuss it later. I'll tell Stiabhan to meet you in your room."

STIABHAN MET AVERY in her room. He brought an older woman with him. One with beautiful auburn hair. Avery was introduced to Aran Llewellyn. Within a quarter of an hour, Aran literally produced a beautiful gown in burgundy velvet from thin air. It was decorated with lacy Celtic designs fashioned in sparkling gold and silver threads.

Avery remained in her robe while Aran styled her hair. She pulled the long strands into a loose bun. Makeup was applied sparingly. Finally, Aran helped her into her gown.

Closing her eyes for a moment, Avery relished the wondrous feel of the cloth against her skin. She had never worn anything so luxurious.

Finally, the time arrived. Aran left her as Stiabhan returned. He looked her up and down. "You're beautiful. You just need one thing." A crown of holly and apple blossoms appeared in his hands. He carefully settled it on her head. "You're much too good for the likes of Duncan Kerr."

Avery bit her bottom lip before she asked, "Am I doing the right thing? What if I'm ruining his life?"

Stiabhan closed his hands over her shoulders. "You are his mate, Avery. At some point, Duncan recognized this. It's one reason he is pushing so hard for the ceremony to be done quickly. Also, when we were unable to contact you, it frightened him as much as it did me. Perhaps slightly more. With a binding, Duncan knows nothing can stop him from being able to communicate with you."

He leaned down and pressed his lips against her forehead for several seconds. When he pulled away, Stiabhan stared into her eyes. "Only you know if you're doing the right thing. As these humans say, it's cliche, but follow your heart. It will never lead you astray. Having said that, if you were to ask me what I think of the two of you together, I would have to admit I heartily approve. But the decision is yours, Avery. You tell me what you want to do."

Avery didn't hesitate. Her heart knew what it wanted. It wanted Duncan. Forever. "I want to marry him."

Stiabhan smiled. "Then let us go see to this binding ceremony." Stiabhan held out his arm.

Avery placed her hand in the crook of his arm. He led her through the house, and to her surprise, headed downstairs to the basement where Darach's rooms were. Gavin waited at the bottom of the stairs. He smiled at them before turning his head and giving a shrill whistle. Harp and flute music flared to life and played an ethereal tune from somewhere further along the hallway.

Gavin stepped back and to the side. With a sweep of his arm, he waved them forward.

Going down the steps, they entered a room about twenty-five feet across. There was a fireplace ahead and to the left, a merrily burning fire inside. Along the outer walls, large candles burned brightly from tall floor sconces. Seats had been set up in two rows, leaving an aisle down the middle.

At the end, in front of the fireplace, stood Duncan. He wore a black, thigh-length tunic and trousers decorated with the same symbols as those on her gown, and in the same sparkling metallic threads. His shiny black hair fell in waves and curled around his head and over the top of his collar. The sheer masculine beauty of the man took her breath away. He smiled. It drew her to him as magnets drew filings.

So focused was she on Duncan that she didn't even notice the man beside him until Stiabhan stopped right in front of him. The older man was only around six feet in height. He had straight black hair, piercing dark eyes, and a sharp blade of a nose. He nodded to Stiabhan before smiling gently at her.

"Avery, this is Pritchard Cathcart. He's my... great-grandfather with too many greats in front to count," Duncan made the introductions. "Pritch, this is Avery Alison Beaton."

The man took her right hand in both of his slender ones. "It is a pleasure to meet you, Avery."

"Pritch will perform the binding ceremony," Stiabhan said. He kissed Avery's left temple. "I leave you in his capable hands." He stepped back and took a seat beside Iona.

The actual ceremony was a blur to Avery. She must have answered appropriately and at the correct moments because it soon concluded with Duncan gathering her in his arms and giving her one of his mind-blowing kisses. Cheers erupted.

Still accepting congratulations, they went upstairs, where Darrach had prepared a celebratory meal and laid it out in the kitchen and casual dining area. Taking their plates and drinks, they settled in the den.

After a few moments, Pritch took Avery upstairs so he could fortify her sigil. It hadn't taken him and Stiabhan long to convince her of the need. She never wanted another experience with a brollochan. Ever. Anything to give her an edge, she would do.

Avery thanked the ancient Sidhe as they returned to the den, where she took a seat beside her new husband.

Two hours sped by. Avery enjoyed it, but after everything she'd been through that day, her energy was gone. She sat beside Duncan on the couch. He put his arm around her shoulders, urging her to lean against his side.

WHEN AVERY SUCCUMBED to exhaustion, Duncan signaled his aunt. Josey began quietly ushering people out. Fifteen minutes later, only Stiabhan remained. Even Gavin and Darach found other accommodations for the next few days.

It wouldn't have bothered Duncan if they'd waited until the next day to leave. Avery would sleep in his bed, but that's all either of them would be doing. Avery was exhausted. Plus, she was beginning to feel more side effects from the wreck.

Duncan was tired as well. Certainly, too tired for his first time with his bride. He wanted to make it perfect for her.

He looked up as Stiabhan came to stand before him.

"Take care of my kinswoman, Duncan Kerr."

Seated, Duncan was at a disadvantage. However, he wasn't intimidated by the Sidhe. "You have my word that I will. I will protect her with my life if need be."

Stiabhan's expression eased. "Let us hope it does not come to that. I am returning home now. If either of you have need of me, call." In the blink of an eye, he disappeared.

"I thought you said they couldn't do that," Avery murmured drowsily, never raising her head from his shoulder.

Duncan smiled. "Certain Sidhe, ones invited in, are able to come and go. They also have full use of their powers. But they must be asked in. We try to be very careful about who is invited. You're safe in the house. Our house, Avery. I promise."

"That shadow..." She shivered.

Duncan slid his arm beneath her legs and lifted her onto his lap. He wrapped both arms around her and held her close. "I'm so sorry that happened. From now on, nothing will be able to block our communications with one another."

Avery leaned back, looking at him in horror. "You mean it will return and try again?"

"I would love to tell you no, but I can't, sweetheart. I just don't know. Omaon wants you and the other Dubh Sidhe monarchs probably either want you themselves, or they want you dead."

"Aren't you a barrel of sunshine? And to think, some people strive to be popular."

Duncan was glad Avery could find humor in the situation. He saw none. "We'll find a way to make you very unpopular with them. But it's late and we can't do it tonight. Let's go to bed." He stood with her in his arms.

"Duncan, wait."

"We'll just sleep, honey. As much as I want to consummate our marriage, I want to do it right. I'm too tired. And I don't mean to insult my bride, but you look exhausted. Do you mind if we save our wedding night for tomorrow?" A shy shake of her head rewarded him.

It was a sign of how tired she was that she didn't say anything about him carrying her into his bedroom. Now their bedroom. He carried her through into the bathroom, letting her feet drop to the floor when he stood her in front of the large walk-in closet.

"Josey and Aran moved your clothes in here. I'll leave you to change. Do you have a preference for which side of the bed?"

"No. It doesn't matter to me."

"Good. I'll take the side toward the windows. You take the door."

Avery nodded, a befuddled expression on her face. He could understand. While she had to be concerned with defense and self-protection, she wasn't used to protecting others. He was. It came natural to him to put himself between danger and his client. He was sure as hell going to make sure he was between danger and his own wife.

"I'll leave you to get ready for bed. I'll be right back." While she changed, Duncan did a run-through of the house. He checked windows, doors, and the security system. Everything was as secure as he could make it. Which, if Stiabhan was to be believed—and Duncan had every reason to believe he was—wasn't as safe as he wanted it to be. As soon as he could, Duncan planned to see if there wasn't something more he could do about that.

By the time he was satisfied and returned to the bedroom, Avery was already in the large bed. She was curled on her side on the near side of the California King. Duncan wondered how long it would take her to get over her shyness.

Before leaving the bathroom, Duncan turned out the light. If Avery was still awake, he didn't want to shock her when she discovered he slept in the nude.

Once in bed, Duncan considered reaching for her, but he thought it might be too soon. He was still feeling relief that she'd agreed to the Sidhe wedding. He didn't want to push for more than she was ready to give.

Lying on his back, Duncan stared up into the darkness. He listened carefully. The house was empty, except for the two of them. All he heard was the sound of the house settling and Avery's breathing. It was even, telling him she was asleep and not simply pretending.

Duncan closed his eyes, a smile on his face. He was happy. Thrilled even. He couldn't remember the last time he'd felt so good.

CHAPTER TEN

When Avery awoke, daylight was peeking around the edge of the drapes. The second thing she noticed was the masculine arm beneath her head. She was curled on her side with a large, hot male body at her back. A second, heavy masculine arm lay along her waist, hip, and thigh. His fingers were curled loosely around her leg just above her knee. Circling her bare thigh. Her below-the-knee gown had risen to mid-thigh.

Those masculine fingers on her thigh flexed and caressed. "Good morning, darlin."

"Duncan?"

His chest rumbled against her back. "Well, I hope you weren't expecting someone else."

Avery laughed, too. "Of course not." She rolled over so she could see her husband. Duncan lay on his side, facing her.

"Good. I don't want you thinking of any other man." He dipped his head and kissed her. Then he kissed her again. And again.

As if there were any other man in her life. Even if there was, Duncan would have eclipsed them into oblivion.

Passion crashed over Avery like a tidal wave, sweeping her along. Duncan was her only anchor. His strength surrounded her, protecting her even as he stroked her body to a fever pitch. She eagerly made a place for him when he rolled her onto her back and moved over her.

Between drugging kisses, he somehow removed her gown. Avery didn't have time to be embarrassed by her nudity. One, because she suddenly discovered Duncan was already naked. Two, because she wasn't allowed a moment to worry about the extra weight she carried because her husband began a tender assault on her lips. Talented hands brushed across her skin, awakening nerve endings where she didn't even know she had any. Every inch of her skin became sensitive to his touch.

When his lips closed around her nipple, Avery would have come off the bed if Duncan's body wasn't essentially holding her down. She was involved, too, running her hands over his neck, shoulders, and back. Tunneling her fingers into his thick, silky hair, she held his head as he suckled first one breast and then the other.

When he began to kiss his way down her stomach, however, Avery tugged on his hair, forcing him to stop. "Kiss me again. Please, Duncan."

He hesitated a moment, studying her. "Honey, I don't think I can wait much longer. This will make it easier for you."

She didn't doubt Duncan was right. He had more experience, after all, but Avery wasn't ready yet for that level of intimacy. "Please, just kiss me."

Duncan moved back up. "Whatever you want." He kissed her. As he did, one hand went between her legs.

Avery's first instinct was to close them. With Duncan settled heavily between her thighs, that wasn't an option. Instead, she clung to him, running her hands up and down his smooth back.

Closing her eyes, Avery gave herself over to the feelings.

They popped open again as Duncan entered her. He was a large man. Apparently, all over. He focused his gaze on her face, watching her intently. Avery kept her eyes locked with his as he rocked, sliding a little farther inside her with each thrust. By the time he was fully in, Avery's fingernails were digging into his skin just above his hips.

Duncan stilled, holding himself on his elbows above her. "Are you all right?"

Avery nodded. She was. She wasn't a virgin, but it had been a long time. For his size, he was surprisingly gentle, allowing her body time to adjust to his. "I'm more than all right. You may move now."

"Thank god." Duncan's grin was part grimace from his restraint. He began to thrust. Slowly at first, but as Avery met his movements, his pace increased.

Soon, Avery wasn't sure if it was pleasure or pain she felt. It seemed just beyond her reach. Something she had never experienced before. Abruptly, she reached the pinnacle. Pleasure as she'd never known crashed over her. She cried out from the force, clinging to Duncan before sinking bonelessly against the mattress.

Duncan shouted out his release. Holding his weight off her with his arms, he rested his forehead against her shoulder as her inner muscles continued to reflexively clutch him. Several seconds later, when he could move, he eased away. "Thank you." Bending, he tenderly kissed her lips and then her closed eyelids.

Avery blushed. It was all she could manage.

Duncan rolled onto his back, hugging Avery to his side. He smiled. Catching hold of the sheet, he pulled it over them both. "Since we have no place to be today, how about we sleep in?"

Staying in bed, holding Duncan, sounded perfect to Avery. She nodded, her cheek rubbing against his chest as she did so. "That sounds wonderful."

Duncan pressed his lips against her forehead once more.

When Duncan next woke, around two hours had passed. Avery was still curled against his side, her head on his shoulder and her long hair spread across his arm like a dark cloak. One arm was bent across his stomach and chest, a small palm flattened against his skin. Plump breasts pressed against his ribs.

Avery seemed to have some issues with her body image. Duncan had none. She was all female. He loved curvy women, and his wife had some gorgeous curves.

Lifting his head slightly, Duncan kissed the top of her head. A rush of tenderness for the beautiful woman in his arms swamped him. Whatever it took, Duncan was going to keep her safe.

Duncan's stomach growled. He glanced at the bedside clock. It was nearly two in the afternoon. No wonder he was hungry. No doubt Avery was, too—or would be when she woke.

Carefully, Duncan eased away from his wife. Avery mumbled in protest. Her eyes fluttered open as she rolled into his empty spot.

"It's all right. I'll be right back," Duncan whispered.

Avery's eyes blinked a few more times before sleep once more took her.

Grabbing a pair of sweatpants, Duncan went to the bathroom. He hurried through his shower and then pulled on his pants before padding downstairs to the kitchen.

There had been a ton of hors d'oeuvres for the after-ceremony celebration. At least half of them remained. He was sure his aunt put those in the fridge. He hoped so. Opening the two doors, Duncan smiled at what he saw inside. Besides the leftovers, there were also two quiches, three casseroles, and a deep pot containing a roast and vegetables.

Duncan removed one quiche and set it on the nearest counter. After putting a kettle of water on to boil, he retrieved two plates and two forks. Slicing the quiche, he put large slices on the plates.

From above, he heard movement. Avery was awake. He took the plates and began the process of heating them in the microwave.

A short while later, Avery padded hesitantly into the kitchen. Damn, but his wife was lovely. She was dressed only in her nightgown, a short-sleeved garment in a cranberry-colored t-shirt material that hugged her curves and made her skin glow. Her legs and feet were bare. Her dark hair fell in shining waves around her shoulders and down her back. Avery looked sexy as hell. Duncan wanted nothing more than to pick her up and carry her back to bed.

But Duncan needed to feed her first. She needed her strength. "Afternoon, Dahlin'. Are you hungry?"

She nodded, looking a little dazed.

Duncan walked around the kitchen island and pulled out one of the barstools. "Come, have a seat. I'm heating water for tea and I'm warming quiche in the microwave."

Avery hesitated. She waved a hand in the direction she'd come. "Perhaps I should get dressed."

Duncan wrapped his arm around her waist. "Why? We'll only undress each other again. Let's keep it simple for today. If you're cold, I'll get you a robe."

Avery shook her head. She was blushing yet fighting a smile. "I'm fine."

Duncan ran one hand down across her hip and over her bottom. Cupping the rounded cheek, he lifted her to her toes. "Are you wearing any panties?" He could feel the answer. He just wanted to see if she would admit it.

His wife blushed crimson. "No." She ducked her head. "I was going to go back and dress after I found you."

He kissed her temple and whispered, "Well, you found me. Don't bother dressing on my account. In fact, as your husband, I prefer that you don't dress at all. At least when it's just the two of us. I might have to kill anyone else if they saw you like I've seen you."

Avery shook her head, swatting him lightly on the arm. "Duncan."

He grinned. He felt good. And happy. So very blissful.

"Come on. Let's feed you." With one arm around her waist, he lifted her off her feet and walked with her to the bar as she clutched his shoulders. "I'm not going to drop you." He pretended to do just that, which earned him a squeak and a harder swat to his shoulder. "I promise you will never come to harm at my hands."

Avery slipped her arms around his shoulders. She kissed his temple before she whispered in his ear, "I never thought you'd drop me on purpose. But I'm heavy. And accidents do happen."

He gently lowered her onto a barstool. "You're not heavy. There will be no accidents for you, my darling. Just a very late brunch." Before he straightened, he put his hands on the arms of the barstool, leaned in, and kissed her. His heart sang when her right hand slipped beneath his hair to cup the back of his neck and hold him while she enthusiastically kissed him back.

She released him, smiling at him with a little shyness and a whole lot of seduction. "Okay, now feed me."

Duncan laughed. He stepped back and gave a small bow. "Your wish is my command, my lady."

Their late breakfast was a happy, learning time for them both. Duncan learned more about Avery's life and her deceased parents and grandparents. In return, he answered any questions she asked. He wanted her to be comfortable with him.

Duncan was extremely cognizant that he'd rushed her into the binding. Necessary for both their sakes, though for different reasons. He felt the need to make up for not properly courting her. Duncan was sure that a mad dash across a Tìr-dhàimhian kingdom, running for their lives, didn't count.

"You need a ring," Duncan commented several hours later. They were once more cuddling in bed.

"What?" Avery tilted her head back so she could look into his eyes.

He lifted her left hand. "Rings. You need them. At least an engagement ring. We can do the wedding bands when we have the modern wedding, if you want."

Avery took a deep breath and let it out slowly. "I don't need a ring."

"I don't care whether or not you *need* one. I want you to have one. Perhaps it's old-fashioned or whatever you want to call it, but a ring marks you as taken. It says that you belong to someone who cares for you. To me. I'm very proud of that, and I want the world to know we belong to each other. I'm buying you a ring. And I'm going to wear my wedding band, with pride, when we get them."

Avery laughed. The movement of her body gently rocked his.

"Would you like to pick it out?" he asked.

She shook her head, kissed his jaw, and then rested her cheek against his bare shoulder. "No. If you really want to get one, I'll leave choosing it up to you."

That surprised him. "You truly trust me to pick out your rings?"

"Of course. Men have been picking out engagement rings for years. You have good taste, Duncan. I trust you."

He kissed the top of her head. Duncan felt humbled. "Do you know your ring size?"

"Nine."

Duncan eased out from under her side.

"Where are you going?" Grabbing the blankets, Avery held them to her chest.

"I just remembered something I need to do." He grabbed boxers from the dresser before heading for the bathroom and the closet.

"Duncan, it's nearly four. It's Saturday afternoon. Can't it wait until Monday?"

He pulled a sweater over his head, grabbed a pair of slacks, and returned to the bedroom. He slipped into his pants before sitting on the edge of the bed to pull on socks and shoes. "I'm sorry, but it can't. I should have done it yesterday." He leaned down and kissed her. "I'll return before you have time to miss me. Get some sleep while I'm gone. You may not get much once I return."

"Promise?" Her eyes sparkled.

Duncan grinned. "I hear your siren's call, but I refuse to answer until I get home. Then I'll fall willingly under your spell. I promise."

He left before he gave into her siren's call. He needed to hurry. Most of the stores closed at five, and he needed perusal time.

Before Duncan left, he called Darach. While he wanted to trust that his home was warded and secure, he was not about to chance it.

THREE BEEPS STARTLED Avery awake, her heart pounding. She had planned on rising after Duncan left, but he had left her so deliciously, bonelessly sated that she fell asleep. Quickly pulling on her nightgown, she slipped into the robe Duncan left. Since it came to mid-calf on him, it didn't make her look as much like a child playing dress up as his long robe.

She was just nearing the bottom of the back stairs when she saw Duncan step in from the mudroom. She leaned against the banister in relief. Until that moment, she hadn't realized how much on edge her nerves still were.

Duncan turned to see her standing on the landing. Apparently, he saw something in her expression. He came to her, enveloped her in his embrace, and pulled her tightly against him. "Are you doing all right? Did something happen?"

Avery hugged him, pressing her palms against his back. He smelled like fresh air and safety, if safety had a smell. "Nothing happened. I'm just jumpy from that encounter with that shadow creature."

"I'll say. You looked as if you were about to faint."

"I already told you; I don't faint." Avery didn't want her husband thinking she was some missish female who was terrified of everything. That wasn't her. She'd been on her own too long to not have developed some backbone.

"Good." Duncan squeezed her. "Because that would upset me, and I don't like to be upset."

Avery laughed. "Well, we can't have that."

"You're supposed to take care of me. You promised. And it's also in the wedding vows we'll be taking soon."

Avery leaned back so she could see his eyes. She could read a lot in Duncan's eyes. "Not upsetting you is taking care of you?"

"It's a large part of it. To help you out, I'll give you a few examples of what upsets me."

"Okay." Avery was interested in hearing this.

"You being upset for any reason upsets me. You being worried about anything upsets me. You not feeling well upsets me greatly. You being hurt or injured in any way would most definitely upset me."

"Duncan, those are all about me. What upsets you?"

Duncan's right hand came up to cup and caress her cheek. "That *is* what upsets me, Avery. Stay well. Stay happy. Stay safe, and I'll be happy. Oh, and kill all the spiders. Those upset me." He shuddered. "I can't stand those silent creepy-crawlies."

Tears filled her eyes. Avery didn't know whether to laugh or cry. Putting her arms around his shoulders and cupping the back of his head, she pulled it down so she could kiss him. Avery adored being able to touch him. What she didn't feel comfortable enough to put into words yet, she tried to put into her kiss.

Duncan didn't break the kiss, but he released her long enough to shrug out of his jacket and toss it over the banister. One muscled arm wrapped around her waist and lifted her off her feet. Instead of heading up to the bedroom, Duncan walked into the den, went to the couch, and lowered them both to the cushions.

When Avery next woke, it was to the smell of mouth-watering aromas wafting in from the kitchen. She was still on the couch, Duncan's robe and a throw covering her. Avery sat up, wincing slightly. It wasn't all the result of Duncan's enthusiastic lovemaking. Most were aches and pains emerging that she could only attribute to the wreck.

"What's wrong?" Duncan asked, startling her. She hadn't heard him approach. Large as he was, Duncan moved with the silence of a big jungle cat.

"Just a few aches from driving into a ravine. That's all. I stiffened up while I was sleeping." She slipped into the robe and wrapped it around her. She had no idea where her nightgown was.

Duncan watched her. He didn't appear appeased by her answer. "The tub in the master bath has massaging jets. Maybe a hot bath with the jets on is in order. By the time you're done, I'll have supper ready."

"It smells wonderful."

"It's just pot roast Aunt Josey prepared. She makes an amazing one. I can't take credit since I'm just heating it." He pulled Avery to her feet and gave her a gentle nudge toward the stairs. "Take your time."

Duncan must have been keeping track of her progress because when she walked out of the bedroom, dressed in jeans and a sweater, he was waiting in the hallway, leaning against the wall. He smiled appreciatively. Instead of the breakfast nook, he ushered her through the pantry into the formal dining room.

At the sight that greeted her, Avery froze. Five candles in a candelabra provided the only light from the center of the cherry dining table. Two places were set perpendicular to one another at one end of the table. Cream-colored plates had pasta bowls sitting atop them.

Leading her to the seat facing the window, Duncan pulled out the chair and held it for her.

Avery stood, staring at the small, emerald velvet box sitting just beyond the place setting.

"Have a seat, Avery. It won't bite."

Avery didn't have to look at him. She could hear the laughter in his voice. She sat automatically, unable to take her eyes off the little green box. Avery didn't understand why she felt so intimidated by it. They'd already had a binding ceremony. Whatever was in the box shouldn't be scary.

Duncan tired of waiting. Picking up the box, he kneeled by her side. Opening the box, he held it out for her to see the contents.

"Oh, Duncan," Avery sighed in a breathless whisper. She stared at the most beautiful engagement ring she'd ever seen. Mounted in a white-gold setting, it held a square, cushion-cut diamond of at least two carats. On each side were two smaller square stones of a half to three-quarter carats each.

"I hope that means you like it." Duncan removed the rind from its pale green satin cushion, took hold of Avery's left hand, and carefully slid the ring on her fourth finger. "I should have at least done this at the ceremony, but I wasn't as prepared as I should have been."

Avery heard him, but she was having trouble taking it all in. She wanted to say something, but the words wouldn't form. It was as if the hand holding hers and the glittering ring he'd place on her hand held her in thrall.

"Sweetheart? Was I wrong? Do you hate it? I can take it back on Monday and exchange it."

Avery closed her hand as if to hold the ring on her finger. It touched her that the big, gorgeous man next to her actually sounded uncertain. Pulling her hand free, she wrapped her arms around his shoulders and soundly kissed him. "It's beautiful. I adore it. It's the most beautiful ring I've ever seen."

Duncan rocked back on his heels. "For that wonderful response, my lady, even if you did nearly give me a heart attack making me wait, I shall feed you."

Avery didn't want to release him. She could have happily hugged Duncan Kerr for the rest of their lives. Reluctantly, she let go and sat back. "Thank you."

"There is nothing to thank me for. It's my joy to buy you things. Especially things that make you happy. What did I say wrong?"

Avery shook her head, swiftly wiping away tears. "Nothing. You say everything right."

"That look on your face tells me it's definitely something." Pulling out his chair, Duncan sat facing her. "Avery, tell me what I said."

"It's nothing you said." When he tilted his head and frowned, she tried to explain. "Not exactly. It's just that I want to bring something to this relationship, too."

"Besides style, grace, and beauty?"

"Duncan, I'm serious. I don't feel I have much to contribute. I don't want it to be lopsided. I can't even cook." Avery tried not to, but she cried harder.

"Oh, sweetheart, this isn't a lopsided relationship. I can't cook either. I can warm up food, but that's it. You see, I don't care if you can cook, clean, or anything. Darrach is a chef—if you don't mind him living here."

Avery shook her head. She didn't care who lived with them.

He gave her a gentle shake. "Do not ever believe for one second you are somehow less in this relationship. There would be no relationship without you. You are my family. Together, we are one. You, Avery, are my greatest gift. *Never* forget that. Without you there is no us, and *us* is pretty special."

It was the closest that Duncan had come to saying he loved her without actually saying the words. Avery was still too timid to tell him she loved him, so she couldn't fault him for not wanting to be the first. It was the sweetest thing anyone had ever said to her. Avery burst into tears once more.

Duncan sat in a chair and tugged her onto his lap. "Don't cry anymore. Please. Angel, you're breaking my heart. Damnit, this is not how I envisioned this meal going."

Avery hugged him tightly. She even chuckled at his disgruntled last comment. "That was wonderful. You're wonderful, Duncan Kerr."

"If wonderful makes you cry, I don't believe I want to be wonderful."

Avery kissed him and then leaned back to meet his gaze. "These are happy tears. You make me happy, Duncan. Delightfully so."

He looked unconvinced at first, but then shook his head once. "Happy tears, huh? I'm going to have to learn the difference because I don't want any other kind." He kissed her leisurely, yet thoroughly. It was several seconds before he set her back in her chair. "If we keep this up, neither of us will get supper. And I worked hard heating up Aunt Josie's pot roast."

CHAPTER ELEVEN

Duncan and Avery spent an idyllic weekend together.

"We'll have a honeymoon, angel, I promise," Duncan told her over bowls of hot oatmeal and fruit on Monday morning. "I wish I could postpone this job, but I can't."

"I understand. You have to do your job and check out any leads on the weapon. I don't need a honeymoon. I just need you." She spooned up more oatmeal. "Besides, I need to get back to work, too. This all happened so suddenly that Iona couldn't have had time to find someone to fill in for me."

Duncan wasn't about to remind Avery that until hiring her, Iona had been running Time Passages on her own. He already knew that his wife felt best when she was helping someone. She thrived on being needed.

"Are you going to drive me to work on your way out of town?"

"I can." After her emotional reaction to her engagement ring, he wasn't sure how she would react to the second gift he'd purchased for her. It had been delivered that morning while Avery was still asleep. "Or...you could drive yourself."

"I thought my car was totaled."

"It was, but there are plenty of other vehicles to be had. Your new one is waiting for you in the garage whenever you want it."

Her expression froze. Rather than get her reaction wrong, Duncan waited.

"What about the shadow creature? What should I do if it returns? Are we sure the necklace is what kept it from taking me?"

Duncan knew she was frightened. While he was almost certain Orla's gift was the reason, he didn't mind adding extra protection. It would make them both feel better. The damned brollochan had come close to killing her. "I'll contact Pritch and see if he can ward the SUV."

"Will he mind?"

"He's my great-ancestor. Now he's yours as well. He won't mind helping, I swear. Finish your breakfast while I get in touch with him."

Duncan kept his gaze on his wife as he telepathically called Pritch. His ancestor was more than happy to help, but it was going to be a few hours before he could arrive.

Avery hadn't finished her breakfast. Instead, she watched him the entire time. Reaching for her hand, he squeezed gently as he leaned over and kissed her cheek.

"I don't want to be such a chicken." Avery shuddered. "I try not to remember what it felt like when that shadow thing enveloped the car, but I can't seem to stop. I don't want to be afraid to go outside."

"I know you no longer feel safe in Caledonia, but you are. Your necklace is powerful, honey. Still, when Pritch gets here around noon, he'll ward the truck against the brollochan and anything else Sidhe that might think to attack it." He could see she wasn't convinced, even though she was nodding in agreement. "What if I get you a bodyguard?"

She shook her head. "No. Absolutely not. I don't need a bodyguard."

The more he considered it, the more Duncan liked the idea. "What if it was Darrach?" Peter was out. He was a computer geek needed by too many people.

"Duncan, don't be silly. He's not going to want to give up his job to babysit someone who shouldn't need it."

It might not be his ideal job, but neither would Darrach mind. There was one man, however, who would love the job. And hardly anyone would suspect this guy's true purpose with Avery, because he looked about as far from the stereotypical bodyguard as one could get. Even so, the man knew at least twenty ways to kill someone with his bare hands. Plus, he was a Halfling, which meant he was familiar with otherworldly dangers as well.

"I know just the man. He's been salivating to work at Iona's for years. This will be the next best thing for him."

"Duncan, really, I don't want a bodyguard. Surely Pritch warding the SUV will suffice."

"Just let me ask him. If you don't like him, then we'll work out something else."

"No. That's a horrible idea. I won't be able to turn him down if I meet him. Then he'd know why he wasn't hired."

"He's a chef who loves to cook and bake. In fact, he's the one who taught Darrach. He could be our chef. He and his husband could move into the maid's suite off the kitchen—if you don't mind more people living here."

"I don't mind, but why would they want to do that? Where are they living now?"

Duncan sensed her weakening. "He moved here from Texas about two years ago. He met Tony DiFiore about six months later. A bit ago, after laws changed, they were able to marry. They had an apartment, but there was a fire in a neighboring unit that caused a lot of damage. They've been living in a motel room since. Tony works for the Pendragon Alliance. He's gone a good bit, so he'd feel better if they lived here."

"Are you making all this up to make me feel sorry for him?"

He laughed. Already she knew him well. "It's all true. Though he's living in a luxury hotel suite instead of a motel. They both really want to move."

Avery tilted her head back and closed her eyes. A couple of seconds later, she looked back at him. "Fine. Call him. I'm not saying that I want him as a bodyguard, but he and his husband are welcome to the maid's suite."

Duncan didn't dare smile. "All I ask is for you to meet him. His name is Brian MacNally."

Avery bit her bottom lip.

"I'll be right back." Duncan wasn't going to call Brian in front of his wife because he needed to make sure Brian was going to be okay with the situation, too. He went to his study and called from the desk landline.

Brian answered on the fourth ring. "It's a little early in the day, so this better be good."

"I got married Friday night. At least Sidhe married."

"Wow! Okay. I guess felicitations are in order."

"Her name is Avery. She's in danger and I could use your help. She needs a bodyguard. If you agree, the maid's suite is yours and Tony's for as long as you want, and you'll have full use of the kitchen. As long as we get to share in the meals. Something else that might interest you. My bride works for Iona. You'd get a chance to see all of Iona's treasures before she puts them on display."

The line was quiet for all of a second before Brian stated, "Bribery will get you everywhere, my friend."

"Can you come over and meet her?"

"She hasn't agreed, has she?"

"Avery believes a bodyguard is too much. I just hope it's enough. Omaon wants her back, and the rest of the Dubh Sidhe either wants her or wants her dead."

"Damn. What can she do?"

"Authenticate an item. I mean, *truly* authenticate them."

"Holy hell, she's a psychometric?"

Exactly how Duncan felt. "Yes. So will you come?"

"Drive or translocate?" Brian was all business now that he understood.

"The sooner the better." Before Duncan finished speaking, Brian stood across the desk from him.

Brian MacNally was an inch under six feet tall with straight, medium brown hair, and bright blue eyes. His seemingly stocky build led many people to assume it was flab. It wasn't. Brian was all compact muscle. He looked like a banker or corporate businessperson. What he did not look like was a lethal bodyguard. It was one of the things that made him so good at his job. People forever underestimated him.

This morning Brian was dressed in a tan sport coat, dark-blue button-down shirt, dark blue khakis, and loafers.

Duncan stood. "If I didn't know better, I'd think you were just sitting around waiting on a call."

"I'm always waiting for a call. Now, where is this paragon of womanhood who has captured your heart?"

"She hasn't—"

"Oh, please." Brian held up his hand, palm out. "Don't even try. You wouldn't have bound yourself to the woman if you weren't in love with her. You just need your brain to admit what your soul knows. Now introduce me."

Duncan's brow creased. "In case no one's ever told you, you're damned pushy, MacNally. Keep those last suppositions to yourself." Rounding the desk, Duncan headed for the kitchen. "Come meet my wife."

Avery stood nervously as they entered.

"Darling, this is Brian MacNally," Duncan quickly introduced them. "Brian, this is my wife, Avery."

Avery extended her arm. "It's a pleasure to meet you, Mr. MacNally."

Brian took her hand, clasping it between both of his. "I'm just Brian to you, and the pleasure is all mine, Avery." He glanced at Duncan. "She's lovely. If I wasn't gay and already married, I'd be upset with you for snapping her up."

Brian often blurted out his sexual orientation to gauge people's reactions. Avery didn't blink an eye at the revelation. She continued smiling warmly at Brian, her eyes sparkling.

Duncan shook his head. "And if you weren't gay, I wouldn't let you within a thousand feet of Avery."

Brian laughed and winked at her. "Duncan tells me a few pesky Dubh Sidhe are trying to cause you problems."

Avery gave a little shrug. "It seems I'm of use to them. May I get you some tea?" She neatly changed the subject.

Brian groaned. "I'm a coffee man, love. Lots of it. If you don't mind me hanging out with you, I'll grab one once we reach town."

As Avery studied Brian, Duncan held his breath.

"I'd like that," Avery said with a shy smile.

Duncan relaxed.

Brian nodded. "Wonderful. When do you need to leave for work?"

She checked her watch and glanced at Duncan. "I should leave now if I'm not going to be late."

"You can let go of her hand now." Duncan wrapped his arm around Avery and pulled her into his embrace. "Pritch will find you in town. He'll make sure the vehicle is warded." Covering the back of her head with his hand, he gently pressed her cheek against his shoulder, where he whispered, "I really wish I could get out of this job, but I promise that I'll be back as quickly as I can. In the meantime, Gavin and Darach will come back, and Brian and Tony will move in. I'm not leaving you alone."

Avery hugged him as if she'd never let go. "It's okay. I was on my own for quite a while, if you remember."

"Never again." Duncan kissed her temple before tilting her face up and claiming her lips. "Come on, let me show you your new ride," he said after several pleasurable moments.

"You really shouldn't have," Avery protested.

"Of course he should have," Brian argued. "Who else should he spend his fortune on if not his wife?" He rubbed his hands together. "Come on, I wanna see."

After holding her coat for her to slip into and letting her grab her purse, Duncan took her hand and pulled her along with him to the garage. Brian followed.

Parked on this side of his own big SUV was a new mid-sized one in dark blue. Duncan led her to the driver's side. Once Avery was behind the wheel, Duncan gave her and Brian a quick run-through of the safety features.

When he was satisfied she was comfortable with the vehicle, Duncan cupped the back of her neck and held her for a kiss that would have to last them until he completed his mission. He then nodded to Brian before closing her door. Watching as she cautiously backed out of the garage, Duncan returned the wave she sent him as she turned the SUV and headed down the drive.

Duncan watched the vehicle until it disappeared from sight before returning to the house to pack.

He wasn't happy having to take a job so soon after being bound. Especially when several factions of the Dubh Sidhe seemed to be targeting his wife. However, a necromancer and revenant weren't beings that could be freely allowed to roam the human realm. He and Nate had dealt with a similar situation a couple of years earlier. Hopefully, they could wrap this case up just as quickly, and he'd be able to get home to Avery in a week.

THOUGH AVERY WAS UNCOMFORTABLE that Duncan spent his money to purchase her a new vehicle, she admitted she loved the SUV. It had everything she could want, plus several amenities she wouldn't have thought of, including a special phone. Brian checked it out as they drove into town. He discovered someone already programmed in all the numbers Duncan considered important. Knowing Duncan did that gave Avery a warm, fuzzy feeling.

Iona didn't bat an eye when Avery walked in with Brian in tow. The older woman put him to work, moving the heavier pieces around and carrying items to cars for customers. Brian didn't seem to mind. In fact, he appeared to be having a ball.

Pritch appeared in the store around mid-morning. He spoke privately with Iona before having Brian show him to Avery's new vehicle. Before he left, he returned long enough to wish Avery well.

After that first day, she and Brian settled into a routine of sorts. Brian and his husband, Tony DiFiore, began moving into the house. Darach and Gavin returned home in the evenings when they weren't off on some assignment. Because Duncan was out of town, Darach tried to make sure he was home early every evening. Though, with Brian there now, he had some leeway.

Duncan called at least twice a day. By the end of the week, she could hear the frustration in his voice. They had found and disposed of one revenant, but they weren't having any luck locating the necromancer. He continued to create more revenants that Duncan and Nate were forced to deal with.

"This isn't how I envisioned our first week of marriage, honey," Duncan told her when he called late Friday night. "Irrational of me, but I rather thought we'd spend it together."

Avery laughed, as she knew he meant her to do. "It's alright. We'll have plenty of time. Brian and Josey are planning a celebratory feast for your return. Darach is making what they tell me is his famous twelve-layer strawberry cake."

"Damn. I don't want to miss that. Nate won't either. Extra incentive for us to find this necromancer and end his work. One way or another, I plan to be home next Sunday at the latest."

"That would be wonderful." Avery didn't want to admit how much she missed him.

"Sleep well, honey."

"Take care of yourself, darling." Avery wanted to tell her husband that she loved him, but she didn't think he was ready to hear it. Plus, she didn't want her first time telling him to be over the phone. She could have done it telepathically, but she still wasn't used to talking with him that way, and it wasn't that different from using the phone. Avery settled for an endearment to try to pass on her feelings.

"I will. I'll call you tomorrow night unless we manage to wrap this up early."

Avery hated to hang up, but she couldn't think of a legitimate reason to keep him talking.

For a long time, Avery lay awake, staring at the ceiling. It was startling how much she missed Duncan. They had only spent three nights together in the same bed—at least since being home—but it was enough that she hadn't slept well since he'd been gone.

There had been no more run-ins with enormous shadows. Nor had she noticed anyone taking a special interest in her—and she had been paying attention. Avery wanted to believe they had been mistaken in thinking someone from the other realm was after her. Brian, Darach, and Angus, Duncan's grandfather, strongly disagreed, however. Unfortunately for her peace of mind, Avery trusted their judgment. She wished she didn't. It left her on edge when she wasn't either home or at Iona's shop.

SATURDAY WAS A SHORT day at Time Passages. Iona closed the store at three PM.

After work, Brian accompanied Avery to several local stores. She wanted to get Duncan something special. He had given her so much, and she wanted to find something for him.

"How do you feel about a spring wedding?" Brian asked when she asked for his thoughts on a gift. "Or maybe a winter one. Say January?"

"I'm looking for something special for Duncan. That's not a present for him."

"I beg to differ. The Sidhe ceremony was to bind you as much for protection and connection as for the marriage part. Duncan wants the regular wedding, so everyone in this world recognizes your union. A wedding ring—one of Celtic design—would be a good start."

Duncan had talked about a church wedding. Except for Stiabhan, Avery didn't have any family to invite. The bride's side was going to look rather empty with only her cousin and Iona occupying the seats. However, that was no reason to avoid the ceremony Duncan wanted.

"Okay. Is there a small chapel we could use?"

"Avalon College has a lovely chapel on its campus. It's small and constructed of stone. It would be perfect."

"Will you help me?"

Brian put his arm around her shoulders and hugged her to his side. "Oh, sugar, I thought you'd never ask. We'll plan it for the first Saturday in January. That gives us roughly two months."

That didn't sound like enough time to Avery. In fact, it sounded like so little time that she felt panic stirring. "Maybe we should do a spring wedding? I have a lovely ring Duncan gave me already." She held up her left hand for Brian to see it.

"No. The sooner the better."

"Why?" Avery didn't understand the rush.

"Because I sense you chickening out. I wouldn't be surprised to learn that's what Duncan fears as well. Ease his mind and marry the poor soul in our world. That would be another present for him."

All of what Brian called presents for Duncan seemed to be just as much presents for her. Avery would go ahead with the January wedding, but she still wanted something that was just for Duncan. The ring part sounded nice. But maybe a ring for his other hand. Or perhaps a pendant. A protection one similar to hers.

"If I got Duncan a pendant, do you think he'd wear it?"

"Darlin', Duncan would wear a puce necktie with big red lips splashed all over it if you gave it to him."

Avery smiled at the image as she looked skyward and shook her head. "I think I'll skip that item. Let's see what we can find."

CHAPTER TWELVE

"Damnit, Nate, we're finding that bastard tonight and neutralizing him. I told Avery I'd be home tomorrow and I'm going to be there," Duncan told his partner as they staked out the cemetery where the necromancer was currently getting his bodies.

"I'm with you," Nate agreed. "This hunt is taking too long. We've put six revenants back in their graves. By now he's got to know Hunters are after him."

"Yet he keeps returning to this specific cemetery." Duncan frowned. "Maybe he's challenging us."

"Then let's take him up on it and ice the bastard."

Both men watched as a truck from one of the local funeral homes drove into the graveyard. The driver parked, got out, and slowly looked around. After a thorough perusal of the cemetery, he headed for a specific plot.

"Crap! We've been watching him come and go for days. He was right under our noses." Duncan was disgusted by his lack of insight.

"Who would suspect the damned gravedigger? It's a necromancer's dream job." Nate's obvious disgust equaled Duncan's.

"Not anymore. Let's get the bastard and wrap up this hunt. I'm past ready to go home to my wife."

"I'm ready to go home to my family, too."

A few hours later, Duncan and Nate delivered a bound, gaged necromancer to a Sidhe enforcer at the nearest tairseach.

With the job complete, Duncan aimed the SUV for home. He drove as fast as he dared without risking a speeding ticket. He could have translocated home, leaving Nate to drive alone. Nate even suggested it, but they began the hunt together; they would end it together. Both of them were tired; and both were eager to get home to their families. Duncan wasn't going to abandon Nate—even if he was eager to get home to Avery.

They were less than thirty minutes from the South Carolina state line when the attack came.

Just as it had with Avery, a brollochan enveloped the vehicle, making visibility nil, and forcing Duncan to slam on the brakes. A yellow gas immediately flowed in through the air vents. Duncan yanked the neck of his sweatshirt up over his nose and mouth. It didn't help.

DUNCAN LAY ON SOMETHING hard. Even before he got his eyes open, he knew he was no longer in his truck. He was stretched out on a wooden bench in a stone-walled, damp, and chilly dungeon. His boots, socks, and shirt were all gone.

Movement through the barred grill in a heavy door caught his attention. Someone had been set to watch for him to awaken.

Swinging his bare feet to the floor, Duncan sat up. While it was cold, he said a thank-you that his feet touched only stone and didn't sink into inches of slime—or worse.

It wasn't long before Cathan Caolin, one of Omaon's enforcers, appeared on the other side of the bars.

"Where is Nate?" Duncan asked, skipping any pleasantries. Nor did he bother to stand.

"Not here. Obviously," Cathan answered smugly.

"Where is he?" Duncan tried to keep the concern from his voice.

"Do not worry about your friend. He is back in your realm. Someone had to deliver the message to your wife since I was certain you would not be amenable to contacting her yourself. Felicitations, by the way." The bastard leaned against the opposite wall of the hall, eyeing him through the bars of the cell door.

Duncan struggled to keep any emotion from showing in his expression. "Do you believe I didn't leave her well-guarded? Besides, Avery is too smart to fall for any trap set by the likes of you."

Cathan's chuckle chilled Duncan's blood. "Ah, but none of that matters if she fears for your life. Does it, Duncan? We are about to discover just how much your mate cares for you."

Duncan gave a slight shake of his head, effecting a calm he was far from feeling. "No. What you are about to discover is that your elaborate schemes to trap my wife are a complete bust." He leaned back against the icy wall. "Might as well either kill me now or get used to me as a houseguest."

Cathan laughed. "Oh, Duncan, we will not kill you. Yet. We will give our scheme a few days and see what happens." The Sidhe straightened away from the wall. "Unfortunately, you missed the evening meal. I will try to remember to inform the cook we have a new guest. I would not want you to miss getting something to break your fast in the morning."

Once Cathan was out of sight, Duncan leaned forward, elbows on knees, and put his head in his hands. He didn't care about food. He wouldn't be able to eat it, anyway. Worry made his gut churn.

Duncan felt he knew what Avery would do. She could come after him if she learned what happened. He was confident that Nate wouldn't tell her and put her in danger. Still, he wished he could contact someone to set up a plan to keep Omaon from sending a messenger to reach her, but the only person Duncan had a chance of contacting was Avery. He could only hope that the others could extrapolate his meaning from what he imparted to his wife.

It was time to discover how well the binding ceremony worked.

"Avery?"

"Duncan? Where are you? You've never contacted me this way before. What happened to your phone? Are you okay? Are you finished?"

"I'm fine. I just wanted to let you know that there's been a slight delay. I had to accompany the enforcer back to Tìr-dhàimh with the necromancer. Phones don't work here. Certainly not between realms." That, at least, wasn't a lie.

"You won't get home tomorrow, will you?"

Duncan could sense her disappointment. He could also tell that Avery was finding something off with what he was telling her. Perhaps the binding ceremony had worked too well. *"No, sweetheart, I'm sorry. I may be here for another week. Maybe two."*

"Then maybe I should tell you that Brian is helping me plan our wedding. We've set it for early January."

Well, hell, Duncan thought. What he said, however, was, *"That sounds perfect. I'll be back by then. I won't miss our wedding. Swear to God, I will not leave you at the altar."*

"Right now, it's a tentative date. We could postpone it. Should we do that?"

"No, of course not. Go ahead and confirm a date."

"As long as you're all right. Are *you all right?"*

"I'm fine. And we're going to get married on January fourth." If he added the date, he figured it would help ease her mind.

"Is Nate with you?"

Duncan didn't like the way she skirted the issue of marrying him in a legally binding Cruinne ceremony. *"No, he's on his way home."*

"What aren't you telling me? Something's wrong. I can sense it."

Well, hell! The binding had worked too well. Avery wasn't supposed to be picking up on his emotions any more than he should be picking up on hers. It was only supposed to facilitate communication. *"There's nothing. I'm fine. I'll be home in plenty of time for our wedding. You said Brian is helping you plan it, right?"*

"Yes. Brian, Josey, and Iona are helping me."

"Great. That sounds wonderful."

"Duncan?"

"Sorry, honey. I have to go. I'll contact you tomorrow." Duncan hated to do it, but he blocked more communication just in case she tried to read him.

NATE OPENED HIS EYES and immediately shut them. His head felt as if it was going to split open. It had to be the residual effects of the gas.

Why had they been gassed, anyway? It wasn't as if they had anything with them that anyone would want to steal.

"Duncan? How ya doing, dude? My head hurts like hell."

No response came from his left. Maybe Duncan hadn't regained consciousness yet. Not prepared to open his eyes again, Nate reached across to the driver's seat. His hand connected with leather.

Nate squinted his eyes open. Crap! Duncan was gone. They had something the Dubh Sidhe wanted after all.

Something caught his eye. Opening them completely, Nate stared at the driver's seat. A leather patch ripped from a shirt sleeve lay where it had been tossed. Snatching it up, he opened his door, which turned on the interior lights. He peered against the brightness to observe the symbol of a bear rampant on the patch. The symbol for the kingdom of Oirthea.

"Damn it to bloody hell!" Getting out of the SUV, Nate shoved the patch in his pocket. Slamming the passenger door shut, he went around and got in the driver's seat. He had to get to Angus Kerr as quickly as possible. Duncan's grandfather could figure out what to do. No way in hell was Nate telling Avery that Omaon had Duncan.

Nate didn't have enough power to translocate both the vehicle and himself home, so he did it the human way—he got in the driver's seat and sped. He made it to Angus Kerr's house in record time. It didn't matter to him that it was nearly two AM. He'd been unconscious for about five hours, as far as he could tell. Too much time had already been lost.

Only no one was home. Damnit, where the hell was everyone?

"Gavin, where's your grandfather?" Nate didn't care if the young man was asleep. This was an emergency.

"We're all at Duncan's. We've been waiting for you," Gavin responded so quickly that Nate knew he hadn't woken him.

Crap, crap, crap! *"How much does Avery know?"*

"None of us know enough. That's why we're waiting for you. All Avery knows is that something is wrong, but Duncan won't tell her what."

Nate got back in the truck and headed for Duncan's house. *"I'm coming. I was hoping Avery was ignorant of any problems."*

"Duncan didn't tell her much. Avery sensed a problem and that he was being less than forthcoming with her."

"Well hell. So, she called everyone in?"

"Yep. She wants something done. As I said, we've been waiting for you."

"I'm on my way. I'll be there in a few."

Before he could knock on the door, Darach yanked it open. "It's about time. What the hell happened?" Darach held up his hand. "No, don't tell me. Wait and tell all of us at once. Come on, we've turned the den into a war room."

Shutting the door behind him, Nate followed his friend to the large den. Avery was perched on the edge of the couch. She jumped to her feet the moment she saw him. He couldn't face the desperate hope in her eyes. He turned to Duncan's grandfather Angus instead.

"Omaon?" Angus questioned.

Nate nodded. Pulling the patch from his pocket, he held it out to the older man. "Yes. it was a brollochan." Out of the corner of his eye, he saw Avery shudder. "Duncan had to stop. Some sort of gas was forced in through the air vents. It knocked us out. When I came to, Duncan was gone, and that was on his seat."

Angus took the leather badge. He frowned at the symbol on it.

"We have to find that knife," Avery stated into the silence, getting everyone's attention.

"They want you more than the knife," Darach said.

Avery canted her head slightly. "They want me because I can tell the real *sgian dubh* of Accalon from the fakes. That's what Omaon ultimately wants. Wouldn't it be better to find the knife and use it to barter for Duncan?"

"Avery, we cannot trade the blade for Duncan," Angus stated. "We cannot allow the Dubh Sidhe to possess it. It must be given to the Mother Guardians."

"What if Omaon just believed the knife we offer is the true one? If we find the right knife, I believe we could do it. After all, they're counting on me to authenticate it."

"That would mean sending you to Omaon. It's too dangerous," Angus stated. "There are more items Omaon and the others want. If he gets his hands on you, he won't let you go. No, we cannot trust Omaon to be honorable. I will not chance losing my granddaughter to get my grandson back."

"We need to mount a rescue," Brian spoke up. "Go and get him. It's the only way. We all know we can't trust Omaon."

Nate watched Angus and waited.

After several tense seconds, Angus nodded. "You're correct. The only way to get Duncan back is to take him. That means the first order of business is locating where they're holding him."

"He won't contact me," Avery told them. "At least he won't answer me when I try calling him. He said he would call me again tomorrow. Well, today now. Can one of you communicate with him?"

"I can," Gavin spoke up, "but he won't answer." He looked at his grandfather.

"Yes, I can, and he damned well better answer me," Angus said, his eyes flashing. "Give me a moment. Let me see what I can find out."

All of them watched Angus and waited.

DUNCAN JERKED AS HIS grandfather's voice sounded in his head. Crap. He'd avoided answering Avery's repeated attempts to speak with him again. Had she realized more than he hoped and called in the big guns?

Duncan had never thwarted his grandfather in his life. Besides the love he had for the old man, he respected him too much. What the hell was he supposed to do now? Duncan felt guilty as sin for not answering immediately. He didn't want to answer, but this was Angus. Duncan had been raised to obey him without question—at least not much questioning.

"Dada," Duncan gave up and responded.

"It's glad I am to know ye're conscious. Are ye well?"

When his grandfather's accent thickened, Duncan knew he was upset. *"I'm fine. A little hungry. A little chilly, but unharmed."*

"Good. Do ye ken where the bastard is holding ya?"

"You already know this is Omaon's doing?"

"Aye. A patch with his insignia was left in your seat. Nate brought it to us."

"Us? Avery knows? Nate didn't tell her, did he?" If he had, Duncan would kill him—slowly.

"Avery kenned something was wrong after speaking with you. She called me, as she should. Nate has only just arrived. What he related,

he did so to all of us. You canna blame the lad for her finding out. Ye should have been honest with her yourself."

"I was hoping to discover a way to escape before she had to learn the truth."

"Any chance o' that happening?" Angus asked hopefully.

"There's always a chance, but the probability is low."

"Well, dinna fash yerself. We have a plan. We just need to know where ye're bein' held."

Duncan liked that they had a plan, but he wasn't going to be able to help them. He had no idea where he was. Except he wasn't in the fortress where Omaon had first held him.

"Sorry, Dada, but I don't know which fortress I'm in. One with a dungeon with multiple cells. I haven't been here long enough to pick up much intel. The only things I know for certain are that it's not where Avery and I were held, and that Cathan Caolin is currently in charge."

"Anything you tell us will help us narrow it down. We have some people to contact. Are ye sure ye're not hurt?"

"I'm sure. I'm fine, Dada."

"Then speak to the lass. I understand ye think to protect her, but ye're only causing her more upset."

"They took me to draw her out because they can't get to her otherwise. I don't want her trying to rescue me. That is exactly what Omaon wants."

"We're all aware of that, Duncan. Avery included. None of us are going to allow the lass to put herself in danger."

Duncan knew that. It only made him feel moderately better, however. *"Thanks, Dada. I'll talk to Avery and try to ease her fears."*

"See that ya do. Take care, me lad." His grandfather broke the connection.

Duncan took a deep breath and dove in. *"Avery."*

"Duncan. Thank God. Please, don't shut me out again."

Avery wasn't chastising him, instead he felt how much he'd hurt her. *"I won't, sweetheart. I promise. I thought I was protecting you, but I was wrong."*

"Yes, you were. Hiding things from me isn't protecting me. Even if I needed protection. Which I do not, by the way. I've been on my own for a while, so there's not much I can't handle. I want to help you. Don't leave me out again, Duncan."

"I'll try not to leave you out anymore." Duncan wasn't going to make promises he might not be able to keep. *"I'd love to have your help, but not if it puts you in harm's way. You're the one Omaon wants. Not me. This is all to draw you out."*

"I know that. He also wants payback against you, don't forget. It's not all about me."

"Perhaps not, but I'm more worried about you."

"And I'm more worried about you," Avery replied. *"Where does that leave us?"*

"Just where we should be, sweetheart. You can help me, but do it by doing as my dada tells you. Or Stiabhan. Promise me. Please."

"Okay, baby. I promise that. Will you promise me something?"

Duncan wanted to promise her the moon and the stars, but he also wanted his promise to be something he could keep. He never wanted to break a vow to Avery. *"If I can."*

"That you won't antagonize them, and you'll stay alive until we can come to help you."

"I will definitely be alive, honey. As for the other, I promise to do my best."

"I'll take that."

Duncan knew she was trying to sound optimistic. He also felt her fear. For him. She could sense his emotions—at least some of them. Duncan hoped they weren't so connected that she could feel them, too. He could handle her fears as long as he knew she was safe.

He didn't want his wife to have more to worry about than she already did.

"Dada says he has a plan. Don't worry, Avery. I'll be home soon."

"I'm going to consider that a promise, too, Duncan. Just so you know."

Duncan laughed. She made him happy.

"Do me a favor, sweetheart. Get some rest. You're probably going to need it."

"I don't want to break the connection. Darling, I'm so afraid to let go."

"I understand. But we're not letting go. Never. If you concentrate, you'll still be able to feel me, just as I can feel you. We'll hold on to that until we're together again."

"That's sounds nice."

"Baby, don't cry."

"I'm not," she denied, even though he could feel it.

In his mind's eye, Duncan could see the tears on her cheeks. *"Okay. Well, see that you don't."* He didn't want to sever the connection anymore than Avery did, but she couldn't spend all night talking to him. *"Get some sleep, Avery. I'll be here. Contact me whenever you feel the need."*

Avery did. Twice more that night. She let him know when Stiabhan arrived. Then she let him know when they all decided to break up and meet again in the late morning.

When she finally settled down and fell asleep, Duncan leaned back against the stone wall. He knew his grandfather and the others, even Stiabhan (because of Avery), were going over various rescue plans. None would work, however, until they knew his location. Stiabhan might be able to help with that.

The best bet for them all was if he could find a way to escape.

Duncan chuckled. That was the best way, but it was also the least likely. Cathan Caolin was no fool. He wouldn't have survived this long in Omaon's employ if he was.

Still, that didn't mean that some of Cathan's flunkies couldn't be tricked. It was strange how bad guys usually hired idiots. Part of the reason the good guys always won—eventually. Duncan would watch for his chance with one of the underlings.

Perhaps the best way wouldn't be out of reach after all. The worst problem was patience. Duncan didn't possess much, and what he had was running out.

Since Cathan had left, Duncan had seen no one. He didn't know how deep beneath the keep he was. What few sounds he heard were distant and so muffled he couldn't tell what they were.

Frustrated, Duncan reclined on the bench. He couldn't overpower anyone if no one showed up.

Some time later, a noise caught his attention. One very nearby. Lying perfectly still, Duncan listened. At least a couple of minutes passed before he heard it again. A scratching sound. Something against stone, and not too far away. Was there someone else being held prisoner?

Slowly shifting to a sitting position, Duncan listened. He still heard it. Almost frantic scraping could be heard coming from somewhere just beyond his door. The only light came from a weak lamp somewhere up the stairs. It allowed him to make his way to the barred opening in the cell door. Peering through the bars, Duncan found it difficult to see through the gloom. From his vantage point, he could see the bars of three more cells. That meant there would be two more on his side and perhaps one or two at the end that he couldn't see.

Standing just to the side of the door, his back to the wall, Duncan listened attentively. The scratching came again. It was determined, but a determined person or a determined rodent. He couldn't tell.

"Hello," Duncan murmured.

At once, the scraping stopped.

After a few seconds of silence, he asked, "Is anyone else down here?"

"Who are you?" a male voice, rough from disuse, asked.

So not a rat.

"My name is Duncan Kerr."

Seconds passed before the man observed, "You're not from Tìr-dhàimh, are you?"

"No, I'm not."

"Daondasidhe then. You're a Hunter."

It was an observation, not an accusation, so Duncan replied, "I am. From Cruinne."

"What the bloody hell are you doing here?"

"It's not by choice, I assure you. I'm bait to capture my wife." Duncan saw no harm in telling his companion that much.

"When did you arrive?"

"I'm not sure. Hours ago. You didn't hear Cathan?"

"I've learned to sleep deeply when I sleep. You need to do the same."

Duncan didn't like the sound of that. "How long have you been here?"

"Too long."

Oh goody. A non-answer answer. "Who are you?"

"Davin Geir, late of Gwyneira."

"Queen Brigina's enforcer. One of them, anyway."

"Yes." The scratching started once more.

Duncan frowned. The name triggered a recent memory. "Four months. Arzur has been searching for you for four months."

The scratching stopped for a moment before resuming with more ferocity. "Four damn months. You would think I would be further along in this escape venture after all that time."

"What is your plan?"

"Digging through the wall to the hall."

Duncan tilted his head back against the wall. Four months of digging mortar. How thick were these walls? He checked the doorframe. Around two feet. Duncan felt along the seams between the stones. The mortar was rough and around an inch thick. With a tool of some type, it would be doable.

"How far along are you?" Duncan asked.

"I need to remove four stones to make it large enough to wriggle through. This is the last one. I have got a side and a half to go."

Duncan had never met Davin Geir, but it sounded as if they were close to the same size. "What about trying to overpower the guards?"

"Guards?" Davin chuckled darkly. "Do you see any guards? Hear any? The only people who venture down here are the old men who bring food and water. They don't open the door. They slip it all through a slot one hand-span high and two wide."

"What about waste? For a dungeon, this room is surprisingly clean."

"Check your cell. They put in a commode. They do not want us to die from disease."

"Why are they holding you? I mean, was it me? Unless you have some value or use, I'd just kill you. Much simpler."

"I have use. Omaon wants to leverage some control over my queen." Again, that dark, humorless chuckle. "He thinks to use me to gain it."

The light went on. "Besides being one of her enforcers, you're a relation."

"Nephew," Davin affirmed. The scratching stopped. "You said they are using you to get your wife. Why is she important?"

"She's psychometric. She can authenticate artifacts. Omaon wants the *sgian dubh* of Accalon. Among other things. There are several fakes. Avery can discern the true one."

"Well shite" After a bit, the scraping started again. "Do you think she will come?"

"If my grandfather and friends don't stop her, she'll give it her best shot."

Duncan heard Davin laugh, a real one this time. "I like your wife already."

Duncan smiled for a moment, just thinking of Avery. Then he sobered. "Is there anything I can do to help?"

"What can you do? I know you are not a glaisr or you would have already unlocked your door. Unfortunately, it's not one of my abilities either."

"Not a glaisr, no. My strongest talents are psychokinesis and thirokinesis."

Davin was quiet again. "How do you feel about rats?"

Duncan shuddered. He did not like the turn of the conversation. "Why?"

"Rats can chew through wood. Lots of rats could quickly chew holes large enough for us to crawl through. More rats upstairs could create quite a diversion, too. Do you not agree?"

Oh, Duncan agreed. Just the thought, however, gave him the willies. "You want me to call in a hoard of rats?"

"Can you?"

"I've never tried, but if enough are near, I should be able to do so."

"Go ahead."

"Damnit. Rats."

"They are not my favorite animal either, but they should get the job done."

"Fine."

Duncan shuddered again. Mentally, he reached out. It took him less time than he wished to connect with a rat. Though intelligent, they were simple creatures. Their primary objectives are eating and procreating. It made them easy to manipulate. It didn't take Duncan long to round up over a thousand of the rodents. Some were already in the stables. He used them to annoy the horses. Hopefully, another distraction.

Sooner than he wanted, Duncan heard a chittering sound that indicated their arrival. He quickly stepped away from the door. As he heard the rats' teeth against the wood, Duncan stepped up onto the bench. He didn't care if people thought he was a wuss. He was barefooted. No way was he standing on a floor with rats.

"Good job, Duncan," Davin called out. "At this rate, we should be able to get out in less than an hour."

Duncan shook his head. He hoped it didn't take that long. Immediately after the rodents' job was done, he was going to send them packing. He'd try to sic them on Cathan.

"Just a little more and you can send your friends to annoy the keep's inhabitants," Davin said over the din of teeth on wood and scrabbling tiny toenails.

Soon, Duncan hoped. "They're not my damned friends. Though if this really works, I may not hate them as much."

"They are vile creatures, but they have their uses."

A dim light showed through the bars and now through an opening at the base of the door. Duncan admitted that until that moment, he hadn't truly believed it would work. Having never spent much time around rats, he wasn't sure what they were capable of—besides spreading diseases and biting.

"Can you tell how far along they are?" Davin asked.

Duncan looked at the base of the door, gauging the size of the hole with the width of his own shoulders. With little effort, he could squeeze through. "I'm good. How about you?"

"I can manage. Time to send your friends into the keep."

"Thank God. And I know just where to send them." Duncan pictured Cathan in his mind's eye. Slowly, the rats began to retreat up the stairs. It was more difficult than he anticipated, forcing himself to step down from the bench.

When Duncan got to his feet after wriggling through the opening, he got his first look at Davin Geir. In Pure terms, he was about five years older, about the same height, and with dark hair and dark eyes. His clothing was shabby and worn, but it still showed signs of quality. It hung loosely on his malnourished frame.

Davin held out his hand. "Well met, Duncan Kerr."

"Same to you, Davin Geir." Duncan shook his hand.

"Let us find some boots and weapons, and get the hell out of here." Davin eased his way up the stairs.

After a couple of turns, they could hear pandemonium above them. Women were screaming. Men shouted, and a few screamed as well. Reaching the top of the steps, David grabbed a warrior as he passed the door, spun him around, and slammed his head into the wall. The man crumpled at their feet.

"Grab his tunic and any weapons. If his boots will fit, take them as well."

Duncan stripped the tunic from the man's body and put it on. As he was removing the boots from the man's feet, Davin repeated the process with a second man.

Soon, they were both dressed, armed, and had commandeered horses from the stables. They galloped away from the castle and village. It was easy since the rodents still caused pandemonium in both.

CHAPTER THIRTEEN

Avery sat at the bar as Brian prepared breakfast. "We need to find Accalon's dagger. That's what this whole thing is about."

"You get no argument from me, but do you know anyone who has a clue where it might be?"

"No, I was hoping you would know someone we could ask. What about Darach? He and Nathan were helping Duncan locate it when we first met. I'm gonna go wake him up."

"Wake who up?" The very person she wanted walked into the room.

Avery turned on her barstool to see the man in question. "You. You and Nate were helping Duncan search for Accalons' dagger. Both of you have still been looking for it, haven't you?"

Darach eyed her warily. He hesitated before admitting, "Yes."

"Well, what have you learned?" Avery demanded after several seconds of silence, waiting for him to elaborate.

Darach shot a quick glance at Brian. "Uh, we're narrowing it down."

"Darach Shanley, you just lied to me. You know where it is."

"No! No, not for certain. It's a new lead. We don't even know if it's going to pan out."

"I can tell you if it's the real thing. You just have to get me to it." Avery stood. "Let's go."

"Whoa! Hold on a minute," Darach protested. "We need to slow down and think this through."

"I have. We need that dagger to get Duncan back, so we're going to go get it."

"Avery, it's in Colorado. If it's even the right one. Peter is also looking at two other possibilities." Darach frantically tried to come up with an excuse.

"You're capable of translocation. So are Nate and Brian. One of you is surely capable of taking me with you." Avery crossed her arms and glared at him.

"Duncan would kill me. And he'd be right to do so," Darach stated.

"Duncan has been taken hostage. He needs help, and one way or another, I am going to help him. Either you join me or get the hell out of my way," she challenged.

Darach looked at Brian.

Brian shrugged. "I'm with her."

Darach blurted a bunch of mumbled, unintelligible curses. Moments later he said, "Get Angus' okay and Nate and I will take you."

Avery frowned. She hoped to tell her grandfather-by-marriage once getting the dagger was a fait accompli. "Don't you think he has enough to worry about with his grandson captured by Omaon?"

Darach crossed his arms, raised one eyebrow, and stared down at her.

"Hells bells." Avery uncrossed her own arms. "Fine. I'll call him." Going to the wall phone, she dialed Angus's number, putting it on speaker.

"Aye," Angus's deep voice sounded through the room.

"Dada, Peter has given Darach and Nate a lead on the dagger. I want them to take me to it. If it's the right one, we could use it as leverage to get Duncan back."

He was quiet for so long that she began to worry, but then he said, "All right, love. Call your cousin. I want Stiabhan to accompany ye. If he agrees, I give my blessing."

Avery had also hoped to avoid contacting Stiabhan. So much for that plan. "I'll call him."

"Now, love." She spun around at the sound of Angus' voice behind her. She looked up into his sun-weathered face. "Duncan would never forgive me if something happened to ye because I allowed ye to try to save him. Nor would I forgive meself."

"I'll call Stiabhan." Avery did so.

A couple seconds later, the Sidhe appeared just off her right. "What has happened?" He reached out and caught her by the shoulders. "Are you well?"

"I'm fine. This is about Duncan."

Stiabhan looked around. "I do not see him. Where is he?"

"Omaon had him taken. They're holding him, but we don't know where," she explained.

Stiabhan looked at Angus.

"Omaon uses Duncan to get to Avery," Angus stated. "We have decided to try to get him back. Steal him back. Tis nae a good idea to pay blackmail."

Stiabhan nodded before facing Avery. "You have a plan?"

"We go to Colorado and see if this dagger is the right one. If it is, we make a very good replica and use it to barter for Duncan's release."

Stiabhan exhaled. "Sweet, that would be fine if what Omaon really wanted was the *sgian dubh* of Accalon. It is not. It would simply be a bonus. What Omaon wants is you. He has plans for you. Lots of plans."

Avery didn't want to know what those plans were. She already knew she wouldn't like them. "You don't believe we can trick Omaon?"

He shrugged. "It's possible, but not likely. He wants you too badly, Avery."

"May we try? Please," she wasn't above begging.

"Of course. Let us go to Colorado and investigate this knife. Perhaps Omaon will be stupid enough to wish to trade." The Sidhe agreed to her plan. It was obvious he had no expectation of it working.

Avery turned to Darach. "When may we go?"

Darach looked from her to Stiabhan to Angus. The older man nodded. Darach nodded back. "Whenever you want."

That sounded better. "Do we need to wait for Nate?"

"I can take Nate's place," Brian stated.

"Fine by me," Darach agreed. "I'm sure his wife doesn't want him to leave so soon after getting home."

"Tell me where we are to go and I will transport us all there," Stiabhan spoke up.

Darach rattled off an address. Avery barely blinked, and they were standing in front of a very nice two-story home.

"What do we do now?" Avery asked. They stood as a group in the driveway. "Do we just go up to the door, ring the bell, and ask to see their antique weapons?"

"Why not?" Stiabhan took hold of Avery's hand and strode for the front door.

Avery went along with him. She wanted to see the dagger as soon as possible. It had to be the right one. They needed it to get Duncan back.

Stiabhan ignored the doorbell. Or perhaps he didn't recognize it. He knocked on the impressive door. They waited a few seconds. When no one came, Stiabhan knocked again. Harder. This time, they heard someone approaching.

The door was opened by a white-haired man in his late sixties or so. He was dressed elegantly, yet casually. About five-foot-ten, he had to look up at everyone except Avery.

"May I help you?" he asked pleasantly enough, but with a slight frown.

"We would like to see your collection of *sgian dubhs*." Stiabhan got right to the point.

"Who the hell are you people?" the man demanded, suddenly wary.

"I am Stiabhan Iorworth. This is—"

"I'm Avery Beaton. Kerr. Avery Beaton Kerr," she interrupted. "We're searching for a very specific *sgian dubh*. My husband was kidnapped. We need it to get him back."

Blue eyes widened. His gaze swung among the men. "Is she serious?"

All three men nodded.

"Deadly," Brian stated.

"How do you know about my collection?" he asked suspiciously.

"We work with The Pendragon Alliance," Darach stated. "Perhaps you've heard of it."

He slowly nodded. A few seconds later, he stepped back and motioned for them to enter. He closed and locked the door behind them. "Follow me and I'll show you my most private collection."

Avery's heart beat faster. She so badly wanted to find the ancient dagger. It had to be here. They needed it to bargain for Duncan.

Gerald Eisner, the owner of the house, introduced himself and then led them to a spacious study on the second floor. The doors were reinforced steel. Security measures were subtle, but Avery had been around enough in her work to recognize them when she saw them.

Once inside the room, he showed them to two one-foot deep, glass-fronted shadow boxes. One held swords of various lengths up to six feet, not counting their hilts. The other showcased daggers, *sgian dubhs*, and other knives.

Avery's focus became super tight. Carefully, she inspected each blade. Her heart sank. Just to be sure, she slowly went over each blade again—even the ones which weren't *sgian dubhs*.

"It's not here," she said in defeat.

"Are you sure? Maybe the glass is blocking it," Darach suggested hopefully.

Avery wanted to cry. "I'm sure." She pointed to one *sgian dubh*. "This one is old. Around eleven hundred. But it's not nearly old enough to be Accalon's. There is now power here. None."

Stiabhan encircled his arm around her shoulders, hugging her to his side. "But this one is old, yes?"

Avery nodded.

"Could you convince Omaon that his is Accalon's blade?" he asked.

If it meant saving Duncan, she would convince Omaon that a butter knife was the *sgian dubh* of Accalon. "Yes, of course. That's why he wants me—to authenticate items. Unless I give him a reason not to trust me, he should believe whatever I tell him."

"He'll be expecting a trick," Brian warned.

Stiabhan studied the *sgian dubh* intently. He held out his hand, palm up. A second later, an exact replica appeared in his hand.

"How the hell did you do that?" their host asked.

"Fairy magic," Stiabhan replied with surprising honesty.

"I'm serious," Gerald said.

Stiabhan stared down at him. "So am I." A bottle of dark amber liquid appeared in his other hand. He held it out to Gerald. "Some whiskey to help you get over your shock."

Gerald accepted the bottle as if in a daze.

"Thank you for your assistance," Brian said politely.

Avery nodded just as Stiabhan translocated them back home to South Carolina.

Angus rose from the recliner he'd been sitting in. "That dinna take ye long."

"He didn't have it," Avery told him.

"Then what does Stiabhan hold?" Angus asked.

"This is a replica of the oldest knife in the man's collection," Stiabhan said. "None of us know what Accalon's *sgian dubh* looks like, so why not convince Omaon that this is that which he seeks?"

Angus looked at the *sgian dubh* and then at Stiabhan. "Why not, indeed."

"I should be able to convince Omaon that this is the right one," Avery said.

Angus frowned at Stiabhan. "Omaon is many things. Stupid isna one of them. While the idea has merit, it canna be implemented by Avery. He is expecting something. We wouldna know if he truly believed her tale or was goin' along with it to trap her."

Stiabhan inclined his head. "You are right. If we try it, it must be someone besides Avery. Someone Omaon knows better than to toy with. Someone like me."

"No. I need to do it," Avery argued. If they did it, the chances of trading for Duncan went down. Omaon wanted her.

Brian, who had been watching her, spoke up. "You didn't believe we'd let you be the one to make the trade, did you? None of us wants you to sacrifice yourself for Duncan. Least of all Duncan."

"What if it doesn't work?" Avery voice her deepest fear.

"It probably willna," Angus said. "Our best option is to go after Duncan and take him back."

"I can find where they're holding him," Stiabhan stated. "It may take a little time, but I will locate him." He pointed to Avery. "Just make sure she stays here."

"Hey," Avery said to thin air. Stiabhan had already translocated.

"I know ye're worried. So am I," Angus told her. Walking over to her, he pulled her into a hug. "We have to remain calm and rational. It will serve none of us well to panic. Duncan will return to us."

Hugging him back, Avery nodded against his shoulder. She had to believe that.

"WHY THE HELL CAN'T I contact my family?" Duncan fumed. "I could reach them in the damned dungeon, but now I can't. It makes no sense."

"Of course it does—*if* you were allowed to contact them for a reason."

"Shite!"

Davin looked back at him. "The block cannot cover the entire kingdom. We must keep moving. Once we are past their range, we both should be able to contact our people."

"Then hurry. I have to contact Avery before she does something foolishly brave to try to rescue me."

"I want to meet your wife."

"As long as you remember that she is my wife."

Davin laughed. "Were I to forget, I'm sure you would quickly remind me."

"Damned straight. I never thought I'd get married. I didn't expect to find someone like Avery. You can bet your ass I'm going to protect her."

"As you believe she will protect you."

Duncan nodded. "She's loyal to those she loves. She can also be fearless."

Davin pointed to their right. "That way. It will get us to the nearest river the quickest. From there, we can follow the river to the crossing. Then we can make it to the border."

"You know where we are?" Duncan asked.

"I believe so. If we find a river where I expect it to be, we will know for certain."

They rode as fast as they dared in the unfamiliar territory. Far from feeling safe, they kept their eyes open for any of Cathan's warriors.

A long while later, through the trees, they caught the glint of sunlight on water.

"I hope that's your river," Duncan said.

"It is," Davin stated merrily.

That his companion was cheerful eased Duncan's tension. He had been skeptical, but it seemed Davin did at least have a rudimentary idea as to their general location.

They soon reached the riverbank. Duncan looked upriver and then down. "Which way?"

"Downriver," David said, turning his horse in that direction. "Stay undercover of the trees as much as possible. By now, Cathan will have men actively searching for us."

It was what Duncan expected. The rats were a distraction. While the rodents had allowed them to escape, both he and Davin knew they wouldn't stop Cathan.

Messing with the man's horses might, however. Duncan had done so. At least, he hoped he had. It was something he'd never tried before, so he didn't know how well it was working. It was why he hadn't told Davin. Duncan hadn't wanted to give his companion false hope.

It was better to assume it hadn't worked and to remain on guard. The last thing he or Davin wanted was to be recaptured. Besides, even though Cathan, or someone, had blocked their telecommunication, the Dubh Sidhe would still be able to contact their people. It meant people all over the kingdom could easily be alerted to search for them. If someone were to capture them, they would no doubt earn brownie points with the king. In Omaon's oppressive kingdom, it would be a powerful incentive.

Davin suddenly pulled his horse to a stop. Duncan immediately moved his into the shade of the huge evergreen beside him.

A moment later, Duncan heard the soft thud of horses on the leaf and pine straw strewn ground. From the sound, he could tell only that there were more than two and less than ten.

And they were headed directly for them.

Duncan eased his sword from its scabbard as Davin did the same. Then they waited.

Ideally, it would be better if he and Davin weren't discovered. By the time they dispatched those approaching, they would have time to telecommunicate his and Davin's location to the entire kingdom. He and Davin waited. Duncan also controlled the two horses they rode, keeping them still and quiet.

Time seemed to stretch. Lengthening unbearably until finally the other riders passed by them almost seventy yards inland. By the time the sound of the other horses faded, Duncan was more than ready to continue.

"Thank you," Davin said, surprising him.

"For what?"

Davin indicated the horses. "Not even a whinny or whicker to greet the other horses or a hoof stomp. That had to be you."

"I wasn't sure it would work." Duncan shrugged.

"It did. Splendidly." Davin urged his horse forward at a canter.

Duncan followed. After several minutes, they increased their speed to a gallop.

It took two days to find a place to cross the river. Word had spread. They dodged patrols the entire way. Finally, they found a man with a boat large enough to carry their horses, and who was willing to ferry them to the other side.

As soon as they were on solid ground once more, Duncan tried to reach his grandfather. *"Dada?"*

"Duncan, where the hell have you been? We've been trying to reach ye for two days."

"I'm sorry. Cathan or Omaon had us blocked. We're out of the kingdom, and this is the first chance I've had. How is Avery?"

"Worried sick. Stiabhan left to find ya, and we haven't heard from him, either. Where are ye?"

"Where are we?" Duncan asked Davin. He relayed the information his friend gave him to his grandfather. *"If you hear from Stiabhan, let him know I'll try to reach him right after I let Avery know I'm okay."*

"Get home as quickly as ye can, aye?"

"Aye, Dada." Duncan cut contact with his grandfather and reached out to his wife. *"Avery?"*

"Duncan. Oh, thank God, Duncan. Are you hurt? Where are you?"

"Easy, honey. I'm fine. Davin and I escaped. We're headed for the nearest tairseach as we speak. It's about a day away. Just sit tight. I'll be home as soon as I can."

"I'll be waiting."

Duncan smiled. His wife made him feel invincible.

"Did you reach your people?" Davin asked.

"Yes. Avery's still at home. They sent Stiabhan Iorworth to find us. I need to see if I can reach him."

Davin laughed. "He's Gwyneiran. He put out a call for anyone else missing someone to contact him. My queen answered. They were conferring on the best way to locate where we were being held. He will meet us at the tairseach."

Duncan nodded. He wanted time to talk to Stiabhan before he got home and saw Avery. Somehow, they had to make his wife more trouble to the Dubh Sidhe than she was worth. Neither he nor Avery could live the rest of their lives with a Dubh Sidhe sword hanging over their heads.

"Stiabhan, I don't appreciate you worrying my wife by not responding to her," he challenged the Sidhe.

"Don't blame me for worrying your wife, you arse," Stiabhan fired back. *"I'm not the one who got myself captured by Omaon. Twice. And disappeared without a word. When I reach you, I just may pound some manners into your sorry hide."*

Duncan laughed. "*You can try.*"

"I should reach you by nightfall. Prepared to hurt." Stiabhan severed the connection.

Duncan laughed again. "Damn, but that felt good."

"What is so funny?" Davin asked.

"My Sidhe cousin-by-marriage, Stiabhan Iorworth. He's threatening to beat me for making Avery worry."

"You find that humorous?"

Duncan nodded. "Oh, yeah. Because I could use a good fight to ease some tension. Stiabhan is just the one to give it to me."

"If that's all you need, I'd be happy to oblige."

Duncan laughed. "I don't feel like fighting you. You helped me escape. Stiabhan, on the other hand, caused Avery to worry, too. He's given me nothing but grief since I met her. He deserves some pain."

Davin smiled. "You like him."

"What? No." Then Duncan grinned. "Yeah, I do. A little. He's not bad. He just comes across as arrogant sometimes."

"I look forward to meeting him. Arzur has mentioned him on occasion. He has great respect for him."

"Are you sure he's met him?" Duncan asked with a laugh.

"How long until he joins us?"

"He said he'd meet us by nightfall."

"That means we only have a half-day's ride to the tairseach," Davin said, pleased.

CHAPTER FOURTEEN

Duncan and Davin found a semi-protected clearing and set up camp soon after the sun went down. They snuggled in their cloaks because they didn't dare light a fire. Omaon still had people searching for them. They were far enough from Oirthea to let their guard down a fraction.

"I'm rather glad it's cold." Duncan leaned his head back against the tree trunk. "At least we don't have to be concerned about snakes and mosquitoes."

"You do not have to worry about vipers," Stiabhan's voice came out of the darkness. "No snake would dare bite you for fear of poisoning itself."

Davin jumped to his feet, his dagger in his left hand.

"Rest easy, Davin," Duncan said calmly. "May I introduce Stiabhan Iorworth? Stiabhan, meet Davin Geir."

In the moonlight, they saw Stiabhan incline his head in greeting. "Well met, Davin. I have the pleasure of meeting your aunt, Queen Birgina."

The dagger disappeared beneath Davin's cloak. "Well met, Stiabhan. I have heard good things about you."

"Of course you have." Stiabhan grinned. "The only ones who hear bad things about me are my enemies. It's only fair to warn them. Knowing how dangerous I am might save someone's miserable life."

Duncan shook his head as he laughed. "You are one arrogant bastard."

"Not a bastard. Also, it is not arrogance if it's the truth," Stiabhan stated.

Duncan looked at Davin and grinned. "This is what I'm stuck with for the rest of my life."

"Which, if you continue to cause my kinswoman worry and pain, will be extremely short. Even for a Daondasidhe," Stiabhan threatened—or promised. Duncan wasn't sure which.

David laughed. "You two fight like brothers."

Stiabhan looked as horrified by that comment as Duncan felt.

"Have you both eaten?" Stiabhan changed the subject.

"No, we were waiting for you," Duncan told him.

Stiabhan looked around. "So, where is the meal?"

"Why do you think we were waiting for you?" Duncan asked. "You're the conjurer. Conjure up some grub, kinsman."

Stiabhan crossed his arms and shook his head. "If I kill you now, I can swear Davin to secrecy and blame your demise on Omaon."

"Avery would never forgive you if you don't bring me home alive." Duncan grinned.

"Unfortunately, true." As Stiabhan uncrossed his arms, a table with three chairs, and laden with food, appeared. He pulled out the nearest chair and sat. "Davin, please join me."

They'd eaten nothing but what nuts and berries they'd been able to scavenge for two days. Duncan knew how little Davin had been given as Omaon's prisoner. The man was probably thirty to forty pounds underweight. Duncan was glad Stiabhan had created a table covered with delectable foods. As hungry as he was, Duncan knew Davin was more so.

He sat down as Davin pulled out a chair and sat to his right.

"Eat," Stiabhan encouraged Davin. "Omaon serves horrible fare. You must be starving. Eat."

"Thank you." Davin filled his plate. "This all smells wonderful." He began eating slowly, but the hunger took over and he was soon eating ravenously.

Duncan quickly joined him. The food was wonderful, and he was also starving. When he and Davin settled on just nibbling, their hunger slaked, Stiabhan produced three sleeping pallets, complete with pillows and heavy blankets. Not only were their stomachs full for the first time in days, but they would be able to sleep warmly and comfortably.

"Stiabhan, if you can take the first watch, I'll take the second," Duncan offered.

"There's no need," Stiabhan said gently. "I brought friends. They will keep watch and alert us to any danger. Go ahead and sleep well."

That was some of the best news Duncan had heard in a while. "Thank you."

Stiabhan inclined his head. "We leave at dawn."

"Fine by me," Duncan agreed. "I'm eager to get home."

That was a first for Duncan. At least the reason he was so anxious was new. He always enjoyed returning home, but knowing Avery was waiting for him added a deeper layer to his feelings.

Lying down on his pallet and pulling the blanket over him, Duncan quickly fell asleep.

AVERY WAS HELPING BRIAN and Darrach chop vegetables for a large salad and the spaghetti sauce for Duncan's welcome-home meal.

"Honey, why don't you let me cut the onions?" Brian asked for the third time.

"It's okay. I'm fine." Her eyes were burning and tears were streaming down her face. She wasn't fine, but this way she could blame her tears on the onions. When Duncan got home, she didn't want him to realize she was such a wuss.

"Baby, you're not fine," Duncan's voice sounded from just behind her.

Avery told herself she would be strong when Duncan got home. It only took hearing his voice for her to lose it. Dropping the knife onto the counter, Avery spun around and threw herself into her husband's open arms. She tried to check him for injuries while simultaneously clinging to him. Duncan seemed to know what she was trying, but he held her so tightly, she couldn't.

"Avery, sweetheart, I'm not hurt. No injuries at all." Duncan held her close, trying to calm her.

She nodded, wanting to let him know she understood, and that she was okay, but she couldn't get the words out.

"We'll be back," Duncan said, right before translocating them both to the master bedroom. He set her on the bed and began stripping off his clothes.

"What are you doing?" she asked in surprise.

"I'm going to show you I'm uninjured." He tossed the clothes he removed to the floor at the foot of the bed.

Avery drank in every inch of beautiful skin he exposed. She had missed him so much. She had also been so worried that she nearly made herself sick. Having met Omaon, Avery had a good idea what he was capable of doing.

Completely naked now, Duncan held his arms out and slowly turned in a complete circle. "See. No cuts. No bruises. Do you feel better now?"

Avery wanted to ease his mind and tell him yes, but she didn't. The fear was too raw—even though she could see he was well.

Duncan kneeled in front of her, taking her hands in his. "Avery, I'm fine. They just kept me locked up." He grinned. "And the food and accommodations left a lot to be desired."

"We should go get you something to eat. We fixed your favorite."

Duncan shook his head. "Not until you smile, and it reaches your eyes. What can I do to make that happen?"

Avery leaned forward and kissed him. She pulled back and stared into his eyes. "Make love to me."

Heat flared in his eyes. "I can do that."

WHEN AVERY AND DUNCAN finally went downstairs, the others were already eating.

"You couldn't have waited?" Duncan complained.

"No," Stiabhan said succinctly.

"The meal was ready an hour ago," Brian stated. "We waited about thirty minutes, but since we didn't know when you two would make an appearance—or even *if* you would—we decided not to wait on you."

"Well, you'd better have left enough for Avery and me," Duncan pulled out a chair at the kitchen table, holding it for his wife.

"We made enough for about fifteen people. There's plenty," Darach said. He served two pasta bowls, passing one to Avery and one to Duncan, who took the empty seat beside Avery.

"Did you tell Angus you're back?" Brian asked as he put a bottle of beer in front of Duncan and a glass of iced tea in front of Avery.

"Of course," Duncan answered testily. "He's my grandfather. Do you think I'd let the old man continue to worry?"

Brian sat down and held his hands up. "Just making sure."

"You can't blame him," Stiabhan spoke up. "From the moment of your return, you seemed to have one thought on your mind."

Duncan glowered at Avery's cousin. "Pardon me for reassuring my wife. Who invited you to come home with me, anyway? It surely wasn't me. Feel free to leave as soon as you wish."

"Duncan," Avery admonished him.

Stiabhan just laughed.

Avery looked around the table. Duncan pretended to be grouchy, but there was an ornery twinkle in his eyes. He and Stiabhan seemed to be getting along better. At least, she thought they were. Glad that Duncan was home safe, she thought she might be reading things into the situation.

Then Stiabhan winked at her and made her think she wasn't imagining things after all.

After eating half of his serving, Duncan looked at Darach. "Any news on finding Accalon's blade?"

"Peter is still working on it," Darach informed him. "We thought we had a solid lead, but it didn't pan out."

Duncan frowned. "You checked it out?"

"Yes. Stiabhan took us out there and I checked," Avery said, surprising her husband. "None of the blades in the man's collection was the right one."

"You went?" Duncan asked in disbelief.

Avery knew he was about to lose his temper, so she tried to diffuse it. "There was a group of us. We popped over, checked it out and popped back home. No problem. Easy."

Her husband glared at her cousin. "You translocated her?"

Stiabhan nodded. "I did."

"How many were with her?" Duncan asked.

"Besides myself, two," Stiabhan answered.

"Duncan, you can see I'm fine. We went out, had a quick look, and returned." Avery felt her husband's tension and sought to ease it.

Duncan covered her nearest hand with his. "No thanks to the ones supposed to be keeping you safe."

"We kept her safe," Stiabhan stated. "We did not undertake the mission without Angus' blessings."

"I'll speak to him as well," Duncan stated.

"No, you will not." Avery had had enough. "I am still in charge of my own life. You will not argue with anyone else about my choices. They are my choices."

Duncan met her gaze squarely.

Avery waited.

After a few seconds, he slowly exhaled. Duncan reluctantly nodded.

"What is next?" Brian asked. "We can't go on allowing Omaon to kidnap people. There must be a way to make Avery more trouble than she's worth to him."

Avery hoped there was. She wanted a life with Duncan. Hopefully, a family, too. That meant stopping the Dubh Sidhe king from continually trying to take her prisoner.

"Short of killing the SOB, I can't think of any," Duncan responded.

"Killing him would only get rid of Omaon," Stiabhan stated. "Besides his heirs, there are more Dubh Sidhe monarchs who would also love to get their hands on a psychometric. While killing Omaon may temporarily make you feel better, it will not solve Avery's problem."

"Great, oh ray of sunshine," Duncan's voice dripped sarcasm. "What do you suggest?"

"I suggest that you and Avery remain in Caledonia. No more missions for either of you until I return."

"Where are you going?" Avery asked.

"To speak with whoever in Tìr-dhàimh can give us answers," Stiabhan told her. "Brian is correct. There must be a way. A special warding. A talisman. Something."

That was the best news that Avery had heard in a while.

"We can do that," Duncan said.

"Be prepared," Stiabhan warned. "You've escaped him twice. Not only is he going to be in a tearing rage, but his honor has also been broken. Omaon will be out for blood. Be prepared for him to attack."

"Here? In Caledonia?" Avery asked.

Stiabhan nodded. "Oh, yes. He will come for you with everything he has. Do not count on him trying to kidnap Avery again. He may try it one more time, or he may just as easily decide to cut his losses and try to kill you both."

Avery glanced at Duncan. He was watching Stiabhan, apparently unsurprised by what her cousin said.

"I will contact Pritch and see if he can beef up the protection—both in Caledonia and here. Especially here." Duncan said.

Stiabhan frowned. "Beef up?"

"Strengthen," Avery clarified for him.

Her kinsman nodded. "An excellent precaution. I would contact him as soon as possible."

Duncan nodded. He was silent for several seconds. "He will come as soon as he can."

Stiabhan finished his beer. Pushing his chair back, he stood. "I'll return as soon as I have some answers. In the meantime, be on guard." He disappeared.

Duncan turned to her. "You're under lockdown, lady."

"The hell I am. I'm going to work tomorrow. Iona is expecting me. I'll remain in Caledonia, but I'll be damned if I'll be a prisoner in my own home." Avery didn't curse often, which let them know how upset she was.

Darach jumped to his feet. "Duncan, glad you're home. Brian, good meal. I'll see y'all later. I've got work to do." After carrying his dirty dishes into the kitchen, he hurried downstairs.

Duncan grinned. "I think you scared him."

"I was trying to scare you," Avery said.

"Oh, you did." Duncan couldn't stop the smile from dancing around his lips.

Avery narrowed her eyes. "Sure, I did."

Duncan laughed. "Perhaps you didn't scare me, but you did put me in my place."

"That's not exactly what I was trying to do." Avery hadn't meant to hurt him.

He gently squeezed her hand. "It's okay. I needed the reminder. I want to keep you safe and sometimes I tend to slip into the end-justifies-the-means mode. That's wrong. I wouldn't appreciate someone forcing me into house arrest. I shouldn't try to force it on anyone else. Especially you."

Turning her hand over, Avery linked their fingers. "I'm not going to take stupid chances, Duncan. I want to share a long life with you."

Raising their joined hands, Duncan pressed a kiss to the back of her hand. "May I accompany you to work tomorrow?"

Avery felt a jab to her heart. She expected something more from him. At least an acknowledgement of her statement. Preferably a reciprocation. Avery wanted to hear that he felt something for her. She knew as well as anyone, however, that it wasn't possible to make someone love you. Perhaps she should have been plainer.

She glanced at Brian. He was glaring at Duncan, but quickly smiled at her when he saw her looking.

To hide the pain in her eyes, Avery looked down, pushing the remnants of her meal around with her fork. "I guess. I don't think Iona will mind."

"How about desert?" Brian asked.

"No, thank you. I'm full." Slipping her hand from Duncan's grasp, she gathered her dirty dishes and carried them to the sink. "I've been working on some items for Christmas presents. I'm going to get back to my knitting."

"Christmas? Honey, that's still a month away," Duncan remarked.

"Knitting takes time. I have to plan ahead." Passing them, Avery went to the family room.

"YOU STUPID JERK," BRIAN whispered harshly.

Duncan, who had been watching his wife, turned to his friend in surprise. "What'd I do?"

"It's what you didn't do, you idiot."

Duncan shrugged, making a face. "I give up. What didn't I do?"

"Avery just basically told you she loved you and you're like 'okay, so can I go to work with you tomorrow.'"

Duncan sat up straight. "I..." Damn! He had done that. He'd been so concerned with making sure Avery let him stay near her that he hadn't paid attention to what she was saying. As a husband, he was failing. "Well, hell."

Brian nodded. He crossed his arms. "What are you going to do to fix this?"

That was the question. The time for telling Avery he felt the same had passed. Any remarks he made now would come across as fake, or as him just saying something but not meaning it.

"There's nothing I can do tonight that she's not going to think is a fabrication on my part."

"You effed up, buddy."

"Thanks for the newsflash, Brian." Duncan knew he'd messed up. What he needed was an idea of how to make it up to Avery. An apology gift might be a start.

The problem was what to get her. Avery didn't seem to care that much about jewelry. The pendant Orla had given her and her engagement ring were all she never took off. She had several pairs of earrings and a diamond solitaire he learned had belonged to her maternal grandmother, and then her mother.

His wife loved history. Duncan had been meaning to get her a weapon—or several—that she could carry on her person at all times. There were hair thingys that hid small knives and lock picks. His aunt owned several. Duncan would check Iona's shop for some. And a tessen. Women didn't carry fans much, but it wouldn't look totally out of place. Duncan remembered seeing some of them at Iona's, too. If she didn't have any, he'd check with Eilish Carstairs. The woman was young, but she made weapons like no one else.

Duncan looked out the bank of windows without seeing the deck or yard beyond. He was still thinking. While gifts were items Avery would probably like, they had the feeling of being as much for him as for her. He would buy her those things, but he needed something that would tell her he cared for her.

Then it came to him. When it grew up, it would also help him, but as a puppy, it would just be for Avery. She never mentioned a pet, but he'd seen her reaction to other people's and to TV ads. He knew she leaned more toward canines than felines. That would work, too.

But where to get a puppy on such short notice?

Duncan looked at Brian. "Know where I can get a cùdrèagon?"

Brian's eyes widened. "Why a cùdrèagon? Why not a cùsidhe?"

"I don't know. Because they're larger. Better intimidation factor. At least when it's grown. In the meantime, Avery has a pet to love and one that will grow into a guard-dog companion for her."

"I thought that was why you invited me to move in?"

Duncan laughed. "Partially. But a pet can stay with Avery in my bedroom at night. You cannot."

"Fine. Why don't you contact Tremayne? Perhaps he knows."

Pritch's son would be a good one to ask. Duncan sent out a telecommunication to his uncle-centuries-removed. Several seconds later, Tremayne replied he had a four-month-old male available. Duncan immediately told him he wanted the puppy.

Tremayne agreed to translocate with the puppy. Duncan didn't want Avery to see what was going on, so he went through the mudroom and out through the garage. He met Tremayne just outside the garage.

His uncle waited with a large black puppy with white paws and a white slash on his chest. When the puppy saw him, he began wiggling in his great-uncle's arms, anxious to make a new friend. He didn't look like he would grow into a guard dog, but that was an innate part of every cùdrèagon.

Avery would adore him.

"He's perfect." Duncan took the squirming bundle of fur.

"Wonderful." Tremayne tumbled the large puppy into Duncan's arms. "I took the liberty of depositing some bags of puppy food in your vehicle shed. If you need anything, get in touch with me."

"Thanks."

Duncan waited until Tremayne disappeared before taking the puppy into the house.

Brian's eyes widened. "That's not a puppy. It's a baby Clydesdale."

The puppy barked as if he was either in agreement or considered it an insult. Duncan wasn't sure which. He quickly carried it into the family room before more barking alerted Avery to his surprise.

She looked up at his approach. Her gaze focused on the wriggling bundle in his arms. She looked up at Duncan, a huge smile on her face. "Who is this?" She eagerly grasped the chubby puppy as Duncan put him in her lap. The puppy began licking every piece of bare skin he could reach, tickling Avery and making her giggle.

"He doesn't have a name yet. That's for you to decide." He smiled, watching them interact.

"Me?" She laughed as the puppy licked her chin.

"Yes, he's sort of a belated wedding present. Something to keep you company when I have to go away for a job."

"I thought that's what Brian was for," Avery said, scratching the puppy behind his ears and along his back, eliciting wriggles of pure bliss.

Duncan glanced in the kitchen to see Brian give him an I-told-you-so nod. He grinned. His wife was perceptive. "He is, but I thought you might want something in our room. That will definitely not be Brian."

Avery laughed. "You know I would be safe with him."

Duncan nodded. "I know, but I don't care. I got you a puppy. Now, any idea what you want to name him?"

"I think Murphy. He looks like a smart, special guy."

The puppy reacted to the name as if he liked it.

Duncan wasn't so sure. "Do you know someone named Murphy?" The question revealed more of his feelings than he wished.

Avery looked startled. "You're not seriously jealous, are you?"

"Of course not." Duncan shook his head. "Maybe. It depends on your answer."

Avery laughed. "There is absolutely no need. Murphy is just the first name that came to me. It's the last name of some friends of mine. A married couple. Feel better now?"

Duncan grinned unrepentantly. "Much."

Avery looked up. "Is there a pet store in Caledonia? One that's still open? We need a collar, name tag, leash, toys, chews, food, a harness, and a bed. Unless he's going to sleep with us."

"Pet store it is. He can sleep in our room, but not in the bed. Tremayne brought food, so we're good on that." Duncan scooped the puppy up from her lap. "Let's go hit up the local pet store."

They returned nearly two hours later with items Avery insisted the puppy needed. As long as she was happy, Duncan wouldn't have cared if she wanted to buy out the entire store.

"Are you preparing for a baby or this puppy?" Brian stared in disbelief at all the shopping bags Duncan carried in. "I brought in the food, by the way."

Murphy sported a dapper blue collar with yellow dog bones on it, and a blue, bone-shaped tag with his name and info on it. Avery put him down. He ran over to inspect Brian's trouser cuffs.

Avery started emptying the bags. She set four bowls on the counter. Next, she pulled out toys and began cutting off the tags. A soft, round bed was put on the floor near the fireplace. Before long, Murphy's bed was set up in their bedroom with a water bowl in their bathroom. His main water bowl was set on a mat in the kitchen, and toys were scattered over the family room floor where Murphy attacked first one and then the next until he wore himself out, curling up with his head on Avery's feet.

Duncan had never had a pet, so he wasn't prepared for the multiple nighttime potty breaks followed by the play time. He and Avery worked out a plan. Duncan took Murphy out because he could translocate them to the yard and back. Avery would play with the puppy until he fell asleep once more. At least Murphy liked his bed and was content to sleep in it.

Brian took one look at Duncan the next morning and burst out laughing.

"What?" Duncan demanded irritably. Going to the coffeepot, he poured himself a large mug.

"I can't wait until you have a baby. Murphy's good practice, but his care is nothing compared to an infant's." Brian grinned.

Duncan sat on the nearest barstool. A baby. He hadn't had time to stop and think about having children with Avery. It was something they needed to discuss. Especially since he'd done nothing to prevent pregnancy. Duncan was pretty sure Avery wasn't on the pill.

Putting his mug on the counter, he headed back to the bedroom. Avery blinked sleepily as he sat on her side of the bed. Raising her hand, she cupped his cheek. "You're frowning. What's wrong?"

"We need to talk about children."

"Oh. Okay." Avery levered herself to a sitting position. "Do you not want children?"

"I do want them. Do you?"

Avery's eyes became soft and luminous as she nodded. "What brought this on?"

"Brian saying that Murphy is good practice for when we have a baby. It reminded me that neither of us has been practicing safe sex."

"Should we be? We're married, and I'd welcome a baby." Avery eyed him, waiting.

Taking hold of her hand, he kissed her palm. "No, we shouldn't. I just wanted to make sure we were on the same page." Leaning forward, he kissed her.

CHAPTER FIFTEEN

"Duncan, what breed of puppy is Murphy?" Avery asked. "I thought Labrador mix, but now I'm not so sure."

Duncan only had a passing knowledge of dog breeds. If Avery thought Murphy was a Lab, he would be happy to go with it. "He is. Mostly. Mainly mutt. Why?" He needed to talk privately with the vet and let her know not to share Murphy's true bloodline. At least not yet.

"Because he's gaining about eight pounds a week. If he doesn't slow down, we're going to have a pony, not a dog." She told him Murphy's latest weight.

Duncan lifted the squirming puppy from her arms. "Maybe we should have named him Horse."

"That can be his middle name."

"Dogs have middle names?"

Avery shrugged. "Why not?"

"Why not indeed. Are we ready to leave?"

"He's had his booster shots. Next is neutering."

Duncan pressed Murphy's ear to his chest and covered his other ear with his hand. "Hush. Don't upset him with talk like that."

Avery rolled her eyes. Taking the puppy back, she headed for the exit.

Duncan hurried to follow.

Stiabhan hadn't returned. Nor had they heard from him. Pritch had come by and boosted the wardings for Caledonia. None of which made Duncan feel better about Avery's safety. He didn't like her out of his sight unless they were home, at Time Passages, or at Kerr Limited.

He'd been back two and a half weeks and there hadn't been one attempt to come after his wife. Everyone except Avery was about ready to jump out of their skins. It wasn't a good situation. It was good for the enemy and bad for them. Duncan wanted to be proactive. Not sit and wait to react to an attack.

At the moment, all they could do was wait.

Murphy's vet appointment had been midafternoon, so Duncan drove them back to Time Passages. Avery wanted to finish her workday. Brian and Iona were already there.

Duncan loved that Iona hadn't blinked an eye at allowing Avery and Brian to bring the puppy to work. Duncan made a four-foot gate with a pass-through to keep Murphy in the private quarters of the shop. It wouldn't do to give the large, gangly puppy free range of a store with so many priceless, breakable objects.

"How is our little guardian?" Iona asked when Murphy ran to greet her as soon as Avery put him down.

"Not so little." Avery told her about the vet's visit.

Iona laughed in delight as she scratched Murphy behind his ears. "So we will have a large guard dog."

"Where is Brian?" Duncan noticed his friend was missing.

"He went to get our afternoon tea. He should be back anytime."

"Oh, I hope she had cherry-almond scones." Avery's eyes sparkled.

"She did, and I ordered some for you." Iona smiled warmly when Avery hugged her.

"What did you order me?" Duncan asked, curiously.

"English muffin with raspberry jam. What was I supposed to have ordered?" Iona arched one white eyebrow.

Bending, Duncan kissed her cheek. "Exactly what you did. You know me too well, Iona."

"Yes, I do. For some reason unknown to me, Avery talks about you a lot." Iona grinned at him as his wife blushed charmingly.

"Probably for the same reason I'm always talking about her." Duncan was happy with the surprised and pleased look on Avery's face.

Iona nodded. "Probably so."

"Hey," Brian called out as the front door chimed its opening. "I'm glad you're back. Come help me with the snacks and drinks."

Duncan went out and took the two sacks from Brian. Helping to set the food out on the table, Duncan noticed an extra bag. Opening it, he discovered a large, dog-shaped biscuit. He held it up for Avery to see. "If he gets one of these every day, it might explain the growth and weight gain."

Avery shook her head. "It's one cookie. That's Murphy's treat for being so nice to the customers. And for just being such a good boy." She turned to Murphy, who was sitting, his unwavering gaze on the dog biscuit. "Because you are a good boy, aren't you, baby?"

The puppy wriggled in agreement, but never took his amber eyes off the cookie.

"Give him his treat," Avery instructed. "That's why he's sitting. He knows he has to sit to get his cookie."

Duncan held the cookie down to him. "Here you go, boy."

Murphy grasped the cookie and went over to the rug where he lay down with the bone-shaped treat and began to munch.

Joining the others, Duncan sat down at the table to enjoy afternoon tea.

As soon as the women finished, they went to a workbench and carefully began to unpack the two crates that had arrived earlier that morning. Duncan smiled at the excitement on his wife's face.

Working with Iona, Avery had honed her ability to control her reactions to the ancient artifacts.

"Duncan." Once Brian had his attention, a slight motion of his head indicated that he wanted to speak to Duncan outside.

Standing, Duncan reached for Murphy's leash, sending the puppy into an excited dance. "Now that he's finished his treat, Brian and I are going to take Murphy for a walk around the block. See if we can walk off our treats."

Iona raised a brow at that pronouncement, but Avery just nodded. Too engrossed in her work, Avery barely acknowledged his comment.

Duncan snapped the leash to the puppy's harness and followed Brian out the backdoor. Instead of heading for the alley, Brian turned to him, a look of concern on his face that chilled Duncan's blood.

"What?" Duncan asked. He let the puppy tug him to a grassy area.

"I think Avery's being watched. There's a stranger pretending to window-shop. He's meandering or pretending to, but his gaze keeps coming back to the shop."

"Crap." It was what Duncan expected. At least something similar, but he'd hoped they had a little more time to prepare. Especially since he had heard nothing from Stiabhan.

Murphy tugged on the lead, trying to pull Duncan toward the alley. "Come on." He walked to the alley entrance with the puppy. "We might as well walk him. I need to think."

"We need to circle the wagons," Brian argued, even as he followed.

"We will. For now, Avery and Iona are safe enough. Besides, we're not going far, but I don't want to return too early. If Avery's paying attention, she'll ask questions."

They walked to the end of the alley, turned, and walked back the way they had come. Duncan wanted to start teaching Avery self-defense. Now seemed like a good time to start. He ran the idea past Brian. "I need to teach Avery ways to protect herself. How does Wing Chun sound?" It was a good martial art for a woman because it didn't rely on size or strength.

Brian frowned. "You know this woman, Duncan. Do you seriously see your wife being able to gouge out someone's eyes with her fingers? Avery won't be good at hands-on fighting. She's going to need distance. At least a weapon. Something she can carry at all times."

Duncan hated to admit it, but Brian was right. Avery wouldn't be able to kill anyone with her bare hands. Even if she thought to try, her abilities would make it horrific for her. That meant a weapon, or weapons. More than the *sgian dubh* he'd already given her. Thinking over his options, he came up with two. He mentioned the first one. "A tessen might work."

Brian perked up. "Yes, but it would have to be newly made."

"Of course." Duncan frowned at Brian. "Do you believe I'd give my wife an old one with all the emotions and history attached to it?"

Brian waved his hand. "I was just commenting. Of course, I know you wouldn't."

"Sorry, Brian. I shouldn't take out my fears by snapping at you."

"What are friends for? Don't worry about it."

"I'm going to have a naginata made as well. One that can be disguised as a walking staff."

Brian looked excited. "Oh, that's a great idea. That would be easier to hide than a tessen. And maybe easier to teach Avery to use. Even closed, a tessen looks like a weapon."

"I hope Iona knows a blacksmith or weapons master who can make one quickly. I thought about Eilish Carstairs, but I want to check with Iona first."

"I'm sure she does. Let's go ask." Brian vibrated with excitement.

Duncan looked down at the puppy, who was happily sniffing any and every clump of grass he could reach. "I need to finish walking this guy. I think I'll walk around the block. See what I can see. See how Murphy reacts if we spot your stalker."

"Do you want me to accompany you?"

"No thanks. If he's still out there, I don't want him to know you've pointed him out to me. Tell Avery I'll bring Murphy back as soon as he's done."

Brian nodded. "Be careful."

Duncan nodded back. He planned to be. He had no plans to be kidnapped again. But he wanted a look at Avery's stalker. And, even though Murphy was only around five months old, Duncan wanted to know if the puppy would react.

Though feeling a certain sense of urgency, Duncan kept to an easy stroll, allowing the puppy to explore as he wished. He didn't want his anxiety to transmit to the dog. Murphy was happily checking out items as they walked past them.

Reaching the corner with the street in front of the shop, Duncan turned as if he hadn't a care in the world. With his sunglasses on, it would be impossible for the man to tell where he was looking.

Duncan and Murphy were about half a block from the shop door when the puppy suddenly alerted. He stepped back, bumping into Duncan's legs and growling low in his throat.

Smiling at the response, Duncan telepathically calmed the puppy. He let Murphy know how pleased he was with him. While Murphy stopped growling, he kept his gaze focused on a man standing in the shadow of a recessed doorway almost directly across from Time Passages' entrance. Duncan could feel the dislike rolling off the puppy. He was going to make sure Murphy got a treat after supper for already showing signs of being the guard dog Duncan wanted.

"Come on, fella. Maybe your mom has some treats hidden in there." He laughed when Murphy's ears perked up at the word 'treat.'

Duncan monitored the bastard across the street as he walked Murphy to Time Passages. Suprisingly, it took him a while. Women kept stopping him to pet Murphy and ask about the puppy. Murphy ate up all the attention. Finally, they slipped in the front door of the store and made their way to the private rooms at the back. Released from his leash, Murphy headed right for his water bowl and began to drink.

Duncan walked over to where Avery was still carefully unpacking crates. Bending over, he kissed her cheek.

Avery turned her head to kiss him on the lips. "Hi, baby. Did you and Murphy have a pleasant walk?"

"He seemed to enjoy it. He sure got petted enough along the last block."

Avery laughed. She laughed so hard she ended up leaning against his leg for support.

"What?" Duncan asked. He was missing something.

Avery plucked at the hem of his sweatshirt and then swatted him playfully on the rump. "You were the draw, stud muffin. Murphy was just their excuse to get close to you."

Stud muffin? Was she serious?

"I wish you could see your expression. You're adorable." Standing, Avery cupped his cheeks in her palms. "I can't blame them, but they'd better keep their hands on the puppy only."

"You're serious?"

"Yes, of course." The question surprised Avery. "You're a handsome man. You draw attention wherever you go. Surely you know that. Don't you?"

Duncan shrugged. He knew he'd never had trouble attracting members of the opposite sex, but he'd never bothered to consider why. "I guess I never thought about it. And now I'm married. To you. Why would they think I'd be interested?"

"For the same reasons men hit on married women. Some are just outright jerks. Some are out of jealousy because someone has something they don't. Others because they're lonely and hopeful." Avery grinned. "And some because they love dogs, and Murphy is a cutie pie."

Duncan grinned. He was ready to change the subject. Duncan needed to find out about getting a naginata made. He also needed to get Murphy's treat. "Do you have dog biscuits somewhere? I promised Murphy one for being such a good boy."

The dog's ears perked up at 'good boy.'

Brian retrieved a box from the cupboard and handed it to Duncan.

After giving the puppy a cookie and replacing the box, Duncan looked at Iona. She sat at the table looking through an old book that had been in the crate.

"Ms. Iona, would you happen to know a craftsman who could make a naginata for me?"

The old lady looked up at him, glanced at Avery, and then refocused on him. "I do. She works quickly, too."

"Excellent. Can you—"

They all froze as Avery made a low, keening cry.

Murphy stood, his hackles raised, and let out both a growl and a whine.

Duncan hurried back to his wife. She was frozen, an old leather scabbard in her hands. It was the expression on her face that frightened him. It was a strange mixture of fear and excitement. Snatching the object from her hand and tossing it on the worktable, Duncan wrapped his arms around her and pulled her against his chest.

Avery breathed as if she had just run a marathon. She was also trembling.

"Honey, what happened? What is that artifact?"

"Accalon," Avery choked out the answer. She shook harder.

The one word was all that was needed to get everyone's full attention.

Brian went to the table and picked up the discarded scabbard. He carried it to the other table and handed it to Iona.

Iona carefully turned it over in her hands, examining it from every side. After several seconds, she met Duncan's gaze and nodded. "It is entirely likely. This leather is ancient. The threads of the stitching are made from extremely old gut cut into surprisingly fine strips. The workmanship is extraordinary."

Avery shuddered.

Duncan rubbed his hand up and down her back. "Easy, honey. I've got you. Can you talk to us yet?"

Murphy came over and leaned against her leg.

"I'm fine. Really." Avery said. "It was just such a shock. I wasn't expecting it. How is this even possible?"

Good question. "Iona, where did these artifacts come from?" Duncan asked.

"I purchased them from an estate sale in Portland, Oregon. Two unopened crates from the attic. I was high bidder on the unopened boxes. They offer items like that often. It's a calculated risk that pays off more often than not. Sometimes handsomely."

"This one may have just paid off in unexpected ways," Brian observed.

"It can't be this easy." Duncan looked at the partially unpacked crate. "You couldn't have accidentally purchased the *sgian dubh* we've been searching for."

Avery raised her head from his chest. She shook hers. "She didn't. The knife isn't here."

"You're sure?" Brian asked before Duncan could.

"Yes. I would have felt it. It's not here," Avery stated confidently.

"Well shi—heck! We could use a break." Brian sank onto the nearest chair.

Avery straightened. "We did get one. A huge one," she argued. "With the sheath, I should be able to track the *sgian dubh*. We can retrieve it and turn it over to the Mother Guardians."

She made it sound so easy. Duncan only wished it would be that simple. The man out front stalking his wife made a lie of that hope. They would try their best, but they were going to need help. Where the hell was Stiabhan? Why hadn't he returned? If Duncan hadn't heard from him by nightfall, he was going to try to contact the Sidhe.

In the meantime, Duncan needed to see about getting the naginata made for Avery as quickly as possible. As he looked at Iona, his wife was holding out her hand for the sheath.

"I need to see what I can learn from this." Avery accepted the leather sheath and sat down on the workbench to study it.

While she was occupied, Duncan got the name and location of the weapons craftsman. It was the very woman he'd first thought of. Even better, she lived nearby. Making certain that Brian knew not to allow Avery out of the building, Duncan went out the back exit to his vehicle and drove off for the home and attached workshop of Eilish Carstairs.

Duncan had never met Eilish Carstairs in person. She was not what Duncan expected. For one thing, she was about thirty years younger. He expected to find an elderly woman built like a linebacker. What he got was a woman in her mid-to-late twenties, tall, shapely, with curly black hair pulled back in a ponytail. Except for her green eyes, she reminded him a little of his wife.

Eilish met him at the door to her shop-cum-studio and introduced herself. She invited him in. Waiving a hand around her shop walls, she indicated the weapons on display. There was a large range from small knives that could be concealed in a palm to huge battle pikes. Weapons representing nearly every period in history were on display.

She drew his attention to a naginata. "I believe this is the specific weapon you inquired about." Reaching up, she took it off the wall and handed it to him.

Duncan took it. He knew of the weapons, but he'd never personally seen one before. It was lightweight, yet the wood was sturdy. The blade was razor sharp, as the neat cut on his thumb proved.

"How long would it take you to make one disguised as a walking staff?"

"Since I have several staffs already, partially prepared, less than forty-eight hours. I made a couple before where the blade was hidden within the staff until needed, so I've already worked out potential problems with release. If you want it disguised as a walking staff, some extra carved embellishments are called for to hide the release and reset mechanism. At least, in my opinion."

Duncan nodded, impressed. "I agree. I'll gladly pay double if you complete it as quickly as possible. My wife is being stalked. While she has bodyguards, she needs a weapon with her."

Eilish frowned. "Does she know how to use a naginata?"

"She will learn as soon as you finish," Duncan promised.

"Who will teach her? You?"

"No. I could, but I'm no expert with the weapon. However, I know a woman at Pendragon who is, however. I've already spoken to her. She'll teach Avery."

"She must already have one. The length is standard. I would suggest you begin your wife's lessons. She'll be that much farther along when I finish."

"Good idea. I'll speak with Henri and see if she can begin tonight."

Eilish nodded. "I'd better get started, then. As soon as I'm done, I'll bring it to you."

Duncan shook her hand. "Thank you."

Eilish smiled. "My pleasure. I love creating beautiful weapons that people actually use."

"No offense, but I hope my wife never has to use it as a weapon. If she does, however, I promise, she will be proficient in its handling."

After shaking her hand, Duncan left, feeling as if some weight had lifted from his shoulders.

"WHERE ARE WE GOING?" Avery asked when Duncan didn't head home after work.

"To begin your training with a naginata. I've already spoken with Henri. She's going to give you lessons in its use. I'm having one made for you. It will appear to be an elaborately decorated walking staff unless you need to protect yourself. Then you'll be able to turn it into a weapon."

"And I need to learn this now?"

"If we plan to go after the *sgian dubh* of Accalon—and I know you want to—then you have to know how to protect yourself. Female Ninja often used this weapon. It's a perfect weapon for a woman. You'll see," Duncan promised.

Avery agreed with that. She needed to learn to defend herself. Beyond the rudimentary self-defense moves Duncan, Brian, and the others had already taught her.

She only wished she'd had a little warning. It was silly, but Avery felt nervous about meeting Henri. She was even more concerned about disappointing her.

And Duncan. She didn't want to disappoint him.

Avery gave herself a mental shake. She was a capable woman. She could do this.

Looking sideways at the man who had become her world, Avery marveled yet again at her good fortune. Being an introvert, she had begun to despair of even meeting a man she could fall for. Then, along came Duncan, who insinuated himself into her life and refused to leave. She couldn't be happier. Avery would do everything in her power to make sure Duncan was happy, too.

Reaching over, she tucked a lock of his hair behind his ear and gently caressed his cheek with her fingertips.

Smiling, Duncan caught her hand in his, bringing it up to kiss her palm. "What was that for?"

"No reason except that I love touching you."

He flashed her a seductive look. "And I love having you touch me. All over. What brought this up now? You're not nervous about tonight, are you? If you don't want me to watch the lesson, I'll wait outside."

Avery's chest tightened. "That would make it easier. At least until I get an idea of how I'll do. I don't want to disappoint you."

This time, he frowned at her, squeezing the hand he still held. "Avery Alison Beaton Kerr, there is *nothing* you could ever do to disappoint me. Get that crazy thought out of your head right now. You're the most amazing person I know. Absolutely nothing will change that."

Oh, how she adored this man. "Thank you for that. It means the world to me."

Raising her hand once more, Duncan kissed her knuckles. "As you mean the world to me, Avery. Always remember that."

She wasn't likely to forget a declaration like that. Ever.

Duncan released her hand to put his back on the wheel as an especially powerful gust of wind buffeted the vehicle. It was only then they noticed the dark clouds skudding in. In the distance, to the west, lightning struck.

"I guess I should have checked the weather," Duncan observed. "Before long, we're going to be slammed."

Avery watched the gathering storm clouds. It would hit them before they reached the Pendragon Alliance headquarters.

"This looks nasty," he said as thunder rumbled over them with a roll that made everything tremble.

Duncan pressed down on the gas pedal, seemingly unconcerned by the possibility of a speeding ticket. He probably wasn't. Besides, when the storm hit, Avery figured the police had better things to do than come after Duncan.

By the time they reached the small complex of buildings and warehouses that held the main offices of the Pendragon Alliance, lightning flashed every few seconds and rain came down in sheets.

Duncan parked in the nearest open parking space. That still left them about fifty feet to cross to the entrance of the building used for training.

"We're going to look like drowned rats. If we're not electrocuted first."

Duncan laughed. "Give me your hand, my lady." He unsnapped her seatbelt before holding out his hand.

Avery placed hers in his.

In the blink of an eye, they were inside the lobby, and Duncan was supporting her until she got her feet underneath her.

"A little warning would be nice."

"Sorry. I thought you understood."

"I never think of translocation as an option. Probably because I'm incapable of doing it."

He frowned. "No one knows why it's usually only male Daondasidhe capable of translocation." With her hand in his, Duncan guided her down a hallway.

He seemed to know where to find Henrietta McLeod. He would, though, since his firm did subcontract work for the Pendragon Alliance.

Partway down a second hall, he opened a door into a brightly lit room with padding on the floor and walls. A woman she knew was only a few years older than herself turned at the sound and came over to greet them, a smile on her face.

Avery had heard of Henri, but this was their first meeting. Henri wasn't what she expected. Avery thought of a stocky woman of exceptional height or a female bodybuilder. The woman before her was about five-feet-eight, slender, with lean muscles. Avery saw the lithe strength in her. She already had two naginatas laid out on the padded floor.

Blonde bangs showcased clear gray eyes. Her straight, long hair was in a long braid down her back.

Avery absently touched her own long hair. She should have braided her own. It would no doubt get in her way.

Henri noticed and smiled. She pulled a band from her pocket. "Here you go. Most newbies don't think about their hair. If you don't mind, I'll braid it for you."

The offer pleased Avery. "That would be nice. Thank you."

"Sure." Henri stepped behind her and quickly braided Avery's hair.

"What do you want me to do?" Duncan asked.

"Wait outside," Avery said immediately.

"Leave," Henri said simultaneously.

"I thought I could just wait over here by the door." Duncan sounded uncertain, but looked hopeful.

"No," both Avery and Henri responded.

Duncan crossed his arms, resembling a petulant child. "I hoped maybe Avery would change her mind and let me watch."

"I can't pay attention to lessons if I'm worried about what you're thinking," Avery said.

"And I don't allow people to observe my lessons," Henri said. "Why don't you pop over to the IT building? I think Peter is working late tonight."

Duncan slowly uncrossed his arms. "Fine. I'll go see what he's doing. When you're finished, just call."

"I will." Avery smiled and then stretched up to give him a quick kiss.

Her husband's expression eased. He kissed her back and then left.

Henri grinned. "I feel like you're a fast learner. Let's see."

CHAPTER SIXTEEN

"They threw me out." Duncan complained to his friend.

Peter laughed. "Of course they did. No one wants someone they love watching them learn a new skill. Did you?"

"I didn't have a choice. Dad taught me nearly every skill I know." He held up his hand when Peter would have said more. "I get your point and I agree." Duncan considered the rest of his friend's words. "Love, huh?"

"Oh, come on. Are you that dense? I had wondered. And you're head over heels for her, too. All of us can see it."

Duncan didn't even try denial. He couldn't. Everyone probably could see what he felt. He didn't care. Except when it came to his enemies. But he and Avery were married, so his wife was already a potential target.

As for Avery, the Dubh Sidhe already wanted her because of the talents she possessed. It didn't matter if everyone knew they were married.

Duncan thought of something else. "There must be security cameras in the training area. Can you pull them up?"

Peter's brows drew together. "There are. And I can. But I won't. Avery told you to leave because she doesn't want you to see. When she's ready, she'll let you know. I am not aiding and abetting you with spying on your wife."

"Fine." Duncan dropped into a chair. "Show me what you're working on."

HENRI WAS PLEASED WITH how swiftly Avery caught on to the ways to use the naginata.

Avery was delighted with herself. She still had a lot to learn, but already she knew the basics. At least enough to give a good showing in a fight.

Which she didn't want to put to the test.

"We're finished. You can come get me when you're ready" Avery barely finished telecommunicating when Duncan opened the door and came into the room.

"I'll see you Wednesday night," Henri said. "Six o'clock."

"I'll be here," Avery promised.

"Thank you, Henri," Duncan said.

The martial arts and weapons master nodded.

Duncan walked them just outside and translocated them back to his vehicle. Rain still fell, but the violent storm had passed.

Once in the vehicle, Duncan faced her. "You look happy."

"I am. Henri is pleased. So am I. She says I have already mastered the rudimentary skills needed to protect myself. At least enough to slow down an attacker."

Duncan winced. "I don't want you to have to do that."

"Me, either." Avery patted his forearm. "But if I do, I plan on being ready. A naginata is a perfect weapon. At least for me. I don't want to get any closer to an enemy than I must."

"That sounds like the best plan. Avoid them altogether." Duncan nodded, starting the engine and pulling out of the parking lot.

Avery laughed. "You make it sound so simple."

"If only."

"Thank you for suggesting all of this and choosing the weapon."

"You're welcome."

"I haven't heard from Stiabhan. Have you?" she asked, changing the subject.

"No." Duncan glared at the road ahead. "I've tried contacting him, but he's not answering.

Hearing that made Avery nervous. What if he'd gotten injured? Would they even know? *"Stiabhan, can you hear me? You're not hurt, are you?"*

"I'm fine, little one. Just very busy. I'll contact you as soon as I can. Don't worry. And tell your husband to stop annoying me."

"I will. Be careful."

"Always."

Avery knew that was a lie, but it wasn't as if she could do anything to force him to be more cautious. She looked at her husband. "I got him to answer. He said he's fine but busy. And he told me to tell you to stop annoying him."

"Annoying him? Next time I see him, I'm going to kick his a—butt."

Avery grinned. Her husband and her kinsman seemed to have a love-hate relationship going on.

Parking in the garage, they heard the puppy's excited barking as soon as they exited the vehicle.

"Someone besides Brian is excited to see us," Avery said.

Duncan laughed. "Brian might be excited to see you, but I don't think he's as excited to see me."

"Shows what you know. I'm not his type. Though I think he's most excited when his husband, Tony, gets home." Avery looked up at him. "I, however, get excited when you come home."

Duncan caught her by the arm and spun her into his embrace. He kissed her with a passion that made her toes curl. When he moved back, he stared into her eyes. "You will always be in my heart, Avery. Come on. We'd better get in there before your furbaby tears down the door."

Avery took a deep breath, realizing she was holding it. Duncan expected her to be able to move after a declaration like that? Her knees barely kept her upright. He caught her hand and tugged her along with him as if he hadn't just told her something she had waited forever to hear.

Avery went along with him because she wasn't ready to discuss feelings with him. Not yet, but soon.

HENRI SMILED. "YOU'RE a natural at this. You're catching on faster than any student I've had."

"Really?" Avery felt she was improving, but what did she know? She'd never seen a naginata used before her first lesson.

"Yes, really. With what you've already mastered, you'll be able to make any attacker have to fight for it."

"That will make Duncan happy. I'm being stalked by a Dubh Sidhe, which has him worried. He has people guarding me when he's not with me, but he's still on edge."

Henri sobered. "I can see why. The Dubh Sidhe are nothing to mess around with. With your abilities, I can see why any number of them would be after you. You would be a great asset to them."

"Even if they kidnap me, that is not going to happen. I have no intention of assisting them in any way."

"Just be careful."

"I am."

"When do you get your own naginata? I'd like to start your practice with your own weapon, so you're comfortable with it."

"It was delivered Thursday. I didn't think about bringing it. I'm sorry."

"No problem. But you need to become familiar with it. Practice with it at home, and we'll meet back here at seven pm on Monday."

Avery nodded. “I will. And I’ll be here.” Avery went into the hallway and let Duncan know they had finished.

Shortly, he entered near her. “How was the lesson?”

“Good. We were both pleased. I forgot to bring mine, though.”

“Next time.” Duncan smiled. “I’m glad it was good.” Putting his arm around her shoulders, he walked them to the exit door.

“Is it going to rain?” The sky was darkening rapidly.

Duncan looked through the glass. He frowned. “The weather isn’t calling for rain. Something’s wrong.” Stopping a few feet back from the outer door, he pulled her partially behind him.

“Pendragon is warded,” she reminded him.

“Yes, but between here and home isn’t.” He took hold of her hand. “Doesn’t matter. We’re going home the expedient way.”

Brian jumped back from the stove when they suddenly appeared in the kitchen. “What the...?”

“Change of plans. Dubh Sidhe were surrounding Pendragon Alliance,” Duncan explained as Murphy barked happily, scampering in from the family room.

Avery kneeled to greet the puppy and try to get him to stop barking. He was loud. His exuberance overbalanced her, and she landed on her rump. Then her back when he got even more excited to have her on the floor. He licked her everywhere his tongue could touch skin. Avery wriggled, laughing as his tongue tickled her.

Duncan caught her beneath her arms and lifted her to her feet. “Down, you crazy pup.”

Avery laughed. She couldn’t stop. Murphy was bouncing all around their feet and legs.

“Wait. Go back,” Brian said. “Dubh Sidhe were surrounding you?”

“They were trying,” Duncan said. “Omaon may be getting desperate.”

“You’re sure it’s him?” Brian asked.

"No, but he does have a head start on all the others. He's not going to want anyone to get ahead of him. Also, he knows where we live."

"He does?" This was the first time Avery had heard that. It sent a chill through her entire body.

Duncan made a face. He looked at Brian and then back at her. "Ah, yes. He's had someone following you for days."

Putting her hands on her hips, Avery glared first at her husband and then at her friend. "I told you I was being followed. You told me not to worry about it."

"Because I was doing enough for both of us," Brian said. "And God knows I've been worrying enough for the entire family."

"You're not supposed to. You're supposed to share your worries and concerns with the family. Not worry yourself sick by keeping everything to yourself." Avery told Brian before turning to Duncan. "Except you didn't keep it to yourself, did you? You told Duncan. Keeping things from me is *not* protecting me. It's not allowing me to know I'm in danger and be on the lookout. I've protected myself for a long time. I spotted the two men that you had tailing me."

Duncan grinned at the memory. "That you did. Surprised the hell out of all of us."

Avery nodded, satisfied by his response. "Don't keep things from me."

Duncan nodded once. "You're right. It's dangerous to keep you in the dark."

"Exactly," Avery agreed. "Is there anything else you need to tell me?"

"Murphy is a cùdrèagon. When he's grown, he'll be able to shapeshift into a dragon as large as a huge mastiff or a pony. I wanted you to have a true guard dog."

Avery looked at him in surprise. She'd heard of cùdrèagon, but she'd never seen one. "Are you serious?" She pointed at Murphy, now flopped across her foot chewing on one of his toys. "Him?"

"Yes, him." Duncan nodded, frowning. "I know he doesn't look like it now, but he comes from a great bloodline. I got him from Tremayne Cathcart, Pritch's son."

"Pronounce it again. A coo-dray-gone?"

Duncan nodded. "Cùdrèagon. It means dragon-dog. Only now he's still a puppy. You've never heard of one before?"

"Yes, but I've never seen one." She was having trouble imagining Murphy transforming into a dragon.

"Connor and Iain both have them," Brian said. "Theirs look like Great Pyrenees."

"Some can also shapeshift into horses," Duncan said. "Not Murphy, but some special ones can."

Avery held up a hand. "Okay, that's enough. Right now, he's a puppy. I'd like to let him stay that way as long as we can. Tell me more about the person or persons stalking me."

"Person," Brian said. His eyes widened as he faced Duncan. "It is just one, isn't it?"

"Yes," Duncan said sharply.

"What does this stalker look like?" Avery asked. "It would be nice to be able to distinguish the bad guys from the good guys."

"It wouldn't hurt to introduce Avery to Somerset and Caledonia's finest," Brian suggested. "You never know when we might need to call on them. It would be best if we can recognize them."

When Duncan looked at her, Avery shrugged and nodded.

"I'll take you to both departments on Monday." Duncan promised. "In the meantime, the bastard I saw out front of Iona's was lean, about six-feet-one or two. Light-colored eyes. Gray or blue. Sandy blonde, short hair."

Avery frowned. She had seen a man like that on several occasions wandering the streets of Caledonia. "He's been hanging around for at least two weeks."

"Crap." Duncan exchanged glances with Brian. "Okay, no more hiding anything from Avery. Especially if we think we're protecting her, because we're obviously not."

"No, you're not." Avery felt the need to reinforce the lesson.

"We need to do something about this guy," Brian said, crossing his arms and leaning his hips against the nearest counter.

"I'd love to. What do you suggest?" Duncan asked tersely.

"Make him disappear. Permanently."

Avery looked at Brian for signs of teasing, but saw none. "You're not kidding. You can't just kill him."

Both men looked at her as if she was the nutty one.

"You can't."

"Why not?" Brian asked. "He's just waiting for a chance to snatch you and drag you back to Omaon, or some other Dubh Side, where they can use you. He's not going to stop and go away if we ask nicely."

When she looked at Duncan, he shrugged. "I'm with Brian. If he makes a try for you, I'll drop him like a rock and feel just as much compassion."

Avery didn't want to go back to Tìr-dhàimh. Ever. She certainly didn't ever want to see Omaon again. But to kill a person.

"Avery, you're not taking self-defense classes for exercise. I didn't have that naginata specially made, so you'll have a conversation starter. Protecting yourself from the Dubh Sidhe means being able to make a hard choice and potentially kill someone. If it's down to them or you, you'd better pick you. You can't afford to hesitate. That can get you killed. Or worse."

"What could be worse?" she asked.

"Hesitation can get you taken prisoner. With all that might entail," Duncan replied succinctly.

"If it's one-on-one, I won't hesitate," Avery assured him. She didn't want to die. She would fight for her life if she had to do so. "But that's not what you two are talking about. At the moment, he's just watching and waiting for an opportunity. Wouldn't it be better—and easier—simply to make sure he never gets the opportunity?"

"Waiting is bad for us," Brian replied before Duncan could speak. "And the simplest way to assure the bad guy never gets the opportunity it to kill him."

Avery couldn't believe Brian said the things he did. She always thought of him as a gentleman. Sort of mild-mannered. She knew Duncan had hired him to protect her, but Avery saw him as more a companion than a guardian.

"Honey, you do understand that I chose Brian because he's unassuming but lethal," Duncan stated, as if reading her mind.

"I can kill with any weapon. Including just my hands. I can also turn anything into a deadly weapon. Even a paperclip. Make no mistake, Avery, you're my friend, and I love you, but you're also my job. As my job, I will protect you to the best of my ability. No matter how my actions might affect our relationship. Which I value dearly. However, I value your life more."

"Just as your life is worth more than that of a lowlife, second-level enforcer sent by Omaon," Duncan added.

Avery realized she wouldn't win this argument. "Will you at least try to handle him some other way?"

Duncan and Brian exchanged glances, probably also telecommunicating. After a moment, her husband nodded. "We can do that. Other Sidhe might find him useful."

At least they wouldn't murder the man, Avery thought before changing mental gears. "We need to find that knife. I need to go back to the store and see if Iona will let me borrow the sheath. I've been studying it while I've been at work. But I'd like to bring it home where there are fewer objects with so much history."

"No." That's all Duncan said. Just that one word.

"If I can study it, I think I can zero in on the current location of the dagger," Avery argued. She'd never done it before, but she'd felt something new with the sheath over the last couple of days. The tooled leather piece seemed to recognize that it was separated, and it seemed to seek its missing part like a homing missile. "That blade is the main reason Omaon wants me. We take away his incentive and we might be able to live relatively normal lives. I'd like to try it."

"She could be right," Brian spoke up, uncrossing his arms and standing straight. "I'll fetch it from the store." He disappeared.

Murphy, who had just padded into his kitchen with one of his toys, dropped it and barked at the empty spot where Brian had just been.

Picking up the Wubba, Duncan tossed it through the dining room into the family room. Murphy hesitated a moment, glancing at the empty spot before turning and bounding after his toy.

Avery looked at Duncan.

Her husband looked at her.

"We need to get that knife." Avery stepped in front of him, curved her palm over his forearm, and waited for him to reach the same conclusion.

"Yes, we do. It was the original mission," Duncan finally admitted. He stared at her seriously. "Finding it and returning it will take care of one problem, but it won't stop the Dubh Sidhe from wanting you. If they learn you found that blade, it may make them want you more because you'll have proved your worth."

Avery shivered. She couldn't argue because she knew Duncan was right.

"How does this work? You using one item to locate another?" Duncan asked when she said nothing. He bent, took Murphy's toy, and threw it again.

"I'm not sure. I'm still learning." Avery explained, "This is new to me. Maybe because all the other items I've dealt with were complete. This is the first time one has been separated into two pieces. Holding the sheath reminded me of holding metal being pulled toward a powerful magnet."

Duncan's eyes narrowed in thought. "It gives you direction. Can you get an idea of distance?"

Avery considered. "I didn't, but I wasn't trying to do that."

Brian reappeared with the sheath in his hand. He waited until Avery held out her hand to offer it to her.

The energy contained in the leather surged through Avery the moment she touched it. She quickly raised her internal shields. She was thankful for the time spent working at Time Passages. It allowed her to experiment with her ability and not only gain some control but also to discover she had shields and how to use them.

She was lucky to have learned before encountering an object with the power of Accalon's *sgian dubh*.

Avery knew the majority of the power was contained in the blade itself. It made her dread touching it. She would deal with that when she found it.

Avery held the sheath in both hands. Closing her eyes, she concentrated, letting her power join with that of the leather holder. Immediately, she felt the tug of the blade for its scabbard. As she waited, the connection straightened—both between her and the items and between the items themselves. Moments later, she had a direction.

When she opened her eyes, she discovered three pairs of eyes watching her, including Murphy's. The puppy sat at Duncan's feet, eyeing her intensely.

"I have a direction, but not a distance," Avery informed them. "It's northwest of here. Not close, but I don't know how far. How do we find it?"

Duncan looked at Brian before facing her. He shrugged. "Arm ourselves to the teeth, get in my truck, and drive where you lead us."

"We need to be smart and plan. We need a good night's sleep, for one thing," Brian stated.

Duncan nodded. "We need a fourth, too. Tony or Darach? Your call, Brian."

"Tony's on a mission for Pendragon. He won't be back for at least four days. I'll inform him, of course, but we'd better ask Darach," Brian said.

"I'll contact him. Gavin and Josie can watch Murphy. If he was grown, we'd take him," Duncan said.

Avery looked at the puppy. She would swear he frowned at her husband. "I don't think he wants to be left behind."

Duncan looked down at Murphy.

Murphy growled.

Duncan's eyes widened for a moment before narrowing into a frown. "Don't sass me, pup. You're not going this time."

Avery fought laughter. Duncan, so big and tall, and the large puppy staring at each other. "Maybe he needs obedience training."

Duncan looked at her. "Maybe. Their protection instincts are innate, but some lessons in manners might be in order."

Murphy ran for the den, coming back with a toy.

Duncan's lips twitched as he bent, took it, and tossed it.

"Let's eat. I made supper while you were in class." Brian began moving pots to the kitchen table. "Afterward, we can get the weapons picked out and do the rest of the packing."

"Pack?" Avery felt stupid for not considering that it might take them more than a day.

"We don't know how long it will take to locate it," Duncan echoed her thoughts. He picked up Murphy's food bowl and began preparing the puppy's supper.

"Let me tell Iona. I hope she doesn't mind. I seem to take off more than I'm there."

Brian pulled a pitcher of tea from the refrigerator. As he set it on the counter, Avery got two glasses and partially filled them with ice. While Brian poured the tea, she got a cold ale for Duncan.

"Honey, you don't need to worry about Iona. That lady adores you," Brian assured her as they sat down to eat. "She is thrilled to have you. She told me so."

"Don't worry about your job. Iona, better than many, understands how important it is to retrieve this particular artifact. She won't have a problem giving you time off."

After they cleaned up from their meal, Duncan took the puppy outside. Brian and Avery got luggage from the basement storage area. Darach arrived home just as Duncan came inside with Murphy. After Duncan explained the situation, they went to the vault in the back of the storage room where the weapons were kept.

Avery grabbed her new naginata, which looked like a wooden walking staff until she pressed a button hidden in the carved artwork. Then a blade shot out. Avery loved it. She hoped she never had to use it like she'd been practicing, but she could if she had to protect herself.

Besides the naginata, Duncan gave her two more knives in addition to the small ones he'd already had her carrying.

Duncan, Brian, and Darach chose blades of several lengths. Since they were staying in their dimension, they also grabbed handguns.

CHAPTER SEVENTEEN

Duncan roused them all just before daylight. After a hearty breakfast, they left a whining Murphy with Gavin and piled into Duncan's double cab pickup. Darach rode in the front with Duncan, while Avery and Brian rode in the back, Avery behind her husband.

Avery told Duncan the general direction in which to head. She had the sheath tucked in the pocket on the back of his driver's seat. That way, it was near enough for her to read the energy without holding it.

They stopped around one o'clock for a potty break, followed by a leisurely lunch. Back on the road with Darach behind the wheel, they drove until around seven, only stopping for fuel combined with bathroom breaks.

Shortly before midnight, Avery finally felt they were close. She informed her companions. Before long, they were winding up into the mountains of northeastern Tennessee. It was nearly one-thirty in the morning when she had Duncan, who was once more driving, pull into a driveway blocked by a heavy gate.

"Whoever lives here doesn't want unexpected guests. The property's fenced and there are surveillance cameras," Darach observed.

"There are?" Avery leaned over Brian to see.

"They've tried to hide them, but if you know where to look, you can spot them," Darach said.

Avery obviously didn't know where to look. She couldn't see them. That Darach spotted them in the dark amazed her. "What do we do now? The *sgian dubh* is somewhere up that driveway."

"Proceed with caution," Duncan stated. He pulled the truck back onto the highway and drove down the road. "The owner may have been alerted to our presence the moment I stopped the truck. That was stupid on my part. I know better."

Darach had his phone out and was searching for something.

"What about translocating in?" Brian suggested.

Duncan shook his head. "Not without knowing who we're dealing with and more about them. The one thing we don't need is to walk into another trap."

"Working on it," Darach stated, studying his phone screen. "County records show the owner to be the Randolph and Letitia Carruthers James Living Trust. Deeded into the trust by Randoph M. James and Letitia Carruthers James twenty-two years ago. It's seventy-one acres. Letitia appears to have inherited it from her parents thirty-seven years ago. It's old family land going back over a century." He resumed searching for records.

"We're about ten minutes from the nearest town. Let's see if we can find an all-night diner," Brian suggested. "I don't know about y'all, but I could use some coffee."

"I'll see what I can find." Duncan pressed a little harder on the gas pedal.

As they reached the outskirts of town, Darach supplied them with more information. "Randolph James died six years ago. They have two children—son and daughter—neither of whom live around here."

"Are they collectors?" Avery asked.

Darach shook his head. "I can't find any evidence of it. One of them could have inherited it."

At the moment, Avery didn't care how or when they'd gotten it. The pull between the sheath and its separated blade strained toward each other to the point their energies were making her dizzy and lightheaded. Now that the two objects were so close together, their energies seemed determined to join. It was a new situation for Avery. She had a difficult time handling it.

CHAPTER EIGHTTEEN

Duncan parked near the door to a brightly lighted diner after following the directions Brian gave him. Darach exited the truck, still looking at his phone screen. Brian, too, got out.

Duncan got out and opened the back door for Avery. She was slow to slide out and then would have hit the pavement if he hadn't quickly caught her by the arms and held her up. His stomach dropped. "Honey, what's wrong?"

Avery gripped his arms tightly. "They're trying to pull together. I'm just having trouble dealing with it. It's making me lightheaded."

Duncan wanted to curse. He couldn't imagine what she was going through. Worse, he didn't know how to help her. "What can I do?"

"Help me inside. Make sure I don't fall on my face. I hope something to eat and drink will help." Avery leaned in, resting her forehead against his chest. "The only thing that's going to stop this weird feeling is getting the blade back into the sheath."

He hugged her. Duncan could work with that. He'd get her some nourishment, and while they rested and refueled, they'd figure out a way to get the blade back. Duncan would not put his wife through this longer than necessary.

Entering, they were shown to a corner booth away from the windows where they could all fully or partially face the room. None of them wanted any surprises. Once they'd given their orders, Duncan had Avery explain to all of them what she felt.

"We have to get that knife," Brian stated when she finished.

Darach finally shoved his phone back in his pocket. "I can't find any mention of anyone in the family—present or past—who collected anything. They may have simply kept it quiet."

"More people should," Brian said.

Duncan agreed. Broadcasting ownership of rare items made people targets. Just as the wrong person learning about Avery's abilities made her a target.

"How do you want to get in?" Darach asked. "We have no idea of the house's layout. We can't even see it from the road."

Duncan shook his head. "It's too dangerous unless we can get a look at the structure. Or house plans."

"Why don't we wait until daylight and see if she'll talk to us? It's only about five hours until seven," Avery said. "However, to be polite, we should wait until later. Maybe around nine."

The way they looked at her made her second guess her idea.

"I don't think she's going to let four strangers into her house. No matter what time," Darach said. "I know I wouldn't."

"We all know you're unfriendly," Brian said. "It might work. If the woman isn't attached to it, we might even be able to get her to sell it to us."

"That would be fantastic." Avery smiled.

So happy to see her smile, Duncan wasn't about to burst her bubble. Personally, he doubted the woman would relinquish the dagger so easily. He wouldn't be upset to be wrong, however.

"What are we gonna do after we eat?" Darach asked. "Sit here for five to seven hours?"

"Not unless you want to draw attention to us," Brian responded. "That's a bad idea in a small town."

"After we eat, we get back in the truck, find a decent-sized cemetery, and see if we can get some sleep," Duncan said. He grinned at his wife's expression of incredulity.

Darach laughed. "Cemeteries are safe spaces from most nasty Dubh Sidhe sent entities. Not that we'll all sleep at the same time."

Brian turned and smiled as the waitress headed their way with a large tray laden with plates of food. They made small talk with her while she served them.

As they ate, they were quiet. They were in no hurry to leave and go back out into the cold, so they ate slowly. Snow began to fall while they were inside. When they finally left the restaurant an hour-and-a-half or so later, the snow blanketed everything in two inches or more of white.

The ground didn't seem slippery, but Duncan kept a firm hand on his wife's elbow to be safe. Soon they were in the truck once more. Darach located a large rural cemetery nearby, and Duncan found a spot near some trees at the back where he parked, pulling in backward so they could make a quick escape if needed.

"Trade seats." Brian opened his door and got out.

That was fine with Duncan. He'd been about to ask, anyway. Getting out from behind the wheel, he passed Brian in front of the truck. "Thanks."

"No problem. She's tired, and I think she might sleep if you held her." Brian continued around to the driver's side.

Duncan got in the back passenger side, closing and locking the door behind him. He opened his jacket and then his arms. A moment later, Avery was in his arms. As she slid her arms around his waist and pressed her forehead against his neck, Duncan wrapped his coat around her. *"Are you okay?"*

"Fine. Better now. How are you?"

"Better now that I'm holding you. Get some sleep while you can." Duncan pressed his lips against her temple. He could feel her heartbeat against them. It wasn't long before Avery's weight settled fully against him, letting him know she'd fallen asleep. After kissing

her temple, Duncan rested his cheek against her head and closed his eyes.

He must have drifted off to sleep, because Darach awakened him. "It's eight-thirty. What do you want to do?"

"Let's get some breakfast. Different place, though. The fewer people who remember seeing us, the better. Afterward, we'll see if we can get an audience with Mrs. James," Duncan responded as Avery roused.

Brian started the truck. "There's a chain restaurant on the other end of town near the interstate. I'll head there."

"Do you want me to try to set up an interview with Mrs. James, or are we just going to arrive unannounced and hope she'll agree to see us?" Darach asked.

"You found her phone number?" Duncan asked.

"I didn't. I contacted Peter, and he found it," Darach said.

"Don't call," Avery said, surprising them. "I think we'll have a better chance if she's not expecting us."

"You heard the lady," Duncan said.

Darach nodded, once again putting his phone back in his pocket.

Less than two hours later, Duncan pulled the truck to a stop in front of the closed gates to the James' property.

"Let me try." Avery got out of the truck and went to the video intercom.

Duncan rolled down the window so he could listen.

Avery pressed the button. It was several seconds before a woman answered. "Who are you, and what do you want?"

"My name is Avery Kerr. I'm here with my husband and two companions. We would like to speak with Mrs. James concerning an ancient *sgian dubh* or knife that we believe she may have in her possession."

"Well, she doesn't want to talk to you," came the snappy reply.

"Move over and give me that thing," the second woman said. "Describe the knife."

"All I can tell you is that it's a *sgian dubh*. I will recognize it when I see it. Also, I have the sheath it fits," Avery told her.

"What did you say your name was again?" the woman, who had to be Letitia, asked.

"Avery Kerr."

"Your maiden name."

Avery hesitated a moment, looking over her shoulder at Duncan.

He shrugged.

Turning back, she said, "Beaton."

"Did you know a Mac Beaton?"

Duncan sat at attention when Avery stiffened.

"If you mean MacArthur Beaton, no, I never knew him, but he was my grandfather."

There was no reply, but a moment later, the gate swung open.

Brian leaned over the back of the front seat. "Hurry and get in the truck before she changes her mind."

Avery rushed back to her seat and closed the door.

Duncan eased the pickup through the gates and followed the winding driveway through the woods. Eventually, it opened onto a snow-covered lawn surrounding an elegant two-story colonial brick house. Duncan stopped at the end of the sidewalk leading to the front door. A front door which opened as they stopped.

A petite elderly woman with a halo of soft white curls stood in the opening. She waited, watching, as they exited the truck. When they reached her, she motioned for them to enter.

Once they were all in the entry hall, Darach closed the front door behind them.

"Come in and have a seat." Letitia waved them into a formal living room on the left.

With his hand at the small of her back, Duncan urged Avery into the room and to the couch. Brian and Darach took up positions in front of two chairs, leaving another for their hostess.

She followed them into the room. "Have a seat. Tell me how you came to be at my gate."

Avery looked at Duncan. They sat, and Avery took hold of his hand. Duncan gently squeezed her fingers as he responded. First, he introduced himself, and then Brian and Darach. Next, he explained their history with the *Sgian Dubh* of Accalon.

Before Letitia James could comment, Stiabhan suddenly appeared in the archway between the living room and the hall. All eyes focused on him.

"It is a good thing I and others impressed upon the Dubh Sidhe how detrimental it would be to their well-being should they continue their pursuit of Avery. Otherwise, I would be angry you put my kinswoman in danger." The annoying Sidhe looked entirely too pleased with himself for Duncan.

However, because Stiabhan's accomplishment thrilled him, Duncan simply said, "Thank you."

Avery jumped up, ran to the Sidhe, and threw herself into his embrace as she thanked him.

Stiabhan hugged her, grinning like an idiot.

Once the greeting was over, Stiabhan followed Avery to the couch and sat on her opposite side from Duncan.

Duncan turned his attention to Letitia to gauge her reaction. That she appeared unphased seemed to prove his theory she was Daondasidhe.

The old woman eyed him. "How else do you think I came into possession of the artifact?" she asked, as if reading his mind. "My family has hidden it for generations."

"Why didn't you just turn it over to the Mother Guardians?" Brian asked what Duncan was thinking.

"Who do you think requested we hide it?" Letitia looked at him calmly. "They told my ancestor that one day they would send someone to retrieve it. When it was time. It wasn't explained why. Nor did my ancestor ask. I believe the current phrase is 'above their pay grade.' We were told we would know when the correct person appeared to take it off our hands. I'm glad that day arrived. I didn't want to have to leave the guardianship to one of my children."

"How do you know I'm that person?" Avery asked.

"Mac told us about thirty-five years ago that his granddaughter would come one day," Letitia answered. "My husband and I met Mac over forty years ago. We became close friends with him and Edna."

"How could he possibly know that? My parents hadn't even met thirty-five years ago," Avery said. She shook her head.

Letitia shrugged delicate shoulders. "I have no idea. Yet here you are. I'll know for sure if you recognize the dagger." She turned toward the arch between the living room and the formal dining room. "Cleo, we're ready," she called.

Moments later, a brown-haired, heavy-set woman in her sixties entered, carrying a glass tray. She stopped beside Letitia's chair and waited.

Avery, who had the sheath in her coat pocket, immediately felt the pull. Standing, she walked over and stared down at the six *sgian dubhs* spread out on the tray. Though she hesitated to touch it, Avery picked up the second from the left. Power vibrated like a shot up her arm.

"You think that's the true *Sgian Dubh* of Accalon?" Cleo questioned, an odd tone in her voice.

Avery raised her gaze to look at the woman. "I don't think it. I know it." She jumped back as the older woman threw the glass tray with the other knives on the floor. As the blades went everywhere and the tray shattered at their feet, Cleo snatched the *sgian dubh* from Avery's hand and ran back the way she had come.

Pandemonium broke out behind Avery. Before she could move, all four men ran past her. She turned to Letitia.

The old woman turned in her chair to look in the direction her housekeeper had fled. She looked up at Avery. "I don't understand what just happened."

"I'm not sure, but I believe your maid may have just stolen the dagger," Avery told her.

Letitia shook her head. "Cleo has been with me for nearly forty years."

"She was working for you when you knew my grandparents?" Avery's mental wheels were turning.

Letitia's gaze sharpened. "Yes. She heard us talking about it. The problem was that none of us knew which of those six knives was the real one. Sometime over the generations, the identity was either deliberately or accidentally forgotten. Perhaps to protect it." She looked into the dining room and then back at Avery. "They may have feared something like this would happen." She shook her head. "I'm so sorry. I can't believe Cleo has been living in my house all these years, waiting." Letitia shuddered.

Avery understood.

They both turned as the men returned. Stiabhan and Duncan held a struggling Cleo between them. While cursing up a storm, the woman tried to kick anyone she could reach. They weren't letting her.

Brian held out the *sgian dubh*. Avery took it, quickly pulling the sheath from her pocket, and slipping it inside. She breathed a sigh of relief when that took the energy to a manageable level.

"Mrs. James, if you have no objections, I will remove this person from your house," Stiabhan said.

"Can you assure me that she will never return?" Letitia asked.

"Most assuredly. I can promise you that you will never see this piece of trash or anyone associated with her ever again," Stiabhan vowed.

Letitia waved her hand. "Take her."

"Wait!" Avery didn't want her kinsman to leave yet. "What do I do with this?"

"Turn it over to a Mother Guardian," Stiabhan replied, as if it was simple.

Avery held it out. "Here you go. You take it to them."

"I am sorry, Avery. I cannot. Call the Mother Guardians. They will send one of their number to retrieve it," Stiabhan replied. He and Cleo disappeared.

Avery stared at the empty space and then turned to her husband. "But I don't know how to contact a Mother Guardian. I'm not sure I even know what they are, let alone the name of one."

Duncan stepped forward, wrapped an arm around her shoulder, and hugged her. "Don't worry. I know who they are and how to contact them. There are nine of them. They are the most powerful Sidhe women I know. Let me send out a telepathic request. One of them should answer shortly."

Avery looked at Letitia. "Do you mind if we're here a while longer?"

"Not at all. You've already done me two favors. You're welcome to stay as long as you need," Letitia replied. She leaned back in her chair. "Besides, I would love to meet a Mother Guardian. They are the stuff of legend."

It seemed the Mother Guardians were as eager to get the weapon back as Avery was to get rid of it. Letitia barely finished speaking when a woman appeared in the middle of the room. She was around Avery's height and wore an ankle-length, loose brown caftan, and a cowl pulled up over the top of her head. Her visible hair was gray and appeared short in length. It was impossible for Avery to tell her age as her face was weathered with lines on her forehead and cheeks, yet she didn't appear that old.

Duncan bowed. "Lady Angharat Brehus, you honor us with your presence."

Her lips quirked. "You have as glib a tongue as your grandfather, Duncan Kerr." She turned to Avery. "Your husband tells me you have something for me."

Avery nodded. "Um, yes, ma'am." She held out the sheathed dagger.

"Thank you, my dear. It is important that we recover these stolen items as soon as possible." Angharat took the dagger. "Do not worry about your safety. My sisters and I will take measures to ensure that you are not bothered by any of the Dubh Sidhe again. We look forward to working with you on recovering more items."

"Thank you so much, my lady." Avery was in awe and wasn't sure how to address the woman, so she followed Duncan's example.

The imposing woman inclined her head.

Duncan linked his fingers with Avery's. "Let's go home."

They said their goodbyes and walked to the front door with Letitia.

"Will you be okay here?" Avery hated leaving the older woman alone.

"You are a dear. I wish you and your grandparents could have known each other. Don't worry, Avery, I'll be just fine," Letitia answered. "My daughter has been begging me to come and live with her and her husband for years. My son and his wife are retiring. The timing couldn't be more perfect. I'll go live with my daughter, and my son and his wife can have this house. It's too large for me. You see, you've been a blessing to me." Leaning forward, she hugged Avery.

Avery returned the embrace. "It was a delight meeting you," she said as they separated.

Letitia shook hands with Duncan and the others before they left.

CHAPTER NINETEEN

They stopped after a few hours for a quick supper. Except for a couple of potty breaks, they drove straight home, arriving after four in the morning. The moment they got out of the truck, they heard Murphy's excited barking.

Duncan kept a supporting hand on his wife's elbow as they headed for the door. Between the stress and the lack of sleep, his poor darling was nearly asleep on her feet. He smiled at Avery's obvious delight in returning home to the crazy pup.

The moment Gavin opened the mudroom door, Murphy bounded out and straight to Avery, who squatted to hug the furball. Murphy was licking her face and bouncing around as if he hadn't seen her in a month instead of just a couple of days.

Duncan stood behind Avery to keep the large puppy from knocking her over. After a couple of seconds, he'd had enough. Catching Avery beneath her arms, he lifted her to her feet. "Come on. We all need to get some sleep. Murphy, inside."

The puppy raced into the house and then turned to wait, his entire body wriggling in excitement. "Has he been out?" Duncan asked his brother.

Gavin hugged Avery before replying. "At bedtime, but I'll take him out again. What happened?"

"Too much to go into now. We accomplished the mission. We'll fill in all the details over brunch. I doubt any of us will be awake before noon." Duncan clapped his younger brother on the shoulder and then ushered Avery toward the stairs. "Let Murphy in our room when he's finished or none of us will get any sleep."

Before long, everyone in the house was slumbering except Duncan. He should be relaxed. The artifact they'd been searching for years had been recovered and turned over to the Mother Guardians. Not only had Stiabhan said Avery was out of danger, but even better, the oldest of the Mother Guardians guaranteed it.

Avery rolled over and snuggled her back against his side. Duncan put his arms around her, curling his body around hers. Murphy hopped up on the foot of the bed and curled up behind Duncan's knees. With his family safe and around him, he could finally fall asleep.

Duncan woke sometime later when Murphy jumped on the bed once more. Avery was closing the door, a tray in one hand. She smiled when she saw him awake. Duncan returned her smile. She made him happy.

"Good afternoon, handsome." As she brought the tray to his side of the bed, he pushed himself to a sitting position.

"Good afternoon, gorgeous." Duncan told her, as he scratched the puppy behind his ears. "What time is it?"

"Nearly three." Avery set the tray on his lap. When Murphy tried to grab a slice of bacon, she tapped the end of his nose with two fingers. "Down!"

Duncan was surprised when the puppy moved to the foot of the bed. He lay down with his head between his paws, longingly eyeing the plate.

Duncan took a sip of coffee. Despite having slept nearly twelve hours, he was still tired. Hopefully, the caffeine would help. He scarfed down a slice of bacon before he asked, "How long have you been awake?"

"About two hours." Avery sat on the edge of the bed, facing him.

"Why didn't you wake me?" He asked between bites of scrambled eggs.

"Because you have been running nonstop for weeks. You needed the rest."

"I guess I did. What I need right now is a bathroom break." Avery moved, and he handed her the tray so he could get up.

When he returned, Avery motioned him to one of the two chairs, so he sat there. She put the tray in his lap. Before she straightened, she brushed the hair from his forehead and kissed it. "Finish your breakfast, honey."

Duncan did. He was hungry. From all the food piled on his plate, Avery anticipated that. He probably shouldn't have, but Duncan saved a bite of egg and of bacon for the puppy. He set the tray on the side table and put his plate on the floor.

Murphy's head popped up, but otherwise he didn't move. "Come on, boy. You can have it."

That did it. He jumped from the end of the bed and gobbled the remnants of Duncan's breakfast from the plate.

"Softy," Avery accused with a grin. "I don't know what I did to deserve you, but I'm thankful I did. You're my greatest blessing."

That startled Duncan. No one had ever called him a blessing before. It warmed his soul. Reaching across the table, he caught her nearest hand. Lifting it, he pressed a kiss to her palm. "You are the best thing in my life, Avery. You are my sun during the day and my guiding star at night."

Tears began to stream down Avery's cheeks. She got out of her chair and came to sit in his lap. Throwing her arms around his neck, she tightly hugged him.

Duncan held her, stroking her hair and back. "Don't cry, sweetheart. I want you to be happy."

"I love you so much!"

"Love you more," Duncan said easily.

Avery leaned back to give him a watery smile. "What am I going to do with you?"

Duncan shrugged. "Have babies with me. Grow old with me."

Her smile grew. "I love that plan. If you're feeling rested, maybe we could work on the babies part."

He laughed. "I'm rested enough for whatever you have in mind."

SO BEGINS THEIR FUTURE

DICTIONARY

Àrdrìgh – High King

Binding Ceremony – a Sidhe wedding. Often performed for Halflings as well. When used with a Halfling and a Pure, it allows the Pure to then be able to communicate through telepathy.

Brollochan – (bro-lock-an) shapeless things; evil; work at the behest of the Duine Olc; can change shape at will; most often appear as shadows with solid form.

Clauditiskinetic – able to manipulate locks.

Coillemuinntir – "forest dweller"; tall & slender & all lean muscle; leathery & wrinkled skin the color of the trees of the forest in shades of brown and gray; over eight feet in height; clothing was the colors of the forest; extremely swift; when they speak their voices sound like the rattle of dry leaves; often malicious. Can be controlled by the Sidhe. Are not affected by the weather—feel neither heat nor cold. Extremely strong; can run faster than a horse. Called "Muinn" for short. One of the leaders who aids Stiabhan is named Edigru.

Cruinne – Sidhe word for the Halfling world. Earth.

Cùdrèagon – dragon-dog; dragons the size of mastiffs or calves; Sidhe guard dogs and trackers; make a sound part bay and part roar; a breed of cùsidhe "fairy dog." Can appear as any dog. Some are also able to shift into horses. Tails have poisoned tips.

Daondasidhe (thee-on-da-shee) – the name for a person with fairy blood; half-Sidhe/half-Human ancestry, no matter how many generations back.

Dubh Sidhe (or Sith) – (doob shee) Dark Fairy; can refer to the Duine Olc or just to a Sidhe they don't like; also known as the Seelie Court.

Enforcer – usually the top warrior in a kingdom; relentless.

Forabuige caora – (four-a-booge kayor-a) – a breed of Sidhe sheep known for its warm, breathable wool. The wool is waterproof because of the dense yarn created from the wool.

Firinn – divination of facts concerning an object or its owner, place or event through contact with or proximity to an object; see also psychometry.

Glaisr – (gleye-zer) able to manipulate locks; see clauditiskinetic.

Gwarthgydde – caged evil; one of the race of Vanir—master of magic and sorcery; Old branch of gods. Neither male nor female—can be either. Can be released from its prison by one of the Pendragon swords. Medraut believes that in freeing it, he can then use it to free his father.

Halfling – term for a person of half-Sidhe/half-Human ancestry, no matter how many generations back. Used as a derogatory term by Dubh Sidhe.

High Council – a group of Sidhe who were in charge of setting the rules and maintaining peace in their new land after they were run out of our world.

Hunter – male or female; usually a Halfling, but sometimes a Pure; possesses some Sidhe talents that they use in their occupation. Some are in the employ of the Sidhe to find missing fae items that have been lost or stolen and ended up in the Human/Pure world. Sometimes also hired to find and return escaped creatures.

Mother Guardians – nine power Sidhe women; they imbued all of the ancient weapons with their power. Angharat Brehus, Enygeus Gahariet, Gudrum Svanhildr, Ganeida aka Iona Gruffydd, Lidoine

Pelleas, Lyonors Dyngannon, Rona Starkadhr, Sigune Launfel, and Tryamon Isdemus.

Mu-dheireadh Stad – (mu-yer-ah stad) The "end of the road." The name of Gwarthgydde's prison and the fortress that protects it. Often shortened to Mu-dheireadh. The fortress is near the top of the second-highest mountain peak. Snow-covered for nine out of twelve months.

Naginata –a blade in the end of a long pole. It was used to keep enemies at a distance and was often a favorite among female samurai. The blades are from 1 to 3 feet long, and the staff is from 6 to 9 feet. The end of the staff often has a sharp end cap which can also be used as a weapon. The blades are often curved at the end, for my use, these blades are straight so they can be hidden inside the staff until needed.

Ogre – An ogre (feminine: ogress) is a large, cruel, monstrous, and hideous humanoid monster, and fiction. Ogres are often depicted as feeding on human beings, and have appeared in many classic works of literature. In art, ogres are often depicted with a large head, abundant hair and beard, a voracious appetite, and a strong body. Man-eating monsters.

Old Ones - the group of Sidhe who first followed the path of the Tuatha de Dannan from the world of Earth to Hy-Brasil. Pritch is one. They stayed behind in the Four Kingdoms when the Dagda took his people on across the Summer Sea to Tir na-Og.

Peadaran – the name of Stiabhan's home.

Psychometry – talent; divination of facts concerning an object or its owner, place or event through contact with, or proximity to the object.

Pure – what Halflings often call a full human.

Realmgate - name given to the stone circles which allow travel between realms; Tairseach.

Sgian-dubh – (skain-doo) resembles the small skinning knife that is part of the typical set of hunting knives. These sets contain a butchering knife with a 9 to 10 inches (230 to 250 mm) blade, and a skinner with a blade of about 4 inches (100 mm). These knives usually had antler handles, as do many early *sgian-dubhs*. The larger knife is likely the ancestor of the modern dirk.

Shapeshifting – native power to all the Sidhe; power to shift to shape of other people was taken away from them eons ago; may only shift to animals; in the humans the power to shift was originally only passed on to the male of the Halflings, and then they may only shift to one animal; though some female Halflings are manifesting the power, too.

Sidhe, Sith, Si – (shee) fairy; any of the magical beings who live in the Realm, an alternate dimension that can be reached through stone circles. Tall, stunningly beautiful. Renowned for their great age, attractiveness, and power.

Talents – term given to the powers developed by Halflings. They begin to appear in males between the ages of 17-22 years; and in females between the ages of 23-28 years.

Tairseach – (tor-she) Sidhe name for a realmgate; often used by Halflings, too.

Telepathy – talent; mind-to-mind communication of thoughts, ideas, feelings and mental images.

Tessen – Japanese war fan used by Ninja. Folding fans made with razor-sharp metal. They could be used to stab or slice, or unfolded to deflect darts, arrows, small knives, etc.

Thirokinetic – able to manipulate and control animals.

Tìr-dhàimh – (teer-dayv) "Homeland," Sidhe name for their new homeland. Also called the Realm.

Translocation – talent; the ability to move from one place to another without external movement.

Tuatha Dé – the race before the Sidhe. Ancestors of the Sidhe.

Wardings – spells used to protect a person or place from magic or magical beings. The more powerful the person placing them, the more powerful the wardings.

PEOPLE

Cathan Caolin – (Cathan Cow-lin) - One of Omaon's enforcers.

Davin Geir – (Dav-in Ger) – The nephew and an enforcer for Queen Brigina of Gwyneira

Dealla Heregeat – (De-alla Hair-geet)

Omaon Heregeat – (O-ma-on Hair-geet) – Àrdrìgh of Oirthea; Dubh Sidhe

Stiabhan Iorworth – (Stev-an I-or-worth) – Sidhe who often helps the Halflings—many of whom are his cousins.

ACKNOWLEDGEMENTS

They say it takes a village to raise a child. For me, it takes a special group of BETA readers to bring the best out in my books. My original three: Nina, Pam, and Brenda. And my newest ones: Eunice and Lisa. They encourage me, give me emotional support, and still tell me when something doesn't seem right in the story. They make everything better.

I have to give a shout-out to my amazing cover artist, Dar Albert. Besides being easy to work with—even when I ask for more tweaking—, she creates attention-grabbing covers. Ones that make the reader look twice and check out the book.

There are so many fellow authors who have encouraged me and shared information with me. Too many to name, but they know who they are. When you find "coworkers" who support you, hang on to them. They're diamonds!

And, finally, my two rescue dogs, Riley and Sawyer. You keep me entertained; remind me there is unconditional love in the world; and make me exercise whether I want to or not.

INSPIRATION

As many of you know, for the Sidhe Hunters series, I use songs for inspiration, if not for the stories themselves, at least for the titles. In case you don't recognize this song, check out Michael Bublé's version of "Hold On." I hope you'll agree it fits with Avery and Duncan's story.

Don't miss out!

Visit the website below and you can sign up to receive emails whenever Sloane McClain publishes a new book. There's no charge and no obligation.

https://books2read.com/r/B-A-UMNJ-TAZND

BOOKS 2 READ

Connecting independent readers to independent writers.

Did you love *Hold On To The Hunter*? Then you should read *Holding Out For A Hunter*[1] by Sloane McClain!

[2]

HUNTERS: Men and women who protect the world from things that go bump in the night.

Cerridwyn Lavaine is hoping a move to a new state will bring a fresh start to her life. When she meets Maxen Maclean, she thinks it just might. He's tall and gorgeous.

Then Cerri's new home gets blown up before she even gets to see it, and she's forced to move in with Max and his four younger brothers. She soon discovers that the magical abilities she supposedly has but never believed worked actually do.

If all that wasn't enough, someone from another dimension wants her for reasons unknown.

---

1. https://books2read.com/u/4A7lMJ
2. https://books2read.com/u/4A7lMJ

Max doesn't even need to meet Cerri to know there's something special about her. Just hearing her voice over the phone is enough. Then he meets her, and it only gets better. At least until he realizes she is in some serious danger. Can he protect her?

Life just got a lot more complicated, but hopefully there's still time for some romance.

HOLDING OUT FOR A HUNTER is a full-length, stand-alone romance with paranormal & fantasy elements. There is no cliffhanger and it ends with an HEA.

About the Author

No big surprise, but Sloane's a romantic. She loves strong Alpha males, but she wants them to have equally strong women for their partners.

The mystery surrounding King Arthur has always been a favorite subject and it led her to wonder what would have happened if there was more to the story. What if the sword, and other swords, were more important? What if he had sons who survived? These questions and more led to the birth of her Sons of Pendragon series. She's also been fascinated by tales of the Fae from Ireland and Scotland. How would they interact with humans? What if they were forced into an alternate dimension and some of them were angry about it? The old, familiar, but still relevant trope of Good vs. Evil. This led to the birth of her companion series, The Sidhe Hunters.

Sloane currently has two very spoiled rescue dogs. She also loves photography. You'll often see her photographs on her social media pages.

You can contact her on Facebook: SloaneMcClainAuthor

BookBub: @SloaneMcClain

BlueSky @ sloanemcclain.bsky.social

Instagram: @pendragonsandhunters
Pinterest: @pendragonsandhunters/
Pendragonsandhunters@gmail.com

Milton Keynes UK
Ingram Content Group UK Ltd.
UKHW011428140724
445326UK00001B/37

9 798224 432134